RAT RUNNERS

RAT RUNNERS

Oisín McGann

OPEN ROAD

INTEGRATED MEDIA

NEW YORK

Copyright © 2013 by Oisín McGann

Cover design by Jason Gabbert

978-1-4976-6580-4

Published in 2015 by Open Road Integrated Media, Inc.
345 Hudson Street
New York, NY 10014
www.openroadmedia.com

FOR MAGS, JENNY, AOIFE, PATRICIA, DAVID, NESSA,
AND ALL THE FANTASTIC BOOK PEOPLE
WHO MAKE CHILDREN'S BOOKS IRELAND WHAT IT IS.

RAT RUNNERS

CHAPTER 1

TAKING THE CASE

NIMMO HEARD THE WHISTLES and immediately stopped what he was doing. People on the ground floor of the tenement were warning those above. There was a Safe-Guard in the building. He looked at his watch, noting the time. Six-fifteen—three hours before sundown. He needed to be gone before seven, or he'd have to leave the job for another night. If the Safe-Guard was just here to wander around, it might take half an hour or more to reach Nimmo's floor. If it had an assignment, it would go straight to the apartment it wanted. There was no way of telling which, without going looking for it. There was no way he was about to do that. In Nimmo's line of work, it didn't pay to get noticed.

He had his trainers off, and was fitting one with the kind of raised insole you used for flat feet, the type with a lump under the arch of the foot to support it. Nimmo did not have flat feet. And he only put an insole in the left trainer, leaving the other one as it was. Putting on the shoes, he walked around until he was satisfied that the arch support was having the desired effect. Taking the insole out, he stuffed both of them into the small backpack he kept near the door. Then he put his trainers back on.

Pulling on his scuffed black leather jacket and his gray woolen hat, he slung the pack onto his shoulders and headed for the door of his dingy but well-kept apartment. A kid his age should not have been living alone, but there was no need for the authorities to know. With his lean, somber face, tall wiry build and close-cut red hair, he could pass for older if he needed to. He had several identities to match. He was reaching for the latch when a knock on the door caused him to freeze. A flicker of thoughts went through his head. Had the Safe-Guard somehow been assigned to him, despite the rules? What then? Stay there and look innocent? Try and bluff his way past? Get out now, by the window?

Nimmo shook his head. If it was the Safe-Guard, it could see through the door. It could see his skeleton, hear his elevated heartbeat. If he'd had dental records, it could have identified him by his teeth. There was no point running. The knock sounded again. He opened the door.

Watson Brundle was standing out in the drab, faded yellow corridor. A few inches over six foot, Brundle was a narrow, angular man with wide cheekbones, dark eyes and a curly mop of black hair. He always had a restless manner, moving with a twitchy energy. His large hands held a small flat leather box out in front of him; it was a little over twenty centimeters square, the kind you might use to hold an expensive necklace.

"Hey, Nimmo. I need a favor."

"I'm going out," Nimmo replied.

"This is a pretty serious favor. I'd owe you a great big fat one."

"Gnarly. Ask me when I come back."

"No. I need you to hide this for me, now." Brundle was sweating as he thrust the case towards Nimmo.

"You want me to *hide* something for you with that peeper downstairs? You think I'm a complete gombeen? No way."

"It's nothing illegal. Not technically," Brundle said softly, desperately. "It's just . . . questionable. Look, I got a tip-off, all right? The Safe-Guard is here for me. It's coming to my place, not yours. Just take this thing from me and I'll let you off a month's rent, OK?"

Brundle owned the whole building, and rented this small apartment to Nimmo for cash, no questions asked.

"What's in it?" Nimmo asked.

"I can't tell you. But they're not looking for it, and it's not illegal. Not really. Look, come on, we haven't much time. That peeper is probably coming up the stairs right now."

"Six months' rent," Nimmo said.

"What? Are you havin' a laugh? Listen, I need to get out of here for a while, just until it's gone. And I can't take this out with me. How about two months, OK?" Brundle looked down the hallway towards the door to the stairwell. The elevator hadn't worked in over a year. The Safe-Guard would have to climb the stairs.

"How about six?"

"Don't be a complete sod. Three months off, and you take this right now, all right?"

"I'll take it right now," Nimmo told him, "when you give me six months off. I don't play the shell game with Safe-Guards, Brundle. Nobody does, if they're smart. So you're asking me to do something stupid when I know better. You're up to no good and looking for company. Six months, rent-free."

Brundle nodded frantically and pushed the box into Nimmo's hands.

"Bloody hustler! OK. Take it!"

Nimmo took it and closed the door. He heard his landlord stride down the hallway. Brundle was probably hoping to hide in one of the other apartments next floor down and let the Safe-Guard go past, and then leg it out and down the street. That was just dumb—he'd only bring suspicion on himself. Brundle wasn't normally dumb.

Having saved himself rent for the next six months, Nimmo could afford to give tonight's job a miss. Dropping his pack on the floor by the door, he slipped off his jacket and hat and hung them on the hook. As he did these things, his mind was searching the apartment for somewhere to hide the box. He tried to open it, but it was locked, and the edge was sealed with some kind of plastic resin. If he forced it, Brundle would know. That wasn't enough to stop him—he didn't normally handle something if he didn't know what it was—but there wasn't time to start trying to crack it open now.

The flat was a small two-bed place, though one of the rooms was little more than a box room. There was a living room with a kitchenette at the back, one large window looking out on the enclosed courtyard six stories below that boasted a run-down playground and a basketball court. The bedrooms were both off to the right, with a large cupboard just to the left of the front door. All the walls were painted an anonymous beige. There wasn't much in the way of decoration—a few film and band posters, some black-and-white framed photos of London landmarks, a few ornaments lying on the sideboard and the mantelpiece. Nothing that would have told you much about the owner's personality. There was no television. The battered Weinbach piano might have come with the flat, but anyone who tried it would have found it perfectly in tune.

Nimmo looked at the box again. There are two main ways of concealing something. Either hide it where it cannot be seen, or put it somewhere it can be seen, but cannot be recognized. If you want to hide something from someone with x-ray vision, the first option is extremely difficult. He flipped the box over, looked at the underside, which was almost exactly like the top, and then turned it back. It didn't look like anything else in his apartment.

Brundle had a number of boxes like this in his laboratory next door. They held various scientific instruments that he used. This was where he spent all his time, although his living quarters were across the corridor. Pulling on a pair of latex gloves, Nimmo wiped any trace of fingerprints off the box with a soft cloth. Then he took a pair of sunglasses from the pocket of his leather jacket, which hung on the hook by the door. Nimmo opened the front door and walked along the hallway. The scientist had knocked through the walls of three apartments on this floor to build himself a large laboratory, and had sealed off two of the doors. The third door looked normal, but Nimmo knew it had a solid steel core. The two locks were pretty standard, however, which Nimmo had always thought was a bit careless. He unhooked the legs of his sunglasses from their frame. This simple disguise was a handy way of hiding and carrying two of his lock-picks.

The two locks took him less than a minute to open, and then he was inside. He had figured out Brundle's alarm code some time ago—the date of his daughter's Bat Mitzvah—and tapped the six-digit number into the keypad hidden in one of the cupboards, disarming the security system.

As he passed one of Brundle's office desks, the sound of a dog barking right next to him nearly made him jump out of his skin. He spun around to find a life-size pug dog toy sitting on the desk. It was the type that could make sounds, triggered by one of those infra-red sensors that detected people walking past. Its head was nodding idiotically.

"Little git," Nimmo muttered, with a grim smile as his heart settled down again.

Brundle loved his gadgets, but this one was new. Nimmo quickly found some variously sized cases of scientific instruments piled on a worktable, coated in a thin layer of dust. He slipped the leather box in amongst the pile, wiped some dust off one of the windowsills and sprinkled it over the leather-covered box to hide its polished sheen. It looked completely at home.

This was the best place for Brundle's 'technically-not-illegal' box. It didn't *look* as if somebody was trying to hide it, and yet the mixture of metal and plastic parts in the other boxes would help conceal its contents from a Safe-Guard's x-ray vision, unless the thing inside was a shape the watcher was specifically looking for. And this way, Nimmo wasn't taking the risk of hiding it in his own apartment.

This lab consisted of a long room, taking up about half of the footprint of the three original apartments. It was filled with computer equipment and workbenches; electronics tools such as soldering irons and phase testers lay among the clutter, along with circuit boards and other bits and pieces. Different types of microscopes stood along one table. Through an airlock door system was a smaller room. It was a 'clean room,' where Brundle did his micro-technology work. No dirt or dust could be allowed in there. You had to wear a coverall 'bunny suit' and a mask to keep the air clear of contaminants. There was an electron microscope in there, and a lot of other expensive gear.

A picture of Veronica, Brundle's daughter, stood in an attractive walnut frame on the desk in the center of one wall. 'Nica,' she preferred to be called. She was dark-haired, dark-eyed and coffee-skinned, like her father, and pretty in an offbeat kind of way. But her looks were marred by the port-wine birthmark over her left eye and the top of her cheek. Her father was devoted to her, but separated from her mother. Nica lived with the mother.

Nimmo only knew a little bit about Brundle's work—the scientist's research was legitimate, carried out for some private client, or so he'd said. It had something to do with RFIDs—Radio Frequency ID tags—those multi-purpose micro-transmitters that were on everything nowadays, from clothes to cargo containers. They had replaced barcodes and added many other functions into the bargain. They were everywhere, and Brundle was working on some way of using them in skin implants or something. That was as much as Nimmo knew.

Quickly resetting the alarm, he had barely slipped back out of the lab and locked the door again, when he heard footsteps on the stairs. Seconds later, he was back inside his own apartment, with the door closed. He recognized Brundle's tread, and someone with him who took shorter, quieter strides. It seemed the scientist had failed to evade the Safe-Guard.

Sitting down on the worn but comfortable armchair in the small living room, Nimmo closed his eyes, and listened carefully as Watson Brundle unlocked the door to the lab, and let the Safe-Guard in.

CHAPTER 2

THE CATERPILLAR JOB

MANIKIN SAT ON A BLACK-PAINTED STEEL PARK BENCH, facing a litter bin ribbed with wood that stood on the far side of the path. Her eyes were on the book she held in her hands, but she kept her attention on the tarmac path that passed in front of her, following the perimeter of the small green area that offered shelter from the rush of the city beyond. The small park was surrounded by tall mature trees, and a dense hedge. A gate opened into the park thirty-five meters up on her left. The mark would come in that way. He would exit the park through the gate at the other end of the lane, off to her right. There was another gate behind her, just visible over her left shoulder. Outside that gate, in the shadow of a multi-story car park, her two partners waited for her signal.

The patch of green was one of the few public spaces in the

city center that were almost entirely obscured from security cameras. Only one camera, on the wall of the car park behind her, watched over this space. Manikin knew that camera would not be working. Her brother would see to that.

She looked at her watch. The guy they were waiting for was late. Manikin realized that she hadn't turned a page of her book in several minutes and did so now. It was at that moment that she saw a Safe-Guard walking down the lane on the far side of the park. Her blood ran cold—if the mark appeared now, they would have to let him pass. Just as she always did when she saw a Safe-Guard, she ran through a check of what she had on her person, in case the peeper looked over at her. Nothing too suspicious. She was wearing a strawberry-blonde wig, but the watcher wouldn't spot that unless it was very close. The same went for the tinted contact lenses that made her eyes look blue instead of green. The pockets of her khaki-colored mac were empty—so that the coat could be cast off in a hurry if need be. Beneath the coat she wore a pair of unremarkable black jeans and a gray wool sweater. Nothing too distinctive. She carried nothing illegal—except for her fake ID, which was of an extremely high quality. She was always careful about that when she was on a job. The work was dangerous enough without doing something stupid like carrying a weapon or some stolen property.

Even so, she felt a chill as the blue-gray, cloaked figure turned the glass visor of its helmet in her direction. She hated the way they moved. They were trained to glide, walking slowly and smoothly. She never saw one looking hurried or agitated. They were taught to show as few human qualities as possible, to be walking surveillance posts and nothing more. They couldn't even talk to you without permission from their Controllers. It didn't look at her for very long, but she still felt that disturbing sense they always gave you—that they could see through you, see anything you were hiding. The stare that said they could tell when you were up to no good.

Then it was gone, leaving through a gate on the far side of the park. That wasn't gone enough for her liking, but at that moment a boy her age appeared through the gate on her left, swerving onto the lane on a skateboard. His lank brown hair hung over a spotty, petulant face, much as his baggy jeans hung off his backside. His tense expression and watchful eyes gave him away. This guy was on duty. He was carrying a cuddly toy under his left arm, a rather hungry-looking caterpillar with a meter-long skinny green body, a large red head and multi-colored legs. It was time to go to work.

Manikin tapped the top of the bench with her right hand. As the skateboarder sped towards her, two people on roller-blades swept out from the gate behind her, coming up on her left. They were going too fast to stop. The skateboarder twisted to avoid them, but the guy with the bleached-blond hair and the ox-blood leather jacket hit the skater hard enough to knock him off the path. The spotty kid might have stayed on his feet if the red-headed girl hadn't fallen over her boyfriend's sprawling legs and slammed right into the unfortunate skateboarder. He collided with the litter bin, dropped his cuddly caterpillar and tumbled onto the grass. The redhead staggered up into a standing position, wobbled on her roller-blades, and stood on the side of the skater's knee. He let out a yell. She fell over onto him again, her elbow hitting him in the face.

"What are you doin'?" he protested. "You muggin' me or do you, like, *normally* skate like a drunk baby? Get off me!"

Manikin was already on her feet, as the guy in the leather jacket stood up on his roller-blades, his face contorted into a snarl. His name was Punkin, and he was a short fifteen-year-old, with a pale, pinched face, premature bags under his eyes and cropped, bleached-blond hair. He stood over the spotty kid, his right hand clenched into a fist.

"Watch where you're goin', you little scrote!" he barked. "You skatin' with your eyes open, or are you, like . . . usin' the Force? Hey, I'm talkin' to you, arse-face!"

The skater was distracted for a moment by Punkin as Manikin picked up the caterpillar. She reached for the litter bin as she walked behind Punkin, who stood between the bin and the skater. The spotty kid stretched to the side, looking past Punkin and focusing his entire attention on the cuddly toy in Manikin's hands.

"Hey, that's mine! Let go of that! Let it go!" he cried, his voice a little too shrill.

"Sure, sure," she said, handing it over as he stood up. "I saw what happened. You OK? It was all their fault, they ran right into you. I'll testify to that if you need to make a claim. Are you hurt? Is the caterpillar OK?"

"Yes! No! Just . . . just leave me alone," the skater said, obviously shaken, and holding onto the cuddly toy like a toddler meeting strange relatives. "I just need to go."

"Hey, this isn't over!" the bleached-blond guy snapped. "You run into me, you're gonna apologize! You and your caterpillar both!"

"Apologize for what? You got a whole park to roll through and you hit the only other person in it? I gotta apologize 'cos you can't steer straight? That what you're tellin' me?"

"Yeah, let's 'ave it!" his girlfriend backed her man up. "You an' that bug gonna show us some respec'."

The girl, whose name was Bunny, was a manic-faced strip of a thing, with a wild mop of ginger hair and near-permanent look of frustration. The same age as her boyfriend, she was slightly more stupid, and just a little bit more of a psycho. She always spoke as if her knickers were painfully tight. Manikin would not have been working with either of them if she hadn't been desperate. Bunny moved forward as if to push the guy, and Manikin stepped into the way. Manikin felt a hard shape under the girl's jacket and frowned. Looking down, she saw the butt of a black plastic handle sticking out of Bunny's waistband. Manikin hid her shock well. Turning back to look at Punkin, she noted the way he held his right hand down near his waist. He was carrying as well, the idiot.

"Leave him alone!" Manikin told them. "I saw the whole thing—you weren't watching where you were going, either of you. You ran him right off the path! I should call the bloody police, although they've probably seen everything already." She pointed at the camera up on the wall of the multi-story car park. "Go on, get the hell out o' here."

But it was the skater who moved first. With one glance up

at the security camera, he kicked his skateboard back onto its wheels, jumped on and rode away down the path.

Manikin spun around, hissing quietly through her teeth: "You could have blown everything, you stupid bloody fools! Guns? You bring *guns* to a *switch*? Are you out of your tiny little minds? Get lost, and meet me back at the van. And try not to get arrested on the way."

"Mind your tone," Punkin grunted, showing her the handle of the automatic he had in his waistband. "I know how to use this."

"Really? 'Cos the only thing that's good for is putting us all in *prison*," Manikin growled. "FX and me brought you in on this 'cos we thought you had savvy. Now, if it's not too much trouble, try and get back to the van without bringing every bloody copper in the city down on top of us. I'll see you there."

"Did you get it?" Bunny asked, ignoring Manikin's expression of disgust.

Manikin reached into the litter bin, pulling out the black plastic bag that sat within it. This was not a garbage bag—she had placed it in there herself. Inside the bag was the skater's green caterpillar. The one he was hurrying away with was a dummy, which she had switched for the real one as she passed behind Punkin's back. She nodded, showing them the toy before closing up the bag and tucking it under her arm.

"That camera's about to come back online." She tilted her head towards the wall of the car park. "Let's move."

As Punkin and Bunny went one way, and she went the other, Manikin was already working over the angles. Her 'partners' had not needed the guns for the job. Manikin and her brother had planned it that way. In a city filled with x-ray cameras and the super-senses of the Safe-Guards, even a complete moron would avoid carrying a gun unless they had a really, *really* good reason. And there was only one reason Manikin could think of.

She and her brother were about to be reesed.

CHAPTER 3

GETTING REESED

FX FOLDED HIS CONSOLE as he saw his older sister approaching the minivan. The server controlling the cameras in the underground level of the car park would stay offline for another ten minutes—plenty of time to get out of there. There was a scattering of other cars parked on this level, but it was late in the evening, and very few people were working in the office block attached to the car park. FX had hacked into, and crashed, the surveillance server seven other times in the last two days, to make sure the security guards who monitored the car park were thoroughly sick of the malfunctioning system before the day of the job. Another crash would be unlikely to cause much alarm. He had also knocked out a single camera, on a separate system. It overlooked the park behind the building—and the lane that ran along one side of that park, where his sister had just finished their latest job.

Now that he could see Manikin coming towards him through the shadowy car park with a black bag slung over her shoulder, he knew it was time to go.

FX was short for his age—as his sister was always keen to point out—and his round face and the spray of freckles on his brown cheeks did little to relieve his youthful appearance. His curly black hair was gelled into a carefully sculpted mess atop his head and his teeth were a little crooked at the front. And he was becoming doubtful that his wiry build would ever be particularly muscular. But then, FX was never going to be the muscle on any job. He was too useful in other ways.

Manikin slid open the side door of the metallic-mustard minivan, dumped the large black plastic bag on the seat and whipped off the wig of strawberry-blonde curls. She pulled the pins out of her own straight black hair, letting it fall over the collar of her khaki mac.

"Gimme the dye pack," she muttered, as two figures hurried up behind her.

"Did you get the thing?" he asked.

"Did you hear me?" she asked back.

"What happened?" he tried again.

"Give. Me. The. Bloody. Dye. Pack. You. Wazzock," she said slowly and softly, in a voice she only used when they were really in trouble.

He drew a wad of twenty-pound notes from his bag and handed it to her. Inside the hollowed-out wad was a type of anti-theft device used by banks. If Manikin had decided to use it, the job had gone badly wrong. She slipped her hand into the top of the plastic bag and placed the bound lump of notes somewhere inside. FX opened his mouth to ask her what had happened, but she cut him off:

"The switch went fine. Punkin and Bunny knocked the mark off his feet, just like they were supposed to. Born to fall over, those two were." She shook her head, color rising under the tanned skin of her face. "While they were all untangling themselves, I switched his caterpillar for the dummy in the litter bin. The courier didn't cop it, I'm sure of that. He whined a bit, and took off holding onto the dummy like his life depended on it."

"So?" FX pressed her. "What's the problem?"

Punkin and Bunny rolled up behind her on their roller-blades, and Manikin looked sourly at them.

"These monkeys brought guns."

FX's jaw sagged open, and he stared at their new partners in disbelief. The arrogant smirk hiding just below the surface of Punkin's face told FX why Manikin had wanted the dye pack. They were about to be reesed.

"That's right," Punkin said, drawing a nine-millimeter automatic from his ox-blood-colored, Italian leather jacket. The guy figured himself for a Mafia-style gangster. "We're done bein' rat-runners. It takes a proper villain to pull off a job like this."

He wasn't pointing the gun at them, but he wasn't pointing it away from them either.

"The wheels rather spoil the image," Manikin said, looking down at his feet. "I imagine they'd spoil your *aim* too, if you had any to begin with. I can't believe you'd be so stupid. Even *you*. Any scan-cam we passed driving in here could have detected those things. And we still have to drive back out. What if we pass a bloody Safe-Guard? They can see right through the van, you tick. If they spot those pieces, we're all going down."

Her face was flushed, but her green eyes were cold. FX could see she was in a spitting rage. He was silently hoping her temper wasn't about to get them killed.

"You don't got no problem then, do yaw?" Bunny said, pulling a snub-nosed six-shot revolver from the waistband around the back of her jeans. She aimed it straight at Manikin's chest. "'Cos you ain't goin' out wiv us. Right, Punkin?"

"You got that right, Bunny," Punkin said with a smile. He crossed his arms, laying his pistol across his left bicep. "You two are stayin' right 'ere. Out of the van, FX. Dolly, hand over the caterpillar."

"Don't call me Dolly!" Manikin snapped at him, as her brother climbed out behind her.

"What are you shouting at him for?" FX said, thumping her shoulder. "You want to get us shot?"

"Shut your face! You should be taking my side," she retorted, pushing him against the door of the van.

"I'm on whatever side doesn't get *shot*!" FX shoved her back, nearly knocking her into Punkin. "You shut *your* stupid face, yeh windbag!"

"Both of you, shut up!" Bunny barked, switching her aim from brother to sister and back again. "Somebody'll hear!"

"Oh, well *shoot* us then," Manikin sneered at her. "That'll cut right down the noise, won't it, you wazzock? I can't believe we got these clowns involved. I mean, how could working with such a pair of pissin' lobotomy cases be anything other than a complete cock-up?"

"Will you please stop dissing the morons holding the guns?" FX cried.

"Who you calling morons?" Punkin snarled. "Knock it off and give us the soddin' caterpillar!"

"When are you going to grow a pair of balls, ya weedy short-arse?" Manikin exclaimed, pushing her brother against the van again.

"When you gonna develop higher brain functions?" he roared back at her, shoving her back hard.

She stumbled, nearly losing her balance, and collided with Punkin. She would have fallen if she hadn't caught hold of his waist. He twisted and knocked her away. Bunny pointed her gun in the air and let out an incoherent shriek. Then she fired her gun three times into the concrete ceiling, and she was almost knocked off her roller-blades by the weapon's recoil. The gunshots were deafening in that hard, echoey space, and dust drifted down from the holes in the ceiling. Everyone stood frozen. Bunny was breathing hard, terrified and ecstatic over what she'd done.

Somewhere nearby, some microphone out on a street would be transmitting that sound to WatchWorld Control. It would be isolated, filtered and analyzed. They would be able to identify the caliber, perhaps even the model of the weapon. And if more than one mike had picked up the sound, they would be able to quickly triangulate, and nail down the location. Seconds from now, a police jump squad would be skidding out into the streets, headed this way.

"Bunny . . . honey . . . pet," Punkin said softly, reaching out to her. "You'd . . . you'd best give me the gun."

She looked at him in hurt surprise and shook her head. He nodded, raised his eyebrows and stretched out his hand. After a moment's hesitation, she reluctantly handed over the gun.

"The bloody caterpillar, now!" he said through gritted teeth, as he pocketed her gun and aimed his own weapon at Manikin's head.

She didn't react immediately, taking the blonde wig from the seat first, and stuffing it into the pocket of her mac. She wrenched the belt tighter around her waist, and reached into the black plastic bag that also lay on the seat. Then she handed over the large cuddly toy. The stuffed, multi-legged creature was over a meter long, and was heavier than it looked. That was because of the wide rubber tube shoved down its body, filled with hundreds of notes in high denominations. Punkin grabbed the toy, gave a grimacing smile, and waved Bunny into the van. FX snatched his console out of the back just before Bunny slammed the sliding door shut. Punkin rolled around the front of the van and got in behind the wheel. He started the engine, over-revved it, spun the boxy vehicle around and headed for the ramp. FX was impressed. It seemed Punkin was well able to drive while wearing roller-blades. Not bad for a guy who was still just a kid. He probably did a lot of joy-riding.

Manikin was already striding towards the stairwell that led up into the office building beside the car park. Going out the front, onto the street, would be a really dumb move about now. They'd have to find another way out. The police would be here in minutes—she could hear the sirens in the distance, getting steadily closer.

"Back to square one," FX said as he caught up with her. "Should have known they were going to reese us. Bloody trolls."

"We had to take the chance," she replied. "We've only got a few days before Move-Easy comes looking for us to make our next payment. I just never thought those clatterheads would be thick enough to bring guns. They probably won't get a hundred meters down the street."

Her phone beeped and she took it out of her pocket, looking at the screen.

"I dunno," FX grunted. "They've managed to stay free so far. Must be blessed with some of that supernatural good luck reserved for fearless idiots."

"Yeah, well, *we're* not, obviously," Manikin said as she pushed open the door to the stairwell. She held up her phone so that he could see the screen. It was a spam email, offering excellent deals on a new drug that treated fungal infections. The email would have been received by hundreds of thousands of people, but only those who worked for the gangster known as Move-Easy would recognize the summons for what it was. She gave her brother a bitter grin. "Looks like he's calling us in."

"Jeez, we're just not getting any breaks, are we?"

"Well, I did manage to pinch Punkin's wallet when I bumped

into him," Manikin replied, smiling as she held up a fold of leather.

"Not bad." FX smirked. "But wait'll you see what I'm going to do to his MyFace page. You'd be amazed what you can do with imaging software and a few pictures of farm animals . . ."

CHAPTER 4

THE PEEPER

NIMMO HAD NEVER BEEN TRACKED by a Safe-Guard—he was too young to be listed on the citizens' register—but he had heard from enough people who had to know what it was like. Right now, right next door, Brundle was expected to go about whatever he had been doing as if the Safe-Guard wasn't there. Every action he took, every little movement or decision he made would be recorded by the stranger in his home. Any radio station he listened to, any television program he watched, anything he ate or drank or smoked, any product he used, anyone he spoke to on the phone or contacted online, any website he visited, anything he said out loud or wrote down would be studied by the Safe-Guard and its supervisors in Control. And it would all be analyzed in great detail by the massive surveillance system that was WatchWorld.

If Brundle wanted to go to the toilet, the peeper had the authority to stand there and watch him doing his business. Once a Safe-Guard was assigned to you, they could observe you until your time was up and then they moved on.

If you refused to let them into your home, you could face a 'Life Audit.' And nobody wanted that. Nimmo listened to Brundle moving about in the lab. It must have grated at the scientist's nerves to be followed around like that—he was reluctant to talk about his work, and only put up with Nimmo being in the lab from time to time because Nimmo was even more secretive than he was.

Having a Safe-Guard next door had put Nimmo on edge, and he couldn't stay still for long. Feeling an urge to get some fresh air, he stood up and opened his front door, stepping out into the hallway and closing it behind him. His apartment was at the end of the corridor, near the door that opened onto the stairs leading to the roof. Opening this door, he started up the steps and then slowed and stopped. His head was just level with the top of the stairs, and he could see the thin line of daylight under the door leading out onto the roof. A shadow passed across the sliver of light. Someone was on the roof.

There was a way on and off the roof without coming through the building. Nimmo had made sure of this before moving into the apartment. You risked being spotted from the street, but whoever was up there now had not come past his door—he was sure of that. So it had to be someone who was trying to get in without being seen. The door at the top of the steps was solid, but would be no obstacle to anyone who was good with locks . . . or a team of coppers equipped with a battering ram. Nimmo made his way slowly down the steps and back to his apartment. He'd moved to this building to avoid being noticed. Now, all of a sudden, everyone was taking an interest in the place.

Closing the door of his apartment, he wondered about the intruder on the roof. Nimmo had enemies, but he was pretty sure none of them knew where he lived. He was very careful about that. Did the intruder know there was a peeper here? Probably. Were they interested in Brundle too? Nimmo would prefer it if they were. It could just be some burglar trying his luck. But if it *was* Nimmo they were coming for, he could make for the front door, go out one of the two windows in the apartment, or fight it out here if he had to. But he hated fighting if he didn't need to. He should leave now, while the Safe-Guard was here, before the intruder came down.

The decision was barely made when he heard Brundle's lab door open. Nobody spoke, but Nimmo could make out the Safe-Guard's footsteps heading down the hall. Brundle had got off lightly—the peeper had stayed less than an hour. The lab door closed and locked. Less than a minute later, Nimmo detected the slightest sound of feet in the hallway. He was impressed. He had not heard the intruder come down the squeaky stairs from the roof. There was a knock on Brundle's door. Nimmo walked across to the adjoining wall in the apartment. His blue eyes were expressionless as he held his head close to the beige emulsion surface.

Both voices were muffled by the wall, but Nimmo could detect the emotions. The visitor was quiet and calm, Brundle louder and distressed. Nimmo heard a question being asked, and Brundle replied aggressively. There was the scrape of a hard object being slid along a table top and Brundle let out a grunt of effort, as if he was swinging something at his visitor. There were only two sounds immediately after that: a short gasp of pain from Brundle, and the unmistakable, dull thud of a body hitting the floor. Then there was silence. Nimmo leaned harder against the wall, his lips pressed together in a thin line. Don't get involved, he told himself. This is none of your business. Don't draw attention to yourself.

His conviction held for about another minute. But then he was swinging open his front door. The door to the lab was standing open. Watson Brundle was lying on his front on the floor just inside. He was deathly still, his head turned to the side; his eyes were half open and vacant, unblinking. Nimmo checked the man's neck for a pulse and then swore under his breath, gritting his teeth and looking up and down the corridor. Darting towards the stairs leading to the roof, he bounded up them, pushed open the door and jumped out. There was no one out there. Either the murderer was blindingly fast, or they had gone out another way. Nimmo trotted around the parapet encircling the roof, looking down in every direction, trying to spot Brundle's attacker, but saw no sign of them.

Perhaps the murderer was playing it cool, taking their time leaving the building. Nimmo raced back down the steps and along the corridor to the main stairwell. He didn't know what the attacker looked like, but if he found them, he'd see *something* about them that would give them away, he was sure of it.

Descending the steps three at a time, he looked along the fifth-floor corridor and then continued on down. There was no one in any of the hallways, and he didn't come across a single soul on the stairs. This wasn't surprising, seeing as a Safe-Guard had passed through only a little while ago. People would be staying out of the way.

"Jesus, who is this guy?" Nimmo muttered to himself as he hurried down the last flight of stairs. "The pissin' roadrunner?"

He wasn't used to being outrun so easily. How could this scrote have disappeared so quickly? Nimmo was steaming over this as he ran through the lobby to the front door, throwing it open to find himself staring straight into the tinted visor that covered the face of the Safe-Guard.

The figure in front of Nimmo was only a little taller than him, but seemed much bigger. Its head was covered by a graphite-colored helmet with a long smoked-glass visor, behind which Nimmo could just make out a mask of lenses and sensors. The helmet was mounted on a sturdy shoulder harness, able to swivel right and left, to save the guard's neck from carrying the weight of all the apparatus. The only marking on the helmet was the WatchWorld logo on the front, and the square white digits of the Safe-Guard's identification number—L489I—on the sides. The logo was made up of two silver, stylized hands on a black background, encircling a red sphere, forming the image of an eye. There were vents in the sides, allowing the figure to hear, but also to detect sounds and signals inaudible to the human ear.

Its height was exaggerated by the length of the visor, and by the long blue-gray cloak, the seams marked in lighter gray in vertical lines. The cloak hid the Safe-Guard's arms and covered its legs down as far as its ankles. There were epaulettes on the shoulders of the harness, also bearing its ID in steel numbers, and a WatchWorld badge on the left breast. But otherwise the cloak had little in the way of features. The Safe-Guards were not meant to be eye-catching. It was their job to see others.

Nimmo had seconds to think. Bursting through a door, breathing fast and looking like you're going somewhere in a rush was the kind of thing that got noticed. Doing it not long after a death on the top floor of the building—a death that would be discovered before long, even if he didn't report it—would set alarm bells ringing in WatchWorld Control. Best to get it all out in the open. Or a version of it, anyway.

"Muh boss is dead!" Nimmo panted, letting his face go slack and his eyes go dull. He let his lip hang as he spoke, giving himself a strong North London accent and slurring his words slightly. "I fink someone's muuuurdered 'im. You got 'o get help!"

The Safe-Guard regarded him for a moment, and Nimmo had to remind himself that there was a human under all that get-up. The peepers were designed to be anonymous, asexual, impersonal. The less human they looked, the more people could think of them as a walking camera, rather than a nosy public official. There was a pause as the figure stood still and Nimmo knew it was waiting for instructions. Safe-Guards could not communicate with the public without permission from their supervisors.

"What is your name?" it asked at last. The voice was electronically modulated. All Safe-Guards had similar voices, to remove their individuality.

"Charles U. Farley," Nimmo replied without hesitation. He had been trained to beat the Safe-Guard's rudimentary lie detectors.

"Who is dead, Charles, and where did the incident take place?" the Safe-Guard inquired.

"My boss, Watson Brundle. I live next door to his place, righ'—you were just there, but I wusn't in the lab. Look, aren't you gonna to go up there? Ah'm telling yaw, he's *dead*. It's only just 'appened. The one who did it must still be nearby!"

"What age are you, Charles?"

"I'm fifteen. Look—"

"You say you live with Watson Brundle? You are not listed as a dependent."

Nimmo sighed and shook his head.

"I . . . I was on the street—homeless, awright?" This was a story Nimmo and Brundle had agreed on. Nimmo paid his landlord for the cover, and did the odd errand for the scientist. Given Nimmo's line of work, Brundle had discovered he could be all kinds of useful. "'E give me a break, took me in. He don't like goin' aht-side much, so he let me work as an assistant in his lab. I got him stuff that he needed from the shops an' that. You're going up there, right? That scrote's gettin' away!"

The Safe-Guard paused for another few seconds, listening to its handlers.

"I have another assignment," it said, and Nimmo could have sworn he heard a reluctance in the impersonal voice. "A police unit will be sent to investigate. You may go back inside, but do not go to the sixth floor or interfere with the crime scene in any way, or allow anyone else to do so."

"How long will they take to get 'ere, the police?" Nimmo demanded.

"They will be here as soon as possible. Thank you for your cooperation, Mister Farley."

That appeared to be the end of the discussion. The Safe-Guard turned around and walked away. Nimmo stared after it, trying to hide the bitterness he felt. He had taken a huge risk, standing in front of this thing, allowing himself to be recorded in order to report this murder, and the bloody drone wasn't even going to bother heading up to have a look at what had happened.

He strode back inside and ran up the stairs. They were sending someone to investigate. Nimmo knew what that meant. Ever since the WatchWorld system had been brought in nearly ten years ago, the number of police on the street had been steadily cut until it was fraction of what it had been. Nowadays, the government relied on surveillance to deal with crime. There were thousands of Safe-Guards on the streets now, but hardly any police officers, hardly any detectives to investigate serious crimes. That unit could take hours to get here, and even then, the investigation might never get off the ground.

Nimmo had chosen to live in this part of town for a reason. It was poor and run-down, with fewer cameras and surveillance towers than the more affluent areas. It was the type of area where there was so much trouble the police didn't bother with the minor stuff. As long as the crime stayed in this area, they paid it little attention. And if something big happened, they came in hard, with Serious Crime Squad officers, riot police, or the heavily armed jump squads. It was the kind of place where you could keep a low profile, if you were careful to stay out of trouble.

A single murder in a dodgy tenement wouldn't score very high on their priorities. Brundle's case might get some attention because he owned the building and had that weird lab of his, but there were too few detectives, and too many other, more important cases.

Charles U. Farley was one of Nimmo's identities, one he might now have to dump after the police interview. The character was designed to explain his nomadic life, while remaining enough of a nonentity to avoid the interest of the police, or anyone else for that matter. He was particularly careful when entering or leaving his home, regularly changing his appearance and using hats, sunglasses or scarves to casually conceal his face. Apart from Brundle, hardly anyone who knew Nimmo knew where he lived.

Farley was just one more uneducated, unmotivated and unremarkable drop-out who'd get put on the register as soon as he turned sixteen. Nimmo had clothes, possessions and ID to go with the identity, just as he had for his others. Each identity took a lot of time to prepare and establish, and he hated having to give one up. But that was what they were for.

Nimmo stood in the door of Brundle's laboratory, gazing down at the dead scientist. He had two options. As the last person, except for the Safe-Guard, to see Brundle alive, he'd be the focus of the police investigation. He should get out now, and never come back. But if he ran, it would make him look guilty. They had recorded his face and his voice. That was more than enough information to track him down, unless he left the country completely—assuming he could. No, he'd have to stay here and ride this out.

And if he *was* the chief suspect, the sooner they had another suspect, the better. Nimmo wasn't the type to sit around waiting for others to decide his future. He moved into the lab, pulling on a pair of latex gloves and taking a few sealable plastic bags from a drawer. As he walked past one of the desks, the stupid pug dog toy started barking again. Nimmo swore at it, but left it on—the less he interfered with things the better. Taking a look around the room, he took a deep breath and went back to the body.

He took photos with the camera on his phone—from as many different angles as he could. He could find no sign of a wound, or blood, or even a recent bruise. He didn't want to move the body too much, but there was no obvious sign of the cause of death. He checked Brundle's eyes and the inside of his mouth. He wiped down the blade of a letter-opener and used it to clean under the corpse's fingernails, putting his findings into a plastic bag. He checked the color of the skin under the fingernails, and photographed the tips of the index finger and thumb of each hand with his phone, to record the fingerprints.

Looking at his watch, he tried to guess how long he might have before the police got here, but there was no telling. He plucked a few hairs from Brundle's scalp and put those in a bag. He carried on moving around the body, gathering as much information as he could for another five minutes and then he decided he'd pushed his luck far enough.

He was turning to leave when he spotted the box that Brundle had asked him to hide. It lay undisturbed, just where he had left it. Nimmo felt a pang of guilt, disappointed that, in his last contact with this man, he had played such a selfish trick.

"I'm sorry," he said softly.

Careful not to leave a trace of his action, he slid the leather case out and took it with him. Brundle had wanted it kept safe, and he'd been scared the peeper would find it. Was it the reason he'd been killed?

Wrapping the case and the evidence in two plastic bags, Nimmo checked the time again and went up to the roof. A hacker mate of his provided him with updates of the movements of surveillance satellites—he always preferred to move around in the blind spots. The sky was a clear blue; there was no sign of surveillance aircraft, or drones either. He taped the packages into the top of a ventilation duct that jutted up at one corner of the roof.

He came back down into the corridor, went into his flat and looked quickly around to make sure there was nothing in sight that would draw attention to his real life. But he was always careful about this, and it all seemed fine.

Then he descended to the fifth floor, where he sat on the stairs and waited for the police. As he waited, he checked his emails on his phone. He had one email address that rarely received anything but spam. He opened them all, and came upon one that was advertising excellent deals on a new drug that treated fungal infections. It seemed Move-Easy had a job for him.

CHAPTER 5

A TOUCHY SUBJECT

LIKE MANY IN THE CRIMINAL WORLD, Scope worked from late in the day until late in the morning. This was not because she was a career criminal herself. She might have been resigned to taking part in the business side of crime, but at least she didn't commit any crimes *against people*—or against civvies, normal people, anyway. For her, it was an important distinction. She did work criminal hours, however, because everyone she worked with did too.

It was nine o'clock in the evening, and she was just beginning work. She was sitting at her desk in a small underground lab, with a magnifying glass hooked over the left lens of her glasses. Scope did not need to close her right eye to see clearly through the magnifying glass, because she was blind in her right eye. There was a little light over the lens of the glass, and she was using it to stare at the rounded end of the piece of gelatin in her hand. It was roughly the size of her thumb, and it had a fingerprint molded into the end of it.

The fingerprint was a man's—some hit man who had tried to shoot her boss. Her boss was an extremely powerful gangster known as Move-Easy. She had taken the fingerprint off a glass that the hit man had touched. What that man would never know was that this glass had been stolen and delivered here to her lab. And then Scope had used a process involving superglue, a digital camera, some photo-editing software, a transparency sheet and a cheap photosensitive printed circuit board to mold his fingerprint onto this piece of gelatin.

Now she would give the lump of gel to her boss, and his men would use it to leave the hit man's fingerprints at a crime scene. This and a few other bits of manufactured evidence would be enough to send him to prison for twenty or thirty years. It was not work that Scope liked doing, but she was good at it, and as long as she did it, her family stayed safe.

"What you do is weird," a voice commented from behind her.

"Are you wearing overalls?" she asked, without looking up.

She knew he wasn't, because she hadn't heard him come in. Scope insisted that everybody entering her lab wear white disposable overalls, and they rustled when you walked.

She sighed, switched off the little light, and lifted the magnifying glass off her spectacles. She took the glasses off, rubbed the bridge of her nose, and then looked at the teenage boy who was addressing her. He had parted the clear plastic curtains that blocked the space between her workspace and the door to the corridor, and was leaning into her pristine workspace. This breach of her rules annoyed her, but he knew that and was doing it anyway.

Tanker was older than her, but they were actually very alike in looks—people commented on it all the time. He was only slightly taller than her; they both had their hair in shoulder-length corn-rows; there were the same well-defined cheekbones, triangular faces, sticky-out ears and lean frames. But while Tanker was proper black, Scope was albino black—paler in every way. Tanker often joked that they were a positive and negative of the same picture, yin and yang. Her skin was a creamy white, her hair was blonde, and her eyes were hazel. Many of the people who lived in the Void and didn't go out a lot were paler than they were supposed to be, but Scope was the only one who looked like she was born to a life underground. It was as if someone had taken an African baby and raised her in a cave.

She only felt that way sometimes, but they were tough times. As a self-confessed nerd, she was a social outcast in the world of crime. As an albino, her appearance cemented her inability to fit in.

Her finger pointed at him like a weapon.

"I just wanted to tell you that—" he began.

She cocked her thumb like the hammer on a gun and pointed again. He sighed and pulled his head back behind the curtains.

"All I ask is that you don't contaminate my space," she called over to him. "And you, my friend, are crawling with contaminants. Why do you always have to push it?"

"Because I like winding you up," Tanker said from behind

the curtain. "And when my own business is slow, I like pokin' me nose into other people's. Boss has got all paranoid again, and shut down my web connection. He wants you, by the way. That's what I came to tell you. He's askin' for his 'Little Brain.'"

Scope sighed again, placed the piece of gelatin carefully in a sealed container, and pulled off her latex gloves as she walked through the curtains. She got out of her own overalls, picked up her toolbox and followed Tanker out of the lab. He was Move-Easy's best hacker, but when it came to chemistry, biology—or anything to do with forensics—Scope was called in. Before joining Move-Easy's 'staff,' she would never have guessed how much chemistry and biology were involved in running a criminal empire. The applications for forensics were a little more obvious.

She spent most of her time here, in Move-Easy's Void. A Void was a speakeasy, any place hidden away from the prying eyes of London's WatchWorld system. It was a place free of surveillance—or at least, surveillance by the Safe-Guards and the police. This one was the largest in London, situated beneath Ratched Hospital, right in the city center. Voids were typically run by criminal organizations, though there were a few hippy communes and artists' refuges around too, like the one where Scope had grown up. None of them were as secure as this one. But then, they didn't run major counterfeit operations either. The rooms she walked past contained people working on producing fake IDs, or hacking firewalls, or running identity theft scams, or online gambling or black market operations. One room was being used to plan a bank robbery. In another part of the complex, men and women with intense eyes gambled their money away in an illegal casino.

As Scope and Tanker walked down the concrete-walled hallway, the boy handed her a 'backscatter' x-ray image printed on an A4 sheet of paper.

"He wants to know what that is," Tanker said, pointing at part of the image.

Scope frowned, puzzled by what she was seeing but not in the least bit surprised. She'd seen all sorts of bizarre things since she'd started working here. The main object was caterpillar-shaped, filled with rectangular shapes. There was a harder, clearer box visible near the mouth end. This was what Tanker was pointing at. The image was still holding her attention as she followed Tanker through a doorway.

"Ah, there's my Little Brain!" an East End accent bellowed. "Come 'ere, my pet, and grace us wiv yor luminescence!"

Move-Easy was orange. If you valued your life, you didn't mention it in his presence. It was a result of spending time on a sun-bed nearly every day. Since establishing himself as one of the most powerful gangsters in London, he had become increasingly paranoid about surveillance, and had sought permanent refuge underground. He had been living underground, without emerging into daylight, for seven years. After the first year, he became concerned about how this lack of sunlight might affect his health, and his looks, so he'd had a sun-bed installed in his quarters. Hence the orange skin. It was a touchy subject with him. The last guy to crack an Oompa-Loompa joke in Move-Easy's presence was now sleeping with the fishes.

The audience chamber, as Move-Easy called it, was a room about twelve meters square. It looked like an interior decorator's dream from the nineteen-seventies: all maroon, white, orange and brown, with geometric-patterned wallpaper, ornate gold lamps and paintings that would once have been considered avant-garde, but now looked hopelessly out-dated. A cinema screen was built into one wall, with a state-of-the-art sound system, and there was a bar in one corner. A snooker table was visible through one doorway, a second door was closed, and the third door admitted staff and guests. Scope came through this door to find that Move-Easy had visitors.

There was a circular sunken area in the floor, its circumference made up of couches. A young man and woman sat on one couch with their backs to Scope. When they turned to look up at her, she recognized Punkin and Bunny. She'd seen them enough times before to wonder why two small-time chancers were being given an audience with the boss. They weren't members of his organization, and rarely had anything of real worth to sell. They were looking pretty pleased with themselves now.

There was a round, smoked-glass table in the middle of the circle. On the table sat a cuddly caterpillar with a green body, a large red head and multi-colored legs. That was new.

"Got yor tools?" Move-Easy asked, gesturing her towards him.

Scope nodded. She descended the three steps to the sunken floor and sat down beside her boss, opening the toolbox on the floor. Move-Easy was sitting on the couch opposite Punkin and Bunny. He had a bulbous, brutish face, a smutty grin and chilly blue eyes. His thinning, dyed black hair was slicked back in a widow's peak from his orange brow. He was wearing an expensive white shirt and navy suit trousers, his wrists and fingers adorned with heavy gold bracelets and rings. A gold chain hung down over the shirt, the gray hairs of his orange chest sticking in a tuft over the open collar at the front. He made her skin crawl, and there were times that he terrified her, but she knew he liked her. As he often said, she was worth her weight in diamonds.

"These two 'ave brought us a present, 'aven't you, guys?" he said, not expecting an answer to his question. "Robbed a cash courier, comin' from another Void. Some poor soul's lost his profits for the week. Still, their loss is our gain, eh? Have to say, I'm impressed, Punkin. Didn't think you had the brains to pull off a job like that, out among all the eyeballs, and get away with it. But my boys tell me you wasn't followed or nuffink. So . . . had some 'elp, didya?"

"It was all us, Mister Easy," Punkin replied casually, throwing a smug smile at Bunny. "What can we say? We got the moves, y'know?"

"You got the moves, eh?" the boss said thoughtfully, working his jaw. "Thing is, my lovelies, you was scanned when you came down, and we found a piece of electronics on you that you didn't declare. Only reason you're sittin' here now is that it's *not transmittin' any signals.*"

Punkin and Bunny looked nervously at each other. Everyone knew you got scanned when you came into Move-Easy's place. It was a standard precaution in any Void, but he ran his place like airport customs. You had a better chance of getting on a plane with a machine-gun than you had of slipping an electronic device into his Void without him knowing. And the penalties for trying could be ugly and painful. Scope could tell from their expressions that they didn't know what he was talking about.

"I'm tellin' you, Mister Easy, we don't know nothin' about—"

"Obviously," the gangster growled, cutting him off. "You 'aven't the balls. But neither of you has more brains than a bird, so I'm assumin' you didn't check to see if the cash had been rigged before bringin' it here. Or did you just not *want* to check, in case you blew it? Was you just tryin' your luck instead?"

They exchanged glances again.

"Was that wrong?" Bunny asked innocently.

"Christ, but you're a proper pair o' wazzocks." Move-Easy sighed. "Scope 'ere is goin' to 'ave a look wiv her sneaky eye, and tell us what you've brought into my 'ome."

Scope was no longer paying any attention to the people in the room. She had work to do, and went at it with her usual fixed intensity. She had taken her inspection camera from her toolbox. This was a keyhole camera on a long flexible tube. She could manipulate the direction of the tube with her index finger, using the joystick positioned like a trigger on the handle. The front of the tube had a tiny camera, connected to a small screen at the on top of the handle. Laying the x-ray printout down in front of her, she switched the inspection camera on, took the lens end of the tube and inserted it into the mouth of the cuddly caterpillar. Then, keeping her eye on the screen, she slid the lens end further in.

The image on the screen showed her what was inside the soft

toy. She knew there was a tube filled with money, but that wasn't what she was interested in. The camera was equipped with an ultrasound scanner. She switched it on and the screen filled with blue-white see-through forms against a dark background. Her attention was on the hard-edged shape near the mouth that stood out clearer than anything else on the image.

"It's a dye pack, sitting at the top of the money tube," she said to Move-Easy. "Doesn't look like there's a transmitter, but I'd have to take it out to be sure. I'd say the trigger is a light sensor. If you'd tried to take it out of the toy, the lights in here would have set it off. But I can deactivate the mechanism with a magnet."

Taking a small magnet from her toolbox, she slid her hand into the caterpillar's mouth and pressed it against the wad of money she could see on her screen. Then she pulled out the bound bundle of notes and held it up in front of Punkin and Bunny:

"You brought a dye pack in here. Banks use them to foil armed robberies. If you'd tried to take out the money, the first wad of cash you'd pull out would be this one. It's hollowed out. Inside, there's a device that, when exposed to the light, would spray a bright pink aerosol dye all over you, while burning at two hundred degrees Celsius."

She taped the magnet to the wad of money and tossed it into her toolbox.

"An' if I got painted, or if I even had to repaint this place 'cos of you monkeys . . ." Move-Easy sniffed as he pulled the meter-long rubber tube of cash out of the caterpillar's mouth, "*you'd* be the ones swallowing *this*."

The two small-time crooks went pale, but Move-Easy had already thrown the tube to Tanker, who took it from the room. The cash would be checked, sorted, counted and absorbed into the business. There had to be thousands of pounds there, but the gangster had hardly given it a second glance.

"Now," the orange-skinned boss said, lounging back on the couch, as Scope packed up her toolbox and stood up, "you've bought yourselves a few minutes of my time. What exactly is you two looking for, in return for this charmin' act of goodwill?"

"We'd like to join your organization, Mister Easy," Punkin said, leaning forward. "We wanna move up; we're done just bein' rat-runners. I know we'd have to prove ourselves, but we've got a line on a big score. I got myself an implant the other day, at a clinic in Soho. It's an underground operation—the surgeons there only deal in cash . . ."

He paused, and glanced up at Scope. Move-Easy looked up at her and tilted his head towards the door. She took the hint and headed out of the room. As she was leaving, she heard her boss say:

"And you want to knock it over, right?"

"The money's there for the stealin', Mister Easy. All we need is . . ."

Scope couldn't hear any more without pausing beyond the door, and she had learned long ago not to be curious about these things. Move-Easy was as paranoid about his own people as he was about the police. As he said himself, "You can never trust criminals."

CHAPTER 6

THE CREW

ONE OF THE KEYS TO MOVE-EASY'S SUCCESS, reflecting the length of time his Void had survived undiscovered, was the confounding means of getting inside. Unless you were part of his inner circle, you didn't get in without being invited. Most of the day-to-day business was done by his people on the outside, whom the boss monitored closely. If you did get invited in—and it was unwise to refuse such an invitation—you entered the maintenance tunnels beneath the massive hospital by a door chosen randomly on the day. You were given blacked-out contact lenses that effectively acted as a blindfold. An actual blindfold would have looked suspicious if you ran into any hospital staff or other civvies who might happen to be in the tunnels at the time.

You were then led by a member of the gang to one of the

steel- and lead-lined doors that opened into the nest of old war-time bomb-shelter corridors that formed the core of his Void. Each time you visited, you were taken in through a different door. Each of these doors was disguised in a different way, and their use was also dictated at random. Even the boss's own people had to change their routes constantly. The WatchWorld computers loved patterns. The hospital complex was monitored twenty-four hours a day, and every member of the hospital staff and every frequent visitor was on file. Anyone else seen going in or out of the hospital on a regular basis would eventually attract suspicion. Move-Easy had built a career on avoiding suspicion.

Manikin was still wearing her mac over black jeans, but had changed to a bobbed red wig. FX was in his usual combats, hoodie and trainers. Blinking over the contact lenses that blinded him, he felt someone take his console bag from him at the security checkpoint, but didn't protest. It would be held until he was leaving. He suspected they'd try and have a look through the console, but was quite certain even Tanker would not be able to break the encryption that protected its contents. There were hackers in Britain who were better than FX, but he knew most of their names, and none of them worked for Move-Easy. It was more his physical safety that concerned him. These gangsters scared him, and whenever he and Manikin came here, he let her do the talking, because he had a habit of mouthing off when he was nervous. Around someone like Move-Easy, that could be a dangerous habit.

When they got the nudge, Manikin and FX plucked out their blacked-out contacts and handed them to the man who had guided them in. They found themselves standing in the gang-ster's audience chamber. He was sitting in the circle of couches, beaming up at them. There was another kid there, about Mani-kin's age, with a slightly blank bony face, but intelligent eyes, and a gray woolen hat, which covered hair that was cut close to his scalp. Dressed in trainers, jeans, T-shirt and a weathered black leather jacket, he was tall and looked impressively fit. He did not seem at all nervous in Move-Easy's presence—unusual for someone his age.

"Manikin, FX, meet Nimmo," Move-Easy said, waving them over. "I'm puttin' a crew togevver for a new job, and you're it."

The three nodded to each other, but said nothing. FX and Manikin sat down on the couch next to Nimmo and waited. There was one other man in the room, standing by the bar, mak-ing himself a Martini. He was an Oriental guy with an expensive hairstyle, a sharp light-gray suit with a cravat instead of a tie, and a set of wireless earphones in his ears. The dapper man had the dead black eyes of a shark. This man's name was Coda, and he was the most dangerous of Move-Easy's enforcers. And he was the only one who didn't wear a piercing in his eyebrow—the means by which the boss monitored his people. Nor did he ever carry anything that could be recognized as a weapon. Rumor had it that Coda only ever killed with his bare hands, or with what-ever happened to be lying around. FX eyed the man anxiously. He had heard that Coda had once tortured and killed someone using only a pair of spectacles. FX could only guess how.

Move-Easy stared at the three kids for a minute, with a fatherly smile that didn't reach his eyes. He had been one of the first gangsters to start using specially trained teenagers for some of his dirty work, and had several on his payroll. The three in front of him were freelancers, but that didn't make much difference. If you lived in London and Move-Easy wanted you to take on a job, you took it. As you were underage, it was easier for you to operate within the WatchWorld system. The system could watch you, but it was forbidden to assign a Safe-Guard to follow you until you were sixteen, and even then there were limits to what they could watch until you were eighteen.

That was why Move-Easy used kids on a lot of his jobs.

"You owe me money," he said to Manikin and FX. "This job will wipe the debt clean. That'll be your payment. Nimmo, you'll be paid on your usual terms. You're all good little players, and as of now, you've got one very simple task. I want you to find this box."

He lifted a remote, pressed the touch-screen surface, and an image appeared on the cinema screen. Manikin, who was discreetly watching Nimmo, trying to measure him up, noticed the slightest change of expression in his eyes as he saw the picture. He was hiding something. The image was of a tall, long-limbed man with a mess of black hair and protruding features. The photo had been taken at night at the back of a tall building, with wheelie bins in the background. It was monotone, slightly blurred and a bit grainy, probably taken with a night-vision camera. But they could make out a slim black box in the man's left hand. It was roughly the size of the kind of presentation box used to hold a necklace.

"So what's in it?" Manikin asked.

"Ten credit cards," Move-Easy replied. "Blue and gold in color—you don't need any more details. Either they'll be in the box or not. The geezer in the picture is the previous owner. Name's Watson Brundle, an' he's dead. He was a civvie. A scientist, engineer or summink—had some private project going, workin' on RFIDs and the like."

"How'd he die?" Nimmo asked.

"You don't care," Move-Easy assured him. "What you care about is that box. We know it was in his lab yesterday, because we saw 'im go in with it, and 'e didn't come out again before 'e died, which was early this evenin'. Bit of a hermit, he was. The old bill went in about an hour after 'e died, and after they were gone, I sent a couple of boys in to fetch it. It wasn't there. If the cops've got it, I'll find out through my people. But I don't think they have. There was some kid who lived up on the same floor as Brundle, 'parently did some work for 'im. We've not had a good look at 'is face yet, but he's the law-abidin' type. Went runnin' right up to a peeper when the murder 'appened. 'E was questioned by the bill today, but we can't find 'im now. We will. That's not your job either."

He touched his remote again, and a new picture appeared on the screen. This one showed a teenage girl, possibly about fifteen or sixteen. She was wearing a blue, gray and white school uniform. The picture looked as if it was a still from a surveillance camera in a school corridor. Tanker had probably hacked in and lifted it from the school's files. The girl's left hand was running through her dark hair, revealing that her sallow-skinned face was tainted by a port-wine birthmark that went from above her left eye, across her cheek, almost to her ear. Manikin was sure that the girl normally covered as much of that mark as possible with her hair. It spoiled what was otherwise quite a pretty face. With hips like that, she wasn't exactly model material, but there was something very attractive about her. She had a spirited expression, and the posture of her small figure suggested a confident personality.

"Veronica Brundle, the boffin's daughter," Move-Easy announced. "The person he trusted most in the world. He was mad about 'er, but separated from the mother. The girl lives with the mother. She visited 'er dad last night. The handbag she had with 'er could have held the case, but we didn't 'ave anyone on the buildin' when she left—there was a Safe-Guard on the street by then—so she could have walked off with the box in her bag without us knowin'.

"Now, her dad told her about us, so if she'd any sense, she'd have brought us that box by now. But she 'asn't. I want you to suss 'er out, check 'er 'ouse and the school. Is she connected? Is she protected? Does she 'ave the contacts to sell the cards? If she's gonna try an' run, I want to know before she does. There's no guarantee she's got 'em, but I think she's our best bet. Tricky bit is, she lives in a two-floor apartment in the Barbican and goes to a private school."

Manikin rolled her eyes towards the ceiling and FX groaned. The Barbican Estate was a mass of concrete structures containing over two thousand flats, some as part of three massive residential towers. It was a maze, and it was riddled with security cameras. And even though primary and secondary schools could not be observed by the WatchWorld system, they all had their own security measures. Private schools were usually the most paranoid and had higher quality systems.

"I presume these cards are worth a lot of money to someone who can use them," Manikin spoke up. "Would she leave something like that in school?"

"Might, if she didn't want her mum findin' it," Move-Easy told her. "Leave no stone unturned, that's what I say. Tanker will give you all the details we 'ave on the girl. You've got three days to find out for sure whether she 'as it or not."

He glanced up at the well-dressed man standing at the bar, who was leaning there with his eyes closed. With those earphones in his ears, it was impossible to tell if Coda was listening to them or not.

"I don't want to 'ave to send in Coda here, or set any of the boys on 'er and the mother unless there's no other way," Move-Easy said. "Let's keep this quiet and hands-off for now."

"If it's OK with you, I'd like to bring Scope in on this as well," Nimmo said.

Manikin glanced at FX, who shrugged. They both knew Scope and trusted her. She wouldn't get in the way, but they couldn't see what they needed her for out on the street.

"What d'you want her for?" Move-Easy asked, frowning. "You've got all the skills you need right here."

"I don't want to go to all the hassle of doing the job, gettin' my hands on those cards," Nimmo told him, "and then find out they're fakes. That's one of the jobs she does for you, isn't it? She spots counterfeit merchandise. Better she do it on the spot than have us bringin' fake gear back here."

OISÍN McGANN

"Awright, she can go with you. But look after 'er, Nimmo. If summink 'appens to my Little Brain, I'd be most put out. Worth her weight in diamonds, that girl is. She's like a friend's daughter to me. Not a hair on 'er 'ead, boy, y'hear me? Not a hair on 'er 'ead."

"I hear you," Nimmo said. "It'll be the safest hair in London."

The three teenagers were getting to their feet when Move-Easy added to FX and Manikin:

"Oh, last thing. Just so the both of you know, Nimmo's in charge. What 'e says goes."

"What?" Manikin looked at Nimmo and then at the gangster. She was pushing her luck and she knew it. But in their business, you couldn't let yourself be walked all over. "That's not how we work, Mister Easy. We're freelance. Nobody's in charge of us."

"I'm sorry, darlin'." The orange-skinned mob boss leveled his cold blue eyes at her and leaned forward. "My ears are a bit funny these days. Gettin' old, I suppose. Did you say summink?"

Manikin met his gaze for a brief moment, before her nerve failed her. "No. No, sir."

"Didn't think so. Go see Tanker. You've got three days to dig up everything there is to know about this girl and find that box. If she passes it on or sells it before we can get 'old of it, or if I 'ave to send in the boys to deal with it, so things get loud and messy, I'm not gonna be a happy camper. And we don't want me losin' the rag, now do we?"

Nimmo, Manikin and FX all agreed, they didn't want him losing the rag.

CHAPTER 7

DEATH BY MISADVENTURE

FOUR TEENAGERS WANDERING AROUND in the early hours of the morning could attract the wrong kind of attention, so once they'd checked in with Tanker to be briefed, Nimmo, Scope, Manikin and FX decided to stay in the Void for a few hours and grab some shut-eye until sunrise. After a quick look through the information on Veronica Brundle, they stretched out on some cots and slept until after sunrise. Then it was time to go to work.

Nimmo stayed awake, his mind racing as he struggled to think through all the angles. He'd been hired to search for something he already had in his possession. This was Move-Easy he was dealing with. He should hand the bloody box over as soon as he could lay his hands on it. But he was damned if he would. At least, not until he'd figured out what was going on.

The decision gave him some peace and his mind stopped whirling, allowing his thoughts to find some order. He grew drowsy, eager now for sleep. His mind drifted back to his interview with the police officer, back in his small flat next to Brundle's lab.

The man, Dibble, was a detective constable, but he fumbled through the questions like someone who hadn't been in the job very long. As Nimmo had suspected, the police weren't giving a high priority to Brundle's murder.

"So, Charles, you were next door when you heard the noise of a falling body," Dibble muttered.

"Call me Chuck," Nimmo said in an overly nervous voice. "Everyone calls me Chuck."

"OK, Chuck. You say you heard a fight. Scraping, thumping, that kind of thing?"

Nimmo nodded. This was the third time they'd been over this, but Nimmo knew that was standard procedure. Ask things a different way each time, see if the story changes. Dibble's short-fingered hand made notes with a stylus on his web-pad. A pudgy young man, his cheeks were already sinking into jowls, and there were wrinkles around the small black eyes that perched close to each other over a sharp, pointed nose. He used the stylus to scratch an itch under his black hair and looked up at Nimmo again.

"Yeah, and then I went out to check on 'im—Doctor Brundle, I mean," Nimmo said. "And 'e was dead. Or at least, I thought 'e was dead. He was really still. And 'is eyes were open. And 'e never leaves 'is door open."

As Nimmo kept up the dull-eyed character of Chuck U. Far-ley, his mind went around the room, ensuring that nothing Dib-ble could see would make him curious enough to poke about. He had given the place the once-over before the police arrived, but you could never be too careful.

"Right." Dibble made another note. His tone remained unin-terested. "At any point, did he cry out? Cry for help? Did he say anybody's name?"

"Nothin' I could hear," Nimmo said. "I 'eard him let out, like, y'know, a grunt. Like he was in pain? But it was all really quick."

"Right," said Dibble, scratching his scalp again.

Nimmo was beginning to wonder how much longer this would take when the detective's phone rang. Dibble answered it and listened for a minute.

"Yeah?" He sniffed, his eyes darting over to Nimmo. "No. Sure, I'm talking to him now. Charles U. Farley—'Chuck,' he says. No, it's fine. OK. Yeah, I'll see. OK, cheers." He ended the call and slipped his phone into his pocket. Doing the same with his web-pad, he stood up.

"Thanks for your assistance, Chuck. Looks like we've got things all wrapped up on this one."

"So, is that it?" Nimmo asked. He didn't like the detective's tone. "D'you know who did it?"

"It seems Doctor Brundle didn't have quite as dramatic an end as you thought, Chuck," Dibble told him. "The coroner's made an examination of the body, and believes your friend's death was accidental—'misadventure,' they call it. You probably heard him stagger and fall, and mistook it for a fight. It'd explain why you didn't see anyone when you came out. I don't have any more details at the moment, but we're no longer treating this death as suspicious."

The body had been taken away not long after the police arrived, less than an hour ago. There was no way they could have done an autopsy yet. How could they have decided this so quickly? Nimmo couldn't hide his frustration.

"But I *heard* another guy here! There was a fight! Someone was here!"

"Don't worry about it. It's not uncommon for witnesses to make mistakes, or to misinterpret what they hear and see," Dibble assured him. "You get hyped up or upset, and your brain starts twisting the facts to suit what you think has happened. Basic psychology, Chuck. That's why we've got the Safe-Guards now. No more doubts about how things happened."

"Except 'e died after the Safe-Guard left," Nimmo snapped. "Where was it when 'e needed it? It was in there with 'im for ages, and when I went after it and told it the man it had just left was *dead*, it did *nothin'*."

"Just bad luck, lad. What can I say?" Dibble shrugged. "Listen, we don't know what's happening with this building now that Doctor Brundle's dead, but I doubt you'll be able to stay here. Have you got somewhere else to go? You were on the street before he put you up, weren't you? Got any family? We'll need to find you somewhere to live, get you back into school. You're too young for us to leave you on your own like this. I have to go, but someone from social services is on their way over. They'll sort you out, OK?"

"Yeah," Nimmo murmured. "Yeah, sure."

With that, Dibble left. Less than half an hour later, the social worker arrived to find the flat empty. Chuck U. Farley was gone, having cleared out his cupboards and drawers, no doubt taking to the streets again. The social worker shook her head, lamenting another young man dropping out of society.

Still bitter about the complacency of the police, Nimmo was back in Move-Easy's Void again, tired but uncomfortable on the narrow, well-used cot in the small underground room. The others were sound asleep around him. Brundle's building had not been Nimmo's only safe-house, but it suited him and his identity as Farley. Living alone as a fourteen-year-old in a city riddled with surveillance was difficult. Brundle had taken him in, trusted him. As Nimmo lay there, he swore to himself that he'd find out the truth about Watson Brundle's death.

CHAPTER 8

THE RAT-RUNS

IT WAS TIME TO GO TO WORK. Scope was allowed to come and go from the Void as she pleased, but the others had to wear the blacked-out contact lenses again on their way out, and had to be accompanied by one of Move-Easy's apes. Blinded as he was, Nimmo used his other senses. As he always did, he counted his steps as the troll led the four of them out through the hospital maintenance tunnels. He memorized each turn, and took note of the noises and smells around him, the sounds of each door and the types of floor that passed under his feet.

It was an almost unconscious process, and as they came out into a corridor whose sounds he recognized—the boilers for the hospital's heating system were off this corridor—he thought about the bizarre situation he'd found himself in. It was the worst possible time to be teamed up with strangers, people he couldn't trust. And there were few enough that he had ever trusted. He had to get clear of them as soon as he could.

Once out of the tunnels, he and the others removed their blacked-out contact lenses, chewing them up and swallowing them. Manikin headed decisively for an exit that would bring them out into one of the alleys at the back of the hospital complex. Nimmo watched her, wondering if she was going to be a problem. He knew her by reputation—they'd even worked on the same job at one point—though he'd never actually met her.

She was supposed to be smart, quick and able to change her appearance and character with the ease of a seasoned actor. But she was also known for being a hot-head. Nimmo didn't like working with people who were liable to get emotional. She was good-looking, but not beautiful, with an expressive oval face and wide, open features. Her athletic frame moved like a dancer's, but there was a nervous energy about her too.

Nimmo had also heard a lot about FX. At twelve years old, the younger lad was already an adept hacker—his imagination, inventiveness and sheer technical brilliance making up for his lack of experience. FX was less comfortable in the villain's world than his older sister, but he had nerve and a level head, and that was enough to be getting on with.

They were all following Manikin towards the exit. FX was trailing behind, checking his console to see if anybody had been interfering with it. Scope was walking alongside Nimmo. Like the two boys, she carried a small pack on her back, and all four put on shades as soon as they went outside. A baseball cap also covered much of Scope's distinctive blonde cornrows. She was happy to be getting out for a bit, even if she was taking the risk of some peeper or copper asking why she wasn't in school. Her parents hated the education system, the way the government ran things. They'd schooled her at home before she began work for Move-Easy, but it still felt strange being out in the city on a school day. Her job rarely took her outside, she spent little time at home any more, and didn't have many friends, so she often got too wrapped up in her work.

Nimmo was relieved to see Scope wasn't wearing a piercing in her eyebrow.

"You bugged?" he asked her quietly.

"No." She shook her head. "Move-Easy doesn't normally bug any of the kids who work for him. He insists they stay free of illegal electronics—the less the Safe-Guards can find on them, the less reason they have to get in the kids' way. He relies on sheer bloody terror to make sure they do what they're told."

"That fits."

He had known Scope for a couple of years—as long as he'd been working for Move-Easy. She didn't spend much time on the street, but then that wasn't why Nimmo had asked for her. He needed her analytical brain—that incisive eye she brought to all her work. Despite her tender age, she had been outsmarting forgers, con men and the police's forensic scientists for nearly three years, and making it look easy. Nimmo was hoping she could help dig him out of the hole he was in.

"So what's your line?" FX asked, as if he had been reading the older boy's thoughts.

"What do you mean?" Nimmo countered, though he understood well enough.

"Mani does deception, I do tech," FX said. "Scope does analysis. What's your specialty?"

"Avoiding responsibility," Nimmo replied.

Out in the alleyway, Manikin was waiting for the rest of them. It was eight o'clock in the morning. Around them, they could hear the sounds of rush hour. The streets would be filled with people on their way to work. She turned to Scope.

"Is he cool?" she demanded, tilting her head towards Nimmo.

"I trust him," Scope responded. "And he can certainly keep his mouth shut. Nobody knows anything about the cagey sod." She thumped his shoulder. "He's got me out of trouble a couple of times. He was the one who helped us out with that thing that time—you know, with the accountant. Yeah, he's cool."

"Okay . . . we're going back to our place," Manikin said to Nimmo. "Move-Easy doesn't know where it is, none of the seniors do, and we want to keep it that way."

'Seniors' was the term for anyone over sixteen. Anyone who could be followed by a Safe-Guard.

"OK," Nimmo said, pushing the pair of sunglasses up onto the bridge of his nose. "But right now, we're standing around in a bunch in this alley. That's looking for all the wrong kind of attention. We gonna move or what?"

"Yeah," FX grunted, as he pulled up his hood. "Try and keep up."

Manikin took off at a run, her mac streaming out behind her. FX and Scope were on her heels in seconds, following her as she turned a corner and bounded up over a parked van. The alarm went off, but like most alarms, it was ignored. Running along the roof, they jumped over a wall, landing on the top of an oil tank and sliding down its curving side into a small courtyard. Nimmo was close behind them as they crossed the square space, leaping to cling onto a chain-link fence and flipping themselves over it.

This was another reason criminals were turning to kids for some of their work. Not everyone could use the 'rat-runs.' These were the routes through the city that were not covered by normal surveillance. It took speed, agility and nerve to make your way along these routes, to stay clear of all the eyes and ears that kept watch in the city. The rat-runs were ruled by the young, often known by their bosses—and the public at large—as 'rat-runners,' or simply just 'vermin.'

Most of the main streets in London were covered by scan-cams, or 'eyeballs'—cameras that could record normal visuals, or film in infra-red, or backscatter x-ray. These images were ana-lyzed using software that could recognize your face, even the way you walked. Directional microphones could record conversations hundreds of meters away, and put names to voices using speaker identification software. RFID scanners could read the radio fre-quency ID tags on clothes, in phones, cars and many other things that people used every day.

And then there were the Safe-Guards. They could wander at will, enter people's businesses and homes without permission, and they were equipped with rigs that included miniature ver-sions of the technology that could be found on the watch-towers or camera installations. There was no telling when you might cross the path of a peeper while traveling along the rat-runs, but kids benefited from one of the few limits to WatchWorld's surveillance. Unless a minor was engaged in a crime, they could not be stopped or followed by a Safe-Guard. When WatchWorld was introduced into London, even a population petrified by terrorism and crime could not tolerate the idea of their children being followed around by the faceless figures.

So while normal people—the civvies—buckled down, struggling to accept the new limits forced on their lives by this all-pervasive regime, professional criminals set about finding ways to beat the system. The WatchWorld slogan was: "If you've nothing to hide, you've nothing to fear." The problem was, most people had things they wanted to keep quiet about. And any unusual behavior, any attempt to keep your business private, would bring a Safe-Guard to your door.

Those with something serious to hide were more likely to have the skills to keep it hidden.

WatchWorld had a consumer-friendly face too. The city was littered with large screens, one on the corner of nearly every major street junction, with selected, edited feed from the system's cameras. They were interspersed with ads that used myriad ways to catch the eyes of passers-by. The same feed could be found online, and on several television channels. Scenes that were considered newsworthy, interesting, or just entertaining were broadcast to the world.

Manikin set a relentless pace, but they had to stop a couple of times to wait for Scope, who had trouble keeping up. Nimmo stayed with her; she was strong and agile enough, but lacked the stamina of the others, the result of too much time spent indoors.

Together, the four ran through alleyways, apartment blocks, climbed walls, cut under railway bridges and through derelict buildings, jumping over or ducking under obstacles, and timing their runs past the sweeping cameras that watched nearly every street in London.

When they finally reached an abandoned warehouse on Brill Alley, near Canary Wharf, Manikin and FX were tired and out of breath. Scope needed to sit down and rest her shaking legs. She took a surreptitious blast of her inhaler, always self-conscious of the weakness that was her asthma. Nimmo was already breathing normally, taking their surroundings in with interest.

"Shouldn't rush so much," he said as he looked around. "The Safe-Guards can get curious if they see someone breathing too hard. The mikes in the streets are tuned to pick it up too."

"Yeah . . . yeah," Scope panted. "We should . . . should definitely slow . . . slow it down a bit next time."

"Or just breathe quieter," Manikin retorted, pulling out a loose brick beside a very solid-looking steel door to reveal a hidden keypad. "This is us."

CHAPTER 9

LIFE IN THE MOVIES

WIDE ARCHED WINDOWS, secured with sturdy steel bars, were spaced sparsely along the three-story-high, brown-brick walls of the warehouse. It was situated in an industrial district that had been on the up just before the Noughties Recession hit, crime sky-rocketed, and one business after another in the area began to collapse. Now Brill Alley was surrounded by empty buildings, beyond which modern apartment blocks jutted into the sky. Those apartments, bought in better times, now looked out on an ugly, neglected, industrial landscape. This was the place Manikin and FX called home.

FX used his phone to send an encrypted message disarming the security system, before Manikin keyed in a code that unlocked the steel door. Nimmo looked on in approval. Two separate systems. And phoning the signal in meant neither Nimmo nor Scope could guess where the security console was when they went inside. Manikin and her brother took their privacy seriously.

"There's no bugs inside," FX told them. "At least, there's none here any time we leave. You never know when a peeper's gonna walk in, or when WatchWorld might send in one of those rats with a pinhole camera on its back. We sweep the inner rooms for signals every time we get home. I'm serious about the rats, by the way. If you see any of our cats, don't bloody feed them anything. Lazy buggers are supposed to be earning their keep."

All four entered, and Manikin locked the door behind them. They all took off their shades and Nimmo followed the others into a large open space that stretched all the way up to the roof. There were old stage-lights on frames mounted below the ceiling. Looking around, Nimmo saw the remains of sound stages: film sets for a medieval castle, a city street, a submarine's interior, a space station. A camera crane stood in one corner, and one entire end of the room was taken up with lighting stands, tripods and sound booms.

"This was a film studio?" he asked.

"What gave it away?" Manikin snorted, as she carried on across the room to another steel door.

"Their parents tried to restore the place and make it work, back when everything was moving towards using CGI in live-action films," Scope explained to him in a low voice, gesturing for him to follow Manikin. "You know, using computer graphics to do all the sets and stuff? They wanted to use old-fashioned sets and staging. It didn't work out, especially after WatchWorld came online. Their folks died a few years ago. Not sure what happened. FX was barely eight years old, Manikin was ten. They were left the building and some money in the parents' will, and placed in the custody of a guardian. Turned out the guardian was a treacherous, two-faced witch. She took the money and did a runner. They've been living here on their own, avoiding the peepers, ever since."

"Hiding from the cameras in a film studio," Nimmo said, smiling slightly.

"They were bein' raised for a life in the movies," Scope commented. "Turns out everyone else ended up on-screen too, so they stepped out of the light. They dropped out of school . . . right off the grid. FX sorted it so that nobody in the system knows there are two kids living alone in a warehouse. Officially, they don't exist."

Walking through the second door, Nimmo and Scope found themselves in a much smaller room, but still large by the standards of a normal house. This was a workshop, filled with benches, angle-poise lamps, computers and other electronic equipment. Everything from robotic arms to children's gadgets lay in various states of dissection around the room.

"This is my space," FX said, picking up a radio signal scanner and switching it on. "Manikin's is over there. You don't go in hers if you don't want your eyes scratched out."

One screen showed the view over the door they had just come in. Nimmo glanced quickly at the image. FX might like avoiding WatchWorld, but he clearly had no problems doing a spot of peeping with his own cameras. The younger boy pointed at the door his sister was disappearing through. The door slammed shut behind her.

"Sorry, she's not mad about anybody telling her what to do," he said sheepishly, casting his eyes towards Nimmo. "Especially someone she doesn't know."

"I can understand that." Nimmo sniffed. "I don't want to be anyone's boss. But we've a job to do, and I want to get it done without any pissing contests. So let's hope *she* understands that everything I do while I'm with you is about the job."

"She'll be fine," FX assured him, as he began to walk around the room with the scanner. "Probably already working up a play to get us close to the mark. Don't be fooled by the moods. Girl's harder to read than a stone playin' poker." He turned away and muttered under his breath, "Besides, in a pissing contest? She'd win."

"All right, let's get started then," Nimmo declared. "FX, see what you can find out about Veronica online. Scope, is there anything else you know about these credit cards we're supposed to find?"

"No," Scope said. "I don't know any more than you."

"OK, then I want you to find out more about what Brundle was working on. See if he's ever published any of his research. Dig up whatever you can."

"How's that going to help us find the case?"

"It's not—not directly, anyway. I'm thinking self-preservation," Nimmo told her. "This guy, Brundle, got his hands on something Move-Easy seems to think is worth a packet. Brundle's a researcher, right? That's not normally a money-spinner, unless you're with some big firm. So where'd he get these cards? Was he given them? Did he steal them? Did he *make* them? My guess is they're payment for something. If they are, I'm betting it's something that wasn't legal—only reason he'd be paid that way. Probably meant to be anonymous—untraceable. Move-Easy seems pretty sure he was a civvie, so what did he do for this payment? Who did he do it for? That kind of info won't be online, but if we knew what he worked on, it might get us looking in the right direction."

"You think he was mixed up in somethin' naughty?" FX asked.

"A case filled with some weird credit cards? Sound like a normal way of paying someone? And who is it likes to keep big payments a secret?"

"The mob," FX muttered, as Scope nodded. "Damn. D'you think we could be messing with one of Easy's rivals?"

"If we are, wouldn't you like to know?"

"Bloody right. Last thing we need is to run into some psycho hit man looking for the same thing. What are you going to be doing while we're doing that?"

Nimmo looked at his watch. Tanker had given them an encrypted data key with Veronica Brundle's details on it. Nimmo switched on the key's wireless signal and connected to it from a computer sitting on one of the desks. He checked the girl's address, then handed the key to FX.

"The mother works during the day and the girl will be at school. I'm going to break into their flat and look for that box."

"Right. Well . . . good luck with that. Maybe you can wrap this up for us before we even get started. My kind of job. And if her computer's not switched on, crank it up for a few minutes, so I can have a look-see. Want me to knock out the security cameras for you?"

"No, thanks. I should be able to get past them. I need the rest of you to stay here for now—let me scout things out in the real world first, while you do the same online. Get a trace on Veronica's phone—and her mother's—as soon as you can. If they're coming home early, I want to know. Don't want to find out Little Miss Brundle's pulled a sickie by having her open the door while I'm looking under her mattress."

"Do people actually hide stuff under their mattress?" Scope inquired.

"No—at least, nothing I've ever wanted to find."

He told FX his mobile number. FX didn't bother writing it down, confident that it was already logged into his mental filing system.

"You can let yourself out the door," he said to Nimmo. "Don't get spotted goin' out, yeah?"

"I'll try ever so hard," Nimmo replied.

Rubbing his hands, FX waved at Scope to follow him out into a corridor.

"OK, come on. The computers in the workshop aren't linked to the web. That's a can of worms I only open when I'm in the Hide."

"The Hide?" Scope frowned, starting after him. "You haven't mentioned that to me before."

"You never needed to use the web here before. We don't

have our own connection, I prefer to hitch-hike on other people's wireless signals. Come on."

He went out into the hallway, and Scope was walking after him when Nimmo stopped her.

"I need a favor," he whispered. "It's a bit dodgy, but it's something I think you'd be into."

"Yeah?" She raised her eyebrows. "What is it?"

"I need your help with a murder."

"Jesus, Nimmo!" she exclaimed in disgust. "You know I don't—"

"No, no! I mean, I'm trying to *solve* a murder. I need you to look over some forensic evidence I took from the scene."

"Oh." Her face brightened. "OK, sure, cool."

"Thanks. I'll get the stuff while I'm out. I'll be back this afternoon."

She waved to him and strode off after FX. Nimmo watched her go, then turned to leave. He liked Scope, and trusted her. But he was reluctant to involve her more than he needed to. He'd have to explain to her how he was mixed up in Brundle's death, but he couldn't tell her that he had the case they had been instructed to find. And he was sure it was the same case. A case that now rightfully belonged to Brundle's daughter, but was being sought by the most dangerous gangster in London. And the longer Nimmo kept hold of it without telling Move-Easy, the more likely the orange-skinned mob boss was to send some seriously violent people out to look for it. Once that happened, Veronica and her mother could easily end up in one of Move-Easy's 'guest rooms.' Bare concrete rooms with steel rings in the walls, tiled floors and excellent sound-proofing. Nimmo's thoughts turned to his parting image of the scientist—a cooling corpse, lying just inside the doorway of his lab.

"This is what I get for doing favors for the neighbors," Nimmo murmured, as he opened the outer door. "What the hell were you up to, Brundle?"

CHAPTER 10

BREAKING AND ENTERING

NIMMO NEEDED TO GET TO THE BARBICAN as fast as he could. Rather than walk and run all the way from the Docklands, he found a quiet spot and sat down to take off his left trainer. The sunglasses and hat would make his face harder to identify, without making him look overly suspicious, but the scan-cams had other ways of picking you out of a crowd. Gait-recognition software could literally analyze the way you walked, and compare it with people it had on file. Nimmo made a point of not getting recorded by the eyeballs too often, but sometimes there was no avoiding it. So it paid to vary your appearance, or even the way you walked, so that the system couldn't easily track your movements. Sometimes it was better to be anonymous and out in the open than hiding in the shadows.

He found the pair of insoles he'd put in his bag the day before—the ones with the arch supports for flat feet—and put the left one into his left trainer. Putting the other one back in his bag, he pulled his trainer on again and stood up, taking a few steps. The arch support under his left foot caused him to limp slightly. It was better than trying to fake a limp, and hopefully was enough to disguise the way he walked.

Canary Wharf tube station was a short walk away. He paid for a ticket with cash and took the Docklands Light Rail train to Bank. While he was on the train, he went online on his phone and looked up the layout of the Barbican Estate. A text from FX confirmed to him that Veronica was in school and her mother was at work. Nimmo turned off his phone and took out the battery. Mobile phones were a pathetically easy way of tracking a person's movements.

Switching to the Northern Line at Bank, he got off at Moorgate. From there, he walked to the Barbican, stopping to take the insole out of his shoe along the way. Flexing his left foot to ease the cramp caused by the arch support, he put his trainer back on and set off again. He was more careful of the eyeballs now, and passed two Safe-Guards along the way, making himself inconspicuous as their surveillance rigs took in everything around them.

As he came into view of the concrete towers that dominated the estate, he walked briskly, looking as if he had somewhere to be and he was late. Standing staring at a building, or even walking around slowly looked more suspicious. As he walked, he casually noted the positions of the cameras. He had been here a couple of times before and it looked like there hadn't been any changes.

He had, of course, considered not breaking into the girl's home at all. He knew exactly where the missing case was—tucked into the vent on the roof of Watson Brundle's building, right where Nimmo had left it. Nobody was getting that damned box until he discovered who had killed Brundle and why. But he knew Move-Easy would be checking on him, perhaps even having him followed—though Nimmo doubted any of the villain's people could do it without him spotting them. Nimmo had been taught that the best way to lie was to tell as much of the truth as possible, and leave out the bits you didn't want to tell.

If Nimmo didn't search Veronica's home, and Move-Easy's heavies went in later and turned the place over, he could be caught in a lie if he was questioned about the place. To keep the truth about the case hidden, he had to pretend he was looking everywhere for it.

The building he was studying had blind spots. In the block where the two-floor apartments were situated, there were several windows high up on an outer wall that weren't covered by any of the cameras. One of the windows was open. It wasn't Veronica's flat, but it was close enough. The window was four meters above the ground, and the wall was smooth. The security firm probably thought that made it safe enough. Nimmo pulled on a thin pair of skin-color latex gloves.

There was a small van parked against the curb of the narrow path, a few meters away from the window. It was old, with a sticker for a fake security system on the window. No alarm, but the ignition system on these vans was hard to crack. That was OK, he didn't need to start the engine. Checking that he was still out of sight of the cameras, Nimmo took a long piece of wire and a steel ruler from his bag. The pack was full of odds and ends, but he kept nothing in it that could get him arrested. He had the driver's door open in a matter of seconds.

After another discreet look around, he took the van out of gear, released the handbrake and pushed it forward until it was under the window. Then he put it back in gear and pulled up the brake handle.

There was a young couple coming up the path towards him. He took out his phone—still disconnected from its battery—and leaned back against the side of the van, pretending to text someone until they had passed. After they rounded the corner, he hopped onto the bonnet, then onto the van's roof, and jumped from there up to the window, grabbing hold of the sill. After a peek inside to make sure there was no one in the room, he climbed in, dropping to the floor and listening carefully. He was in a bedroom, standing by a double bed covered in a flowery bedspread and scattered with old-fashioned embroidered cushions. There was someone upstairs in the living room—two people, having a lively argument, by the sound of it. He winced, and dropped quietly to the floor. There were times when you just had to go for it.

He walked across the small, pine-paneled bedroom, down the hall past the bathroom door, and silently let himself out the front door. He put it on the latch, so it wouldn't click when he closed it. They could wonder about that all they liked.

Casually coming out of the front door of a flat made him look like a resident. He was on camera out here, but he doubted anyone paid much attention to this part of the building. Coming in the normal way, you had to walk past a bunch of other cameras to get here. He was now on the corridor leading to the Brundles' apartment. The camera was at the end of the hallway, behind him. Hobbling as if on an old man's stiff legs, he hunched his shoulders, tilted his head down and made his way slowly to Veronica's front door, which opened onto the other end of the corridor.

As he walked along with the camera on his back, his thoughts turned, as they so often did when he was on a job, to his mother and father. He could imagine what they would have said if they saw him now.

"You're taking too many chances, not checking it out enough. Not thinking it through," his father would say.

"Acting like a bloody amateur," his mother would say. "Did we teach you nothin'?"

They'd made a lot of sacrifices to keep him safe—to hide his existence from their enemies, but they'd still left him alone, hadn't they? And now Brundle's death had rattled him more than he wanted to admit, and he was being forced to work with a new crew, just when he needed time on his own to work the angles. He was rushing into this. He'd been in too much of a hurry to get away from the others and do something, *anything*, to lay out a proper plan. But he was stuck into it now, and had to follow it through.

People living in apartment blocks such as these tended to

mind their own business, but there was no one in the corridor anyway. Peering through the glass in the door, he looked for any sign of a passive volumetric sensor in the hallway—the tell-tale box with a little red light. But he saw nothing. He took the arms off his sunglasses and used the lock-picks to open Veronica's front door.

Slipping inside, he heard the faint squeak of a floorboard under his foot. He waited a few seconds with the door open, while listening for any other sound, his eyes searching the door-frame for any sensors. Nothing. A quick look into the first couple of rooms confirmed what he'd suspected. No burglar alarm. The WatchWorld system had reduced casual burglaries, particularly in places like this. That meant fewer people spending money on expensive security systems. There was a silver lining to every cloud. He closed the door.

This was an apartment laid out over two levels, stretching from the front of the building to the back. Nimmo tucked his sunglasses away and had a quick look around the place before he did any digging. At the entrance level was a hall, with the main bedroom to the right. To the left, past the bathroom, was a second bedroom that looked out the front of the building. The stairs went up from just inside the door. The upper floor had a living room at the front, a kitchen in the middle, and a dining room at the back. After checking these, he came back downstairs. Veronica's room was the obvious place to search first. This was the smaller of the two rooms, down the hall past the bathroom.

Most of the apartment was laid with semi-solid beech-wood flooring, with the walls finished in white or pastel colors, but

Veronica was clearly at that stage in her life where everything was about making a statement. Two of the walls were bright green, the other two were purple. It wasn't a big room. Nimmo wondered how she spent much time in here without getting a headache. There were a few posters on the walls—the usual bands and film stars a girl his age would be into. There was a computer on a small desk facing the door, and a dressing table beside it, under the window. A single bed with a deep orange-patterned duvet stood against the wall to the right. A sound dock sat on a sideboard in front of him, beside a small television. Nimmo picked his way across a floor littered with clothes, shoes and books. He made a mental picture of the room. When he left, he wanted to be sure there would be no sign that he'd been there. The computer was switched off. He switched it on, and continued his search while it warmed up.

Even though he couldn't find what he was here to search for, his thief's instincts took over, and he began assessing the value of the things around him. On a whim, he had a look under the mattress first, and to his amusement found a diary there, covered in girlie stickers. He left it there for the moment. He could go back to it later. There were plenty of guys who would have had a good laugh to themselves poking around a girl's bedroom, but Nimmo was working. A quick search through the wardrobe beside the door turned up nothing of interest. There were no hidden spaces that he could find. Her jewelry was mostly of the cheap student variety, with a few more valuable pieces that were probably presents. They lay in and scattered around two open jewelry boxes on the small dressing table. After checking under the bed, he looked through the various drawers, bags and boxes tucked out of the way around the edges of the room.

He poked about, looking for hidden panels in the walls, floor, ceiling and in the furniture. Nothing. If she had a place for hiding her secret things, it wasn't here. Nimmo had to be thorough—the story he told Move-Easy might depend on it.

The computer was now up and online. FX would probably be rooting around in it right now, but Nimmo took a data key from his pocket anyway, connected by wireless signal to the computer, and set the PC to copying all of its more recent documents, photos and other files onto the key. That would take a while. He'd come back to it.

He was flicking a last look across the bookshelves over the computer desk, when his eyes caught on the title of one of the books. *Fahrenheit 451*, by Ray Bradbury. He tilted his head, gazing at the spine. It was a dangerous book. He was surprised her mother let her keep it. Veronica shouldn't leave it sitting out where someone might see it.

Leaving her bedroom, he tackled the rest of their home. It wasn't even eleven o'clock, but the longer he was here, the more chance there was of somebody walking in on him. Just because the two who lived here were accounted for, he couldn't be sure they didn't have a cleaner, or a friend or neighbor who had the run of the house. Nimmo normally didn't do break-ins without studying the target for at least a few days, but he was on the clock now. Again, he could imagine his parents' dismay if they knew how sloppy he was being. His mother, in particular, would be muttering curses under her breath. The risk of being caught always gave Nimmo a buzz, but it knuckled the pit of his stomach too, and he was getting it worse than normal.

He searched Veronica's mother's bedroom next; a more mature, yummy-mummy style with lots of cushions on the bed, interesting fabrics, driftwood ornaments and abstract artwork in box frames. There were lots of ethnic-craft boxes from Eastern and African cultures for her bohemian jewelry. There was every chance the ex-Mrs. Brundle would have known about the case, and could have hidden it herself, so he looked here too. No joy, of course. The living room and dining room were decorated to the mother's tastes, but offered little in the way of hiding places. There was no attic or basement.

The small cupboards in the bathroom held only the mass of toiletry and cosmetic bottles, facial packs, make-up pads and other bits and pieces you'd expect with a teenage girl and her mother competing for space in the apartment. There was a slight give in the teak bath panel when he pushed against it, and he noticed there were faint scrapes on the tiles near the base of the panel, and those at right angles to it.

He pulled at the bottom and the panel came off. It seemed Veronica, and possibly her mother, had their own little Void going on. In the space under the bath, wrapped in plastic bundles, were more dangerous books. Nimmo noted some of the titles: *Brave New World*, *A Clockwork Orange*, *Catch 22*, *One Flew Over the Cuckoo's Nest*. All books that the publishers had voluntarily pulled off the market because of the risk they posed to society. He sat back on his hunkers, regarding this stash with thoughtful eyes. It was a clumsy hiding place, but if Veronica or

her mother were going to hide the case anywhere in the house—
if they'd had the case—Nimmo would have bet that it would be
hidden here.

He took a couple of pictures with a small camera he kept in
his pack, and put the panel back in place, careful to make sure it
was just as he'd found it.

Trotting quietly down the stairs, he checked his watch and
turned to go back into Veronica's room, to have a look at her
diary. He was stepping over the mess on the floor towards her
bed when he heard a key turn in the lock of the front door.

CHAPTER 11

THE OTHER THIEF

HE COULD TELL BY THE SOUND of the tread on the hall floor that it wasn't the girl or her mother. The steps were careful, but the semi-solid wood floor creaked, as if under a heavy weight. The door was opened and closed quietly. It was the sound of an intruder, and Nimmo had to assume they were here for the same thing he was. They would search the place . . . and find him.

The computer was still copying the files onto his data key. He pulled the power cord out of the back of it and the screen went dark. There was a cushioned stool under the dressing table. He pulled it out into the middle of the floor. Grabbing an aerosol deodorant from the table, he moved quickly across to the wardrobe and silently opened the door. It didn't squeak. Careful not to rattle the hangers on their rail, he slipped in, crouching among the hanging clothes. Closing the door after him, he pulled the clothes together in front of him. He wasn't kidding himself that he'd be hidden if the wardrobe door opened. But that wasn't what he was about.

The guy did a quick recce of the flat first, just as Nimmo had, before beginning his search. When Nimmo heard him go upstairs, he considered making for the front door, but he couldn't be sure of making it, and besides, this way he'd get more answers.

Like Nimmo, the intruder began his search in earnest in Veronica's room. Through the white slatted doors of the wardrobe, Nimmo watched him try and switch on the computer. The guy checked the plug, reconnected the power cable, switched it on, and placed a data key down beside Nimmo's, linking it to the PC. Then he came over to the wardrobe.

As he opened the doors, Nimmo was holding the aerosol ready. He sprayed it into the guy's eyes and lunged forward. The man staggered back with hardly a sound, one hand at his burning eyes, the other raised in defense. Nimmo kicked him hard in the stomach. The man fell backwards, toppled over the stool in the middle of the floor, and cracked the back of his head on the dressing table. It wasn't enough to knock him out, but he was stunned, flailing around, trying to fend off an attack he couldn't see coming. He was up on one knee when Nimmo moved in behind him, got a head lock on in one smooth motion, and squeezed, cutting off the blood to the man's brain. There was a thin line between rendering someone unconscious and killing them with this technique, but Nimmo's father had taught him well.

The guy's body slumped, and Nimmo checked he was

unconscious by listening to his breathing. The man had a face like a Mexican gunfighter, complete with horseshoe mustache. He was dressed in the uniform of a security guard—the company that guarded the estate. Nimmo looked for identifying marks on his face, neck or arms and found a tattoo of a cat on the inside of his right forearm. A symbol used in prison by professional thieves. He took a photo of the stranger's face and his tattoo, then tied the man's wrists and ankles with two pairs of Veronica's tights and covered his eyes and mouth with black electrical tape from his own backpack. Then he dragged him out into the hallway. Searching the man's pockets, he found a single key, one hundred and thirty pounds in notes and change, a multi-tool and a phone.

Nimmo also found a WatchWorld ID card. But WatchWorld did not employ ex-convicts. The name on the card was Frank Krieger. He put all of the items into his own pockets.

A small pouch strapped to the man's belly under his shirt held several tiny bugs in plastic cases; microphones and cameras with miniature transmitters. They were still switched off. No doubt they were to be planted around the apartment. The pouch went into his backpack. Then he went back into the bedroom, clicked out of the crash alert that was displayed in the middle of the computer screen, switched it off properly, and put both data keys in his pocket.

The man was regaining consciousness, letting out a soft groan, then looking around in alarm as he discovered he was bound, gagged and blindfolded. He struggled until Nimmo started speaking in a near-whisper.

"You shouldn't be here, but then, neither should I. I'm gonna leave. I presume you won't give me answers unless I ask hard, but I don't have time. I suggest you leave too. You're in the hall near the door. Your penknife will be on the stairs, on the fifth step. Use it to cut yourself loose, and then get out of here. If you're smart, you'll clean up any sign that either of us was here. I'll give you five minutes before I make a call to security, and send them down here. Don't bother tryin' to come after me. By the time you free yourself, I'll be long gone."

He was.

CHAPTER 12

NO ONE

FX HAD A QUIZZICAL LOOK ON HIS FACE as he stared at the central screen on his computer desk. It wasn't often that he went online and ended up with more questions than answers. He had been working for more than three hours, fueled by mug after mug of milky coffee. There were coffee rings on his desk beside his keyboard, and Scope, who was sitting at a much smaller, less sophisticated PC on the other side of the room, was itching to tell him to wipe them up. Or just clean them herself. To her eyes, his workspace was disgusting.

There were faint traces of spills and stains everywhere. FX was obviously careful to prevent dust getting into his machines, but she wondered when he had last swept or vacuumed the floor. The room—his 'Hide'—was equipped with enough servers and screens to run the traffic control for a small airport and, situated in the very center of their film studio home, it had no windows and only one door. Some of the technology was there for online access, but most of it seemed devoted to protecting FX from the perils of the web in general and WatchWorld in particular. Scope was no chimp when it came to computers, but even she could only wonder what half this stuff did.

FX was the fidgety type. Much like a pigeon whose feet could not walk without making its head bob, he clearly could not use his brain without moving some other part of his body at the same time. Scope was not normally prone to wild displays of emotion, but the constant tapping of FX's pen on the edge of his desk—possibly due to agitation or caffeine, or both—was threatening to drive her to violence.

Her own investigation into Brundle's work wasn't providing many answers, and she watched FX's growing state of bewilderment for a while before her curiosity got the better of her. She stood up and came across to him, placing her hand on his improvised drumstick.

"OK, what?" she asked.

"I've been checking out this guy, Nimmo," he said. "I just wanted to know who we're working with, yeah?"

"Aren't you supposed to be digging up stuff on Veronica Brundle?"

"Yeah, I'll tell you about that in a minute," he said, waving towards another file he had open on-screen. "That's a whole other kind o' strange. But this guy . . . I mean, the more I look, the more confusing it gets."

"This is not the job, FX. We're not supposed to be digging up dirt on each other."

"Yeah, yeah. But me an' Mani don't like workin' with people we don't know. So I've been checkin' him out. There are loads of hits for 'Nimmo' on the web, but nothing to do with him that I could see. I had to get hold of something I could use to check his ID. Like his iris scan."

"And how exactly did you scan his eyes?" Scope demanded.

"Remember in the workshop, I had that laptop? It showed the view from the camera in the alley, over our front door?" FX replied, gesturing towards the laptop that now sat to one side of his desk.

"I spotted that camera over the door," Scope said. "You couldn't have got a scan off that. Nimmo was wearing shades. Besides, he didn't look straight into it—neither did I. Just reflex."

"No, but he did look at the *screen of the laptop* when he came in. Everybody does, to check out the angle of the camera—at least, if they're a player. That's a reflex too. I've a camera—an iris scanner—set into the top of that screen."

"You mean you have my iris too?" Scope was scowling at him now.

"It takes the picture automatically, but it's not like, y'know . . . we use it for anything." He shrugged. "We're just bein' careful, y'know? Gettin' reesed is an occupational hazard, Scope. We just like to know who everyone is."

Scope felt uneasy about this. They lived in a suspicious world, and even if she didn't know much about Nimmo, she felt she knew his character. Nimmo was sound. The iris of a person's eye was unique, like a fingerprint. These were used increasingly for the purposes of identification. Scanning Nimmo's eye without him knowing was an invasion of his privacy, even if the Watch-World cameras did it as a matter of routine as you walked along the street. The four members of this team were supposed to be working together.

"Maybe you should let this go," she said to FX.

"No, listen to this," he said, holding up his hand. "Just listen. I got into the national insurance system and compared his iris scan with the files. Nimmo's scan came up with an English guy named Charles Ulrich Farley. The photo matches—he's the right age, right size, right description. I've checked Farley's school records, his membership of sports clubs, his national insurance number and all that, right? Every detail is there, it looks like this is our guy. Except on file, he's a real underachiever—low IQ, poor academic record, nearly illiterate, no registered address. His parents are dead. I did a pretty thorough search here."

"OK, fine. He's not book-smart, but maybe he's a natural-born thief. So what?"

"So most people would stop looking right there," FX told her. "But I used an analysis of his photo to do a search on databases in other countries . . ."

"Jesus, man!"

"No, listen! I found two more identities that came up a match, both of whom *also* look like our guy. One Irish and one American. The Irish one lists his age as nineteen, which I'm bettin' is fake. The weird thing is, his *biometric* files are different. The finger-prints and iris scans don't match on the different IDs. He's got no criminal record, he's not listed on the WatchWorld database, but he's got a PPS number from Ireland and a social security number from the States. And he's got registered addresses and schools for both of the foreign IDs. And I'd bet my back teeth he hasn't been to school in years."

"So, he's thorough," Scope said. "That's good, isn't it?"

"You don't get it," FX said. "These are just the ones I've found in the *last hour*. If I didn't know he was connected, I'd have stopped looking when I found the English one. And the deeper I look into each identity, the more I find—school records, summer jobs, social networking sites. These aren't just false IDs, these are proper *legends*."

"What do you mean? What's a legend?"

"A complete false life, covering every recorded detail right back to the birth certificate," Manikin said from behind them. "It's how the intelligence services set up the agents they put into deepest undercover. The cops use them too, when they're infiltrating the mob. Just creating *one* is hard. You hardly ever hear of someone who can switch between different ones. That's serious tradecraft. I mean MI6, *secret agent* level of serious. He can't have done it on his own."

"Yeah, like . . . who is this guy?" FX exclaimed. "I mean, he's our age, isn't he? He's too young to have a mysterious past."

"I don't know," Scope muttered. "That's the problem with having access to so much information sometimes—if you look hard enough, you can find anything. You're not focusing properly here. You're not finding what we're supposed to be looking for. I think we should—"

"All I know is, FX has checked this guy out," Manikin said, "and we still don't know who we're working with. And now, because you gave him the thumbs-up, we've let him into our home. That makes me nervous. The Irish or American thing would fit with that accent of his—it's subtle, but the way he rounds his 'Rs' is a giveaway. Nimmo . . . that's a handle that could suggest lots of things. Could be from 'pseudonym'—you know, like the false name a writer uses? Or from 'nemo,' which means 'no one' . . ."

"Or it could just be *his name*," Scope said firmly. "D'you know what makes *me* nervous? A psychopath Oompa-Loompa with a bunker full of guys who think with their fists. We've got a job to do, and we're on a deadline. How about we stop pokin' around Nimmo's underwear drawer and get back to work?"

The brother and sister regarded each other for a moment and nodded.

"You want what I've got so far on the girl?" FX asked.

"Save it until our lord and master returns," Manikin replied. Her black hair was scraped back over her head and pulled into a tight ponytail. She pulled on a navy suit jacket over a white shirt and a gray skirt that stopped beneath the knees, and put on a small, stylish pair of rectangular spectacles. She had used make-up on her hands and face to give her skin a paler color, and even some freckles on her cheeks. Scope noticed her eyes were now blue. Tinted contact lenses.

"I'm going out," she said.

"Nimmo said to stay here till he got back," Scope reminded her.

"It can be our little secret," Manikin told her. "Or you can tell him, if you like. Whatever. Move-Easy said they'd checked

Brundle's apartment, but I want to talk to his neighbors, see what I can find out."

"OK, cool. I'll go with you," Scope said. "I'm not getting much here. I need to have a look at his lab."

"No offense, Scope, but I want to keep this low key," Manikin said. "You kind of stand out, y'know? Got a pretty distinctive look goin' on there."

"You might want to hold off on that anyway, sis," FX said to her. "We're not the only ones with eyes on Brundle's daughter."

"No? Who's cuttin' in on our dance, then?"

"Still trying to find out. But it could be official." He opened a minimized window and pointed to a page of code. Scope only understood some of it, and Manikin even less. He ran his finger under some of the lines. "Her computer and MyFace page are loaded with spyware. Nimmo switched on her PC while he was in the flat, started downloading the contents of her hard drive. Naturally I did too. He got cut off before he could finish, but I was faster. The drive was riddled with worms. I had to be really careful to hide the fact that we'd both accessed it. And see this? That's part of a Trojan horse—"

"You going to be getting to the point anytime today?" Manikin asked.

"What, you want the dummy's guide, like usual?"

"Yeah, 'cos I don't have time for a conversation with *bloody Wikipedia*. What's the bottom line, short-arse?"

"Someone's running an operation on her, and they're professionals," he said sourly. His sister rarely showed any appreciation for his skills. "Everything's been hacked. Her computer, her phone, her mother's phone, her MyFace page, her school's server, her mother's work computer. This is more than just dataveillance. I'd be surprised if there weren't mikes and cameras in the flat too. This is no kludge—it's high end. Some of this is definitely WatchWorld code—I mean, hackers rip that stuff off all the time, but it could be a covert unit."

"OK, so the police could be eyeballing her too," Scope muttered. "We need to get this finished before it starts getting too crowded."

"Then the sooner I do my rounds the better," Manikin added. "Scope, give me what you've got on Brundle's work. Let's see why his daughter's suddenly so popular."

CHAPTER 13

THE ENVIRONMENTAL HEALTH OFFICER

MANIKIN WALKED WITH HER BACK RAMROD STRAIGHT, her low heels clicking on the concrete of the path, a slim-line console tucked under her left arm. A large handbag swung from her right shoulder. When adopting a disguise she preferred to rely more on her ability to assume different character traits rather than make-up, wigs or prosthetics. When you were being surveilled by the WatchWorld cameras, the less that was fake about you, the better. Her posture and movement made her look several years older, as did her business-like style of dress. Right now, she looked every bit the regulation-quoting bureaucrat. Her obvious youth just made her appear more fearsome—a young fanatical believer in the system. One look at her would have convinced almost anyone that time spent in this young woman's company would involve filling out forms.

OISÍN McGANN

She approached the building where Brundle had his laboratory, set on a grimy trench of a street lined with buildings whose windows were laid out in regular, Georgian, waffle-shaped fronts. She was surprised to see Punkin standing at a bus stop about fifty meters down the street. Manikin wondered how long it had taken for him to realize she'd stolen his wallet. Bunny was leaning against a litter bin a few meters away, staring at her phone and trying too hard to look casual.

Both Punkin and Bunny were wearing new piercings in their eyebrows. Manikin suspected the ball on each of those rings had a tiny video camera inside. It was Move-Easy's favorite way of keeping tabs on his own people, though he didn't normally bug his rat-runners. It looked like Punkin and Bunny were working for Easy now, but he was keeping them on a short leash.

There were also two men within sight that Manikin identified as being too attentively inattentive to what was going on around them, and both had face piercings. Move-Easy was clearly keeping a close eye on the lab.

Manikin walked past all of them without any sign that she had noticed them, and walked up to the front door of the tall, yellow-brick building. Out of the corner of her eye, she spotted another figure—quite different from the others. It was dressed in a long gray coat, and was wearing a helmet she knew was equipped with state-of-the-art surveillance technology. The upright, dehumanized shape of the Safe-Guard stood on the corner of the street, taking it all in. Manikin felt small cool beads of sweat at her hairline, felt her pulse quicken slightly. Her disguise was geared to play on human nature, not to beat the technological tests of

WatchWorld. If the asexual figure decided to stop her and question her, it wouldn't need to check her identity card, which was a high-quality fake.

The Safe-Guard would be able to examine the contents of her pockets, see the fillings in her teeth and discover that her glasses did not have prescription lenses. Even with her colored contacts in, it might still be able to scan her irises; it could record and analyze her voice and look for identifiable signs of old injuries in her skeleton. And all simply by standing in front of her. She turned her attention back to the door of the building, checked the screen of her console, and pressed the second button in a column of buttons, buzzing the apartment directly below Brundle's lab. A tetchy woman's voice answered, and Manikin went to work:

"Is that Mrs. Caper? Mrs. Caper, I'm sorry to bother you. My name is Matty Bennell. I'm an Environmental Health Officer. I'm speaking to all of the residents in your building in connection with the death of Doctor Watson Brundle. I wonder if I might have a word? It's very important and I'll only take a few minutes of your time."

Three minutes later, she was being ushered into an apartment on the fifth floor. Mrs. Caper was a weaselly woman with black eyes that suggested she knew she was a bit dim, that it was a source of constant frustration to her, but that she didn't know what to do about it. Her hands were held poised perpetually in front her, as if she were drying her red nail varnish, or about to dip her hands in a sink. Looking at those inquisitive eyes, Manikin knew Mrs. Caper would use every minute of their time together to try and bleed her visitor of gossip on Brundle's death. That was fine—gossips were a rich source of local information.

"I knew something waren't right up there," Mrs. Caper said, almost before Manikin was in the door. "I mind me own business, but that Brundle character was an odd sort."

"Is that right?" Manikin raised her eyebrows. "How so?"

She was ushered into a living room that looked to have been furnished entirely from a budget flat-pack catalog. She sat down on a stained fabric-covered sofa, facing her host, who perched on the edge of a recliner.

"Comin' an' goin' at all hours, he was," Mrs. Caper said. "Only there was less of that over the last few months, since that kid moved in. The lad did some of his running around for him, so Brundle went out less. Here, what's a health officer doin' investigatin' a death, then?"

"It's a regulatory requirement, because of the circumstances of the death," Manikin replied. "I'm not really at liberty to give out any details. I do need to know who was in contact with Doctor Brundle. Who was this boy? A friend of Brundle's? A relative? Why was he living alone? Why wasn't he in school?"

"Think he was a charity case," Mrs. Caper said helpfully. "Just some kid. Think he was homeless before Brundle took him in. So, was our friendly neighborhood scientist doin' some dodgy experiments then, eh? That why you're here?" The woman gave Manikin an exaggerated conspiratorial look. "I can keep a secret. Was it summink dangerous? I saw in his door a couple of times, when I went up to tell 'im stuff—he had all sorts of stuff in there.

Gadgets . . . tools . . . *chemicals*. I mind me own business, but he was up to some strangeness, I'll be bound."

"I'm not at liberty to say," Manikin said again. "Tell me more about this young man. Did he have a name? Can you describe him to me?"

"Didn't get his name. He didn't talk much. He was about thirteen, fourteen, fifteen or sixteen or so, maybe a bit older. Normally wore a hat, but his hair was cut short. Not sure of the color. Average-looking. Not too tall, but not short either. He a suspect, is he? The police haven't been around here yet, askin' any questions. Brundle get his ticket punched, did he? Someone do him in?"

"It's under investigation." Manikin pretended to enter the anonymous kid's details on her console, as if they might be helpful. "Was he pale or dark?"

"Pale. But not really white."

"Eye color?"

"No, don't know. Why's this important?"

Mrs. Caper was looking increasingly frustrated with her visitor's refusal to share any scandal, twisting her mousy brown hair and narrowing her eyes. Manikin needed to ensure her cooperation.

"It's very important that I learn who was in contact with Doctor Brundle in the days before he died. It's the only way we can hope to trace the source of the contamin—" Manikin pulled herself up short and her expression turned to one of embarrassment.

"The source?" Mrs. Caper said. "The source of what?"

Manikin's apparent embarrassment quickly worked itself into a state of distress. "I . . . I'm sorry, I shouldn't have said that.

Nobody's supposed to know." She leaned forward, speaking in a lower, more urgent voice, vulnerability showing in her eyes. "If I tell you, do you promise to keep this to yourself? I'm . . . I'm still new in this job. I could get in terrible trouble."

"It'll be safe with me, love."

Manikin shifted uncomfortably on the sofa, pausing for effect and to play on her host's burning curiosity. She was very good at lying, but you had to choose the right time for it. Lies had a tendency to get out of control if not used with care.

"Doctor Brundle contracted an infection, and we believe it was this that killed him. We don't know where he picked it up, but we don't believe there is any immediate risk to the other residents in the building, as it can only be passed by direct contact—person to person."

"What was it?" Mrs. Caper asked in a tone of morbid fascination. "That killed him, I mean. What was the infection?"

"FX syndrome," Manikin whispered. "It gets up your nose and causes a rot in your brain. It's commonly associated with people who work with keyboards and pick their noses. If you don't catch it early, the damage is irreversible."

"That sounds horrible."

"It is," Manikin assured her. "So you can see, we need to track down everyone Doctor Brundle has had contact with in the last few days. It's the only way we can trace the source of the contamination, and find anybody else who might have it, before they can pass it on. I'd be particularly interested in finding this young man you mentioned. Is there anything else you can tell me about him?"

"No, not really. And the only other person I've seen up there is Brundle's daughter. The one with the mark on her face. She's in every few days. They get on well . . . I mean, they *did* get on well, I suppose. She'll be very upset at her dad's death, God love 'er."

"Yes, we have her details," Manikin said. "There's nobody else you can think of? It's absolutely vital we speak to anyone who had recent contact with Doctor Brundle."

"No, that's the only ones I know about . . ." Mrs. Caper said, the disappointment obvious in her voice. She knew she was coming to the end of her usefulness, and therefore the end of the conversation. Her face brightened slightly. "Unless you count the muggers."

"What's that?"

"Well, Brundle was mugged a couple o' weeks ago. I think that kid upstairs scared them off, but Brundle got a bit beat up—had his bag nicked. Shook 'im up, I reckon. He didn't look very *sick* after it, I 'ave to say. More *angry*. Heard him kickin' stuff around his place a few times after that. He was a devil for gettin' hisself worked up at the best of times—I mind me own business, but you know what these intense fellas are like. Anyway, this was worse. I reckon he could've done with a bit of counselin'."

"I see." Manikin pretended again to add these details to her console. "And do you know if he reported this incident to the police?"

"Nah, I doubt it. He weren't a great fan of the police. In fact, I 'eard him rantin' out in the hallway: 'All these bloody cameras and we're no bloody safer! Useless, intrusive shower of spying wazzocks are never around when you need them!' Or summink like that. Anyway, I'm pretty sure the police never showed up

here, although there was that peep— . . . that Safe-Guard what
came 'ere. I can hear anyone who goes up the stairs here, and the
elevator doesn't work."

"Well, that's all very useful, Mrs. Caper," Manikin said, getting to her feet. "Thank you very much for your assistance,
and . . . and I'd really appreciate it if you could keep my little
indiscretion to yourself."

"It's as safe as the bank," Mrs. Caper assured her.

"I'm very grateful. Oh, would you happen to know when Doctor Brundle's daughter was last here? We just want to confirm
her movements."

"That'd be last Friday night," Mrs. Caper said. "She stayed
over. Usually does when she's been out on the town. I mind me
own business, but there's her, not even sixteen and she's drinkin'
already. Daddy must be . . . *must have been* . . . a softer touch
than her mum. She always stayed out late when she slept over
here on a weekend. God love 'er, there'll be no partyin' for her
for a while."

After winding up her interview with Mrs. Caper, Manikin
went on to talk to as many of Brundle's other neighbors in the
building as she could, but they had little to add to her picture
of the scientist's last days. When she emerged from the building, Move-Easy's two apes were still visible—as were Punkin and
Bunny, still in their same positions, still failing to look convinc-
ingly casual. She saw the Safe-Guard was also still on the street,
standing in the same place. Manikin resisted the urge to look
skywards, wondering what other surveillance had been placed on
the area. There was no way of telling if the Safe-Guard was here

to watch the building, or just on a random posting. Remembering what FX had said about Veronica Brundle being the subject of some kind of WatchWorld-style investigation, Manikin felt a quiver of nervousness. She and her brother had never dealt with that level of heat before.

She strode right past Punkin, confident that he wouldn't recognize her and keen to test the effectiveness of her disguise. Turning the corner, she carried on down the street towards the nearest tube station. There was a WatchWorld display screen on the path, showing a group of teenagers having a melodramatic shouting match outside a chipper. It wasn't the kind of thing that would normally have made the screens, but three of the girls obviously had implants. Their hair glowed in shimmering primary colors that changed every time they tossed their head. There was a lot of head-tossing going on. A figure stepped out from behind the screen, and Manikin's heart missed a beat as a hand caught her arm and a voice asked:

"What are you doing here?"

CHAPTER 14

MUGGED

IT WAS NIMMO. Leading her to the doorway of a derelict shop, he didn't look happy. But with a face like his, it was hard to tell. For all Manikin knew, that could have been his party face.

"I'm sorry, who are you?" she asked.

"Spare me the act," he said. "It took me a minute to figure out who you were, but I did, so somebody else could too. I'll ask you again: what are you doing here?"

She cast her eyes around, deciding this was a safe enough place to talk.

"I was talking to Brundle's neighbors, digging up some information. You have a problem with that?"

"Move-Easy put me in charge. I don't like it any more than you do—I prefer to work on my own—but that's the way it is. I told you all to stay put." He waved at her changed appearance, at the street around them. "This isn't staying put."

"Wow. Do you get paid extra for stating the obvious? No, I didn't stay put. I'm getting on with the job. If it's all the same to you, I'd like to get it done before my bloody hair turns gray. Move-Easy didn't hire us to wait around."

Nimmo stared hard at her. He dug his hand into his jacket pocket and pulled out a gray plastic disc smaller than a penny.

"Know what this is?"

She looked at it.

"It's a bug. A microphone and transmitter. Short range, I'd say," she replied.

"It's a *WatchWorld* bug," Nimmo muttered sternly. "I ran into a guy in Veronica's apartment. I surprised him before he could get started, wrapped him up, but he was loaded with kit like this. Probably meant to put them in her clothes, shoes, her phone, everything. This is heavy-duty stuff—you can't get this kind of kit in the underground, not that I've ever seen. I got a phone off him too, but it's locked, so it's not giving me anything. If the bill are monitoring Veronica, and they have a Safe-Guard hovering outside Brundle's building, d'you think they might have eyeballs or ears on his neighbors?"

Manikin felt a tightness in her chest. What if they did? She'd walked right in there. Having got through several years of dodging the police, she might have planted herself right in their sights. They could have her face, her voice. She had been careful not to leave her fingerprints in the place, but it was very hard not to leave DNA without covering yourself from head to toe . . .

"I . . . I was just trying to—" she began.

"I know what you were trying to do," he cut her off. "The same thing I was. And to be honest, I got lucky. I got in before they did. But the less we're poking around without knowing the score, the better. And I don't think I left any traces. What about you?"

"No—at least, I don't think so," she sighed. "But it's a bloody murder case. If they're looking hard enough . . ."

"It's not a murder case," Nimmo said, shaking his head. "They reckon Brundle's death was accidental. Or they're not treating it as suspicious, at least."

Manikin felt a lift of relief. No crime meant it was less likely that there were cops hanging around. She hoped.

"How do you know that?"

"Friends in low places. Come on, let's get back to your place— figure out what to do next."

Manikin was about to nod in agreement when she frowned. "Hang on. What are *you* doing here?"

"Trying to get a view of our competition. Didn't see anybody I'd connect with the guy I met in Veronica's place, but I made two of Move-Easy's drones and two I've seen before but don't know: a guy with a bottle-bleach-job in a leather jacket at the bus stop and a redhead with a face like someone suckin' a lemon."

"Punkin and Bunny, yeah." Manikin sniffed. "I don't know what they're doing here, but they're not serious players."

"Too small-time for the competition?"

"Time doesn't get much smaller. But I'd steer clear of them. They're just big enough to trip up everyone around them. See anything that might actually be *useful*?"

"I saw you. I stopped lookin' around then."

"What, did I distract you?" she asked with the hint of a smile.

"I just thought you looked familiar, and I don't know any Environmental Health Officers. So . . . what is 'FX syndrome' anyway?"

Manikin turned to stare at him, a look of thinly disguised fascination on her face.

"Who the hell are you?"

"I was just thinkin' the same thing," Punkin asked from behind them. They turned to find him standing at the corner, his face raised slightly, his eyes holding them with a suspicious gaze. Bunny was behind and to one side of him, resting her chin on his shoulder.

"You," he said, nodding towards Manikin, "you, I know from somewhere, I just can't place your face. And you"—he looked at Nimmo—"I don't know who you are, but I've seen you in one of the Voids. Tubby Reach's, maybe? You're a player. And here you are, hanging around the edges of a big game. And this trollop was right in there, pokin' her nose around, if I'm any judge. What you doing here?"

"Minding our own business," Nimmo retorted. "You should try it."

"Look at 'em, Punkin," Bunny said in a whisper that everyone could hear. "They're up to summink, I can feel it. They *know* summink. Nobody else has seen 'em yet. They're *ours*. This is good."

Punkin nodded. He pointed towards a narrow alleyway that led off the side street they were standing in.

OISÍN McGANN

"OK, you two. Step into my office—we got some questions for you. Answer up quick and it'll be easier all around."

"Who are you?" Manikin asked, putting on an anxious expression, and gripping her console tightly to her. "Why would we walk into some alleyway just 'cos you say so? What's going on here?"

Punkin sighed and held up his right hand. He twisted the silver ring on his thumb and from the back of his hand an eighteen-centimeter blade slid out of a sheath implanted beneath the skin of his forearm.

"Like Wolverine's," he said with a twisted grin. "Like it?"

"Wolverine has *three* blades," Nimmo pointed out. "On each hand."

"I could only afford the one," Punkin snapped, looking somewhat hurt and defensive. "I'm savin' up for the rest. Now that I'm workin' for Mister Easy, I'll have 'em in no time. This is high-end kit—slides right in along the bone so it's hard to see on x-ray. It's sharp enough to shave with."

"That'll be well handy . . . once you're old enough to shave," Manikin observed. Then, determined to stay in character, she added: "Who's Mister Easy?"

"Into the alley," Punkin growled. "We can be polite, or we can get nasty. It's up to you."

Bunny's hair was pinned up in a loose bun, and she reached up to draw the two pins out and shake her hair loose. Each steel pin was nearly sixteen centimeters long. The way she held them made it clear she knew how to use them as weapons.

"What did you think of Chelsea on Saturday?" Manikin asked quickly.

"What?" Punkin scowled.

Manikin looked pointedly past him, towards the main road at the end of the street. He glanced back and saw the Safe-Guard walking slowly past on the far side of the main road. Bunny gave a soft gasp.

"Don't fancy their chances in the semi-final, with their form," Nimmo commented.

With its highly sensitive mikes, the Safe-Guard could hear what they were saying, but it wasn't looking their way . . . yet.

"You don't know what you're talkin' about," Punkin said, hurriedly holding his knife down against his leg. "Chelsea are going all the way. They'll take the Champions League this year."

"In your dreams!" Manikin scoffed. "That bunch of hairdressers haven't got a straight foot between them. They were lucky against Spurs—they'd have been trounced by a full-strength side."

"You a Spurs fan?"

"Arsenal, till the day I die."

"Poor choice of words," Punkin sneered, casting his eyes back to check that the peeper had carried on down the street. He raised his knife again. "All right. Down the alley, and let's have a chat. I want to know what you're doin' here. And if we're not happy with the answers, Bunny here's gonna start givin' you the needle, you get me?"

Bunny brandished her stiletto-like pins with a disturbingly eager expression. Nimmo's eyes met Manikin's, and a silent signal of agreement passed between them.

"I'm done waitin'," Punkin said through gritted teeth.

Nimmo shook his head and turned into the alley. Manikin followed. Punkin and Bunny followed them. They followed too closely.

Nimmo stopped abruptly. Punkin put his left hand on Nimmo's shoulder and brandished the knife, to remind him of the threat. Nimmo scraped his foot down Punkin's left shin, slamming it down onto the top of the Punkin's foot. He deflected the knife strike he knew was coming, caught the hand and bent the wrist in hard against the forearm, forcing a cry of pain out of Punkin. Then he drove Punkin's blade into the wooden door beside him. Punkin tried to pull it free, but it was stuck. With the heel of his right hand, Nimmo struck Punkin on the elbow to jam the blade in a bit more, then a couple of times in the ribs, knocking the wind out of him.

Bunny let out a squeal of outrage, turning on Nimmo with the steel spikes. Manikin pulled a plastic and steel rod from the edge of her console and jammed the tip of it into Bunny's side. There was a crackle, Bunny's body went rigid, and then she collapsed back against the wall, dropping the pins.

"What was that?" Nimmo asked, as he pushed Punkin back into the same wall.

"One of my brother's little numbers," Manikin said, holding it up. "A shock-stick—gives you an electric jolt. You only get a few shots, but it's not bad for what it is." She looked down at Bunny. "Handy for prodding cattle too."

He was about to respond when she put a finger to her lips, slipped the rod back into place in her console, and sat down beside Bunny. She straightened Bunny's head up, and held up her console as if to show the stunned girl something on the screen. Nimmo glanced towards the main road and saw the Safe-Guard was walking past on the far side of the street. It was looking straight ahead, but if it turned, it could see right down into the alley. Punkin still had his blade jammed in the door, and Nimmo leaned back against the wall beside him to make it less obvious, blocking Punkin's contorted face from view. Putting Punkin's other wrist in a painful arm lock, he aimed his own gaze at Manikin's console, pretending to show Punkin what was on the screen—just four friends discussing a picture or a piece of video. As the peeper passed by, it looked briefly in their direction, but then carried on down the road.

"Time to go," Nimmo said softly.

"Bloody right," Manikin murmured.

Standing up, she faced Punkin, who was still struggling to get his breath back.

"These two reesed us the other day. It was his left foot you stood on, wasn't it?"

"Yeah," Nimmo said, as he released the wristlock that held Punkin in place.

Punkin squealed in pain as Manikin stamped on his right foot with her low, but sharp, heel.

"That's for packing guns on a job, you monkey," she snapped, knowing Easy was watching through the camera hidden in Punkin's eyebrow piercing. "And for the caterpillar. You reesed the wrong chickens, wide-boy. This is the second time you've crossed me. Try it a third time and I'll feed you your *eyeballs*, you got me, you wazzock?"

Turning to Nimmo, she straightened her jacket and patted her hair down.

"Now," she said. "Shall we?"

CHAPTER 15

HAZARDOUS MATERIALS

WHEN MANIKIN AND NIMMO GOT BACK TO THE WAREHOUSE on Brill Alley, they found Scope vacuuming the floor under the desks of the Hide, and FX making cries of protest.

"Stop!" he shouted over the noise of the vacuum cleaner. "There could be important stuff down there!"

"Then why would it be *lying around on the floor*?" Scope sniped back, as she pushed the head of the nozzle in among the mass of wires and plug sockets.

"That's just where stuff falls sometimes. Normally there's no rush picking it up—it's not going anywhere!"

"This place is a like a cattle shed! How can you live like this?"

"You're talking about my home!"

"I'm talking about a bloody health hazard!"

"Will you please *stop cleaning up!*"

Manikin walked into the room, took one look around, and walked back out again. Nimmo hovered for a little longer, waiting to catch Scope's eye. But she was too engrossed in her domestic mission. He blew his cheeks out and pulled his bag from his back. Looking at one of the printers, he saw that FX had printed out Move-Easy's files on Veronica. Picking them up, he turned his back on the drama and followed Manikin towards the kitchen.

She already had the kettle on. He dropped his bag beside the door, where he could keep his eyes on it.

"FX'll need coffee after that trauma," she quipped. "But then, he always needs coffee."

"He seems a bit put out all right," Nimmo commented, studying the files. "Scope's a little OC—but it kind of comes with her job. Nothing here about what Brundle was working on. I didn't find anything in the apartment either. If Veronica was involved in any way, I didn't find any sign of it."

"And I presume you didn't find the case?"

"Hmm?" Nimmo looked up at her.

"The case? The box we're supposed to be looking for?" Manikin pressed him, as she spooned coffee into two mugs, then remembered her visitors, and added another two mugs. "You didn't find the case, I take it? You seem to be really interested in Brundle and his work and what happened to him. But it's a pretty simple job we've got here—find the case, and get paid. We don't need to know what Brundle worked on, or who killed him. We just have to find that box. You want coffee?"

"No, thanks. Just a glass of water. I like looking at the bigger picture. We're messing in something that's more than just Move-Easy. Whoever these other guys are, they're serious. And whether they're players or coppers, we could get out of our depth before we know it, just by looking for a box that somebody else wants."

He was reading a page of Veronica's medical records. She'd had laser surgery to treat the port-wine birthmark that covered part of her face. Nimmo's eyes opened a fraction wider as he studied the before and after photos. The birthmark she had now was still disfiguring, but the surgery had reduced the original mark by nearly half. The file said the doctors had serious doubts of Veronica's birthmark ever being completely removed without the risk of serious scarring. And the mark would most likely get worse from here on in, thickening, darkening and possibly developing lumps as she aged. Nimmo could only imagine what kind of effect it must be having on her.

Now that he thought about it, he remembered Brundle mentioning something about research he'd once done on repairing scar tissue. Something to do with connecting nerve endings—or disconnecting them. Nimmo wished now that he'd paid more attention.

"One of the neighbors mentioned the guy who lived on the same floor as Brundle," Manikin told him. "They confirmed what Easy told us: that he was the one who discovered the body. I didn't get a name, but the neighbors think he was dodgy. They reckon he did some work for Brundle, but nobody knew much about him. He hasn't been seen since Brundle died. That's pretty interesting."

Nimmo said nothing for a moment. If they found out Chuck

U. Farley's name, they'd find a picture, and then he'd have to start answering some awkward questions. But there was nothing he could do about that now.

"We can check him out, but the daughter's still our best bet," he muttered. "We need to get into her life—see what she knows."

"She goes clubbing on a Friday night," Manikin said. "Or at least she did, when she could crash at her dad's. I could get in with her that way. And she's underage, which means she uses a fake ID. Makes her vulnerable. We can use that. Now we just have to find out where she likes to hit the tiles."

"Club Vega," FX spoke up from behind them. They looked around to see him standing in the door, a bundle of discs, paper manuals and electrical bits and pieces cradled protectively in his arms. "Didn't even have to hack it. It's up on her MyFace page. She thinks that only her friends can see it, but, like most people, she's got her privacy settings cocked up. It's up there for anyone to see. Even got pictures from her nights out. If her mother ever saw them, she'd be grounded, like, for ever. She'd be grounded into the afterlife. Girl's a messy drunk. Vega is her favorite hangout. No surprise, really—the typical bouncer there wouldn't know a fake ID if someone drew it on his face with a crayon. She's going there tomorrow night."

"That's our way in," Manikin said, cupping her hands around the hot mug of coffee. "Veronica's about to make a new friend."

"I'm delighted for her," Scope said, appearing behind FX with a dustpan and brush in her hand. "Nimmo, can you get me into Brundle's lab? I need to see his work first-hand—I'm getting nowhere here. And I need to get out of this slob's space before

I catch foot-and-mouth disease or something. I found a bloody laundry basket in behind an old set of speakers. The stuff had *mold* on it. I need to see Brundle's lab, Nimmo. It's either that or I set fire to this place to prevent an epidemic like the world has never seen."

"I've told you about the goddamned laundry," Manikin gasped as she handed her brother a mug of coffee and walked out of the door. "She's right, you're a pissin' slob. Come on and show me these pics of the girl—let's see what she's into."

"There is one thing I found in the apartment," Nimmo said abruptly. "She's into books. Dodgy ones. There's a stash of pirate editions of recalled books: *A Clockwork Orange*, *Catch 22*, *One Flew Over the Cuckoo's Nest*. She even has *Fahrenheit 451* sitting out on a shelf in her room. I don't know if the mother's involved, and the books could be for personal use, or the pair of them could be dealing."

He didn't say anything more. As the WatchWorld motto went: "If you've nothing to hide, you've nothing to fear"—but everyone had something to hide. The possession of these kinds of pirate books wasn't a criminal offense, but it was the kind of behavior that could attract a Life Audit—the kind of investigation and surveillance of every aspect of your life that everyone dreaded. And nobody wanted all their secrets dug up; nobody lived a perfect life.

The other three were looking at each other. Nimmo saw a wariness on their faces. The expression a person wore when they had discovered dirt on someone, and were weighing up whether to use it or not.

"If that's as serious as she's got, she's just dabbling in the game," FX said, flicking his eyes towards his sister. "But if Move-Easy finds out, that's a bad habit he could blackmail her with. That's how he gets a hold on people."

"And once he's got his claws in her, he'd drag her into his world," Manikin sniffed. "That's how he got us. We thought he was doing us a favor, when we needed help. We did a job for him, and then he had us. He pulls you in, and twists it so that you're always in debt to him, you're always working it off. Let him get a piece of you, and you're a criminal for life."

Scope nodded, her eyes trained on the floor.

"My family lives in a Void," she said in a subdued voice. "But they're not hardcore criminals—they just want to stay out of the way of WatchWorld. They're pretty organized, but just a bunch of new-age hippies, really, who make their living from selling art. I was home-schooled by my parents and my gran, before she died. Science was more my thing, and Gran used to work in forensics, so she taught me a lot about that side of it.

"What we never knew was that my gran also worked for *Move-Easy*. He could've taken over our Void, but he left us alone because she helped his men fool the police forensics teams. Gran also used to fake evidence to put his rivals in prison, or collected real evidence against anybody he wanted to control. Move-Easy has dirt on coppers, judges, WatchWorld officials, but especially other criminals. He's a master blackmailer—that's how he's stayed out of prison so long.

"A few years ago, my gran died. A couple of days after her funeral, some of Move-Easy's apes showed up. Without Gran

— 120 —

working for them, we were going to have to pay protection money. If we didn't pay, they'd burn the place down. We weren't criminals—we were terrified of these guys. They knew we wouldn't go to the police. Right then, my folks knew Easy was going to bleed them dry of all the money they had. I was too big for my boots. I wanted to help.

"I spotted that two of the trolls had contact lenses with fake irises covering their eyes, and like the good girl I was, I explained the flaws in the lenses. Not ones my gran would've made. I told them how to make the irises look more real. Shouldn't have opened my mouth. They checked up on me. Found out some of the stuff I'd done. They picked me up one night, and got me to examine some counterfeit money they'd printed. I found the flaws in that too—I mean, the foil wasn't even woven through the paper properly. After that, Move-Easy decided I was going to be working for him. As long as I do, he leaves my family alone. When Dad tried to argue, they broke his arm.

"I'm so far in now, I can't see a way out. I don't want this to happen to anybody else." She gazed at Manikin. "You're right. Give that scumbag any kind of hold on you, and he'll have you for life."

"So we're all agreed?" FX asked, looking pointedly at Nimmo. "We don't tell Easy about the book thing?"

Nimmo nodded, glad of their decision. And as he did, he wondered if he should just tell Manikin and FX about his connection to Brundle, that he had the case, and that the scientist's death had most certainly not been accidental. As it was, he was going to have to let Scope in on it. But in his short life, Nimmo had trusted very few people, and half of those were dead or in prison. He had stayed alive and free by keeping his secrets, so he stayed silent now.

"Good," Manikin said. "Come on, bro', show me what you've got on Veronica. Time to get into character. By tomorrow night, I want to be the best friend she's never met."

"What about getting into Brundle's lab?" Scope asked.

"Let's see how we do at the club. There's a lot of eyes on the lab," Nimmo said. He took the phone and bugs from his bag, the ones he'd taken from the other intruder in Veronica's flat. Handing them to FX, he said: "I picked these up from one of our competitors. See what you can find out, will you?"

"How the hell did you get these?" FX said, staring at the objects he took from Nimmo.

"I hid in a wardrobe with a can of deodorant," Nimmo replied. "Get what you can out of them, soon as you can, yeah?"

FX glanced at his sister, who was pretending not to be intrigued. She peered discreetly over her brother's shoulder, following him as he hurried out of the room towards his workshop.

Nimmo checked to make sure the pair were walking away down the corridor, then he reached down for his backpack, opened the top, and handed Scope a plastic bag containing a bundle of other plastic bags.

"Here's that stuff from that thing I was telling you about. I'll talk you through them," he said. He chewed his lip and cast another look at the kitchen door. "Look . . . I need to be straight with you here, Scope. This murder I'm looking into? It's Brundle's. I knew him. I was the guy who lived on his floor. Apart from his killer, I was the last person to see him alive. I found the body. I reported the death to the police. I'd be the main suspect in their investigation, only they've decided that his death was accidental. Which it wasn't—I heard him die."

"Holy sh—" Scope began to say.

"I really need you *not* to tell all this to the others—at least until I get to know them better," Nimmo pleaded. "I'm up to my teeth in this mess, Scope, but I can't let the coppers brush this death under the carpet. Something's badly wrong with all this. I need your help."

"Bloody hell, Nimmo," she said in a hushed tone, looking down at the package in her hand. "I mean . . . *bloody hell.*"

"How about it?" he urged her for an answer. "I know I'm asking a lot, but . . ."

He shrugged, unable to give her a good enough reason to help him. She met his eyes and smiled faintly. There were times when Scope struck Nimmo as being too innocent for this game—but then, when she gave him a look like she did now, he saw the piercing intelligence that gave her that curiosity, and that ability to interpret the smallest details so as to make sense of the world around her.

"You've got the case, haven't you?" she said.

"Yeah," he replied.

CHAPTER 16

THE KING OF THE GETTERS

MOVE-EASY'S WAS ONLY ONE of many Voids in London. And while he ran the most powerful organization, it was Tubby Reach you went to if you needed what couldn't be got. Reach was the biggest and best getter in London. But like Move-Easy, he was very particular about security. Nimmo was one of very few people outside Reach's inner circle who could enter the Void without an escort, as the King of the Getters had known him since he was a baby.

One of the entrances into Reach's Void was through a door marked 'Staff Only' in a pedestrian tunnel in Victoria Station. This door was not watched by a camera, but you had to be careful to only use this door when the tunnel was crowded with commuters making their way from the Underground to the main line station.

Mingling with the normal morning crowds on their normal way to their normal jobs, Nimmo opened the door and slipped through as the press of bodies hurried past him. He walked down a steel staircase into a narrow utility tunnel, to another door, flanked by a bank of metal compartments housing electrical breaker switches. Instead of going through this door, Nimmo stopped in front of it and whistled the first few bars of Scott Joplin's "The Entertainer."

The bank of aluminum lockers slid aside to reveal a hidden doorway, and a very large Asian man with careful eyes ushered the boy inside. Nimmo made his way along the bare concrete corridor, past several different, discreetly situated scanning devices.

Two more locked doors were opened to him, and he found himself in an ante-chamber that resembled the waiting room of a wealthy doctor, complete with nondescript classical music, modern art prints on the wallpapered walls, and an inoffensive range of reading material on the large coffee table that sat between the two rows of antique cushioned chairs. A closed pair of elevator doors was set into the wall to his right. Half a dozen people of widely varying appearance sat waiting for an audience with Tubby Reach.

There was another door on the far side, this one a teak-paneled affair, rather than a heavy-duty steel slab. Entrance through this door was controlled by a lean black guy in a plum-colored designer suit. He sported an impressive Afro and a pair of sunglasses, which looked somewhat incongruous, given that he was several stories underground. A tall, sporty-looking girl was talking at him. She had an Irish accent and hair the color of a stop sign. She was trying to talk her way past the doorman, but wasn't having much success.

"But I have an appointment!" she pressed him. "My name's on the list: Caragh Boland. Check the list!"

"He'll see you in good time, Ms. Boland," the doorman replied in a tone that was polite but firm. "In good time. But you've got to wait your turn. Everyone here needs to see Mister Reach, but he's a busy man."

"But I've got those books he wants! He's still in the market, isn't he?"

"He is—and he'll get to you eventually. But for now, you need to sit down and wait your turn like everybody else."

Nimmo walked up to them, nodding to the doorman, who nodded back and opened the door for him.

"What? Who the hell was that?" the girl protested, as Nimmo stepped through. "How come he gets in so easy?"

"That's nobody you need to worry about," the doorman assured her as he closed the door again. "Nobody at all."

Nimmo found himself in a hallway that led to a room which could have been the members' area in a high-class nightclub. It was broken into different levels, linked by wide steel and glass staircases, with low, multi-colored lighting around the edges of the space, the odd area picked out by spots. There were comfortable leather seating areas, an array of screens, and a well-stocked bar. The only things that jarred with this club image were the state-of-the-art computer gear occupying one corner of the room, and the enormous, semi-circular office desk that dominated one of the highest platforms. The desk curved around the tremendous girth of the man with the slick businessman's haircut and carefully manicured nails, who owned the Void. Tubby Reach roared a greeting and waved Nimmo up.

"Nimmo, my boy," the massively obese Asian man wheezed in the accent of an Indian who has learned his English from the Cockneys. Slow of speech, but quick of mind, and wise to the ways of London, Reach kept himself surrounded by family, and believed in good hospitality. "You're just in time for some of Mum's nahiri. Be ready any minute. She does the beef so tender, it'll crumble in your mouth."

"Thanks, Tub," Nimmo replied. "But it's seven o'clock in the morning. Bit early for dinner."

Tubby Reach raised his eyebrows in surprise, rotating his bulbous head towards one of his brothers, who stood to one side. The man—almost as large, but built of muscle instead of fat—nodded to confirm the early hour. Like Move-Easy, Reach was wary of going above ground, although he did venture out on special occasions. Much of his legwork was done by his brothers.

The youngest, and by far the most dangerous, of those brothers stood to one side of his desk, shoulders, chest and arms bulging inside a black rugby shirt. His eyes were hidden by a pair of sunglasses, his close-cut hair and goatee framed a bull-dog face. His name was Gort, and he handled much of Reach's security, and did a lot of the debt collecting. The rings on his fingers were not just for decoration; they were the controls for the implants that were set beneath Gort's skin, all over his body. These implants provided him with a range of abilities, from making subtle changes to his skin color to being able to extend needles from his fingertips.

They were extremely useful, but Nimmo knew they were also a liability. Illegal implants were one of the biggest parts of Reach's business, and even though Gort's would be the most advanced on the market, they could still be detected by Safe-Guards. So they could attract an awful lot of unwanted attention. The circuitry in those rings was like flying a flag. Nimmo also knew that Reach and Gort had on-going arguments about the risk of that kind of attention. Deep down, Gort wanted to be famous—a celebrity gangster. Reach wanted nothing of the kind.

"Sorry, boy," Reach said to Nimmo, shrugging his wide, sloping shoulders. "We been pullin' an all-nighter. Lost track o' time. One of our implant clinics was knocked over last night, and we're tryin' to track down who did it. Got a lot of peepers on our turf too, pokin' around. Havin' to step lively."

Nimmo came up the steps, taking an envelope from his jacket pocket. He handed it to Reach, who nodded his acknowledgement, and then dropped it into a drawer of his desk without giving it a second look.

"How they doing?" Nimmo asked.

"About the same." Reach made a so-so face. "Your money helps, of course, but your mum's finding it tough. Handling it like a veteran con though—you'd never guess this was the first time she's been locked up. The worst thing for your dad is that he's always worrying someone'll find out his missus was once a copper. Now that he's settled in a while, he's got a couple of rackets going, as you'd expect, but he's missin' her like crazy."

"Shouldn't have got caught then, should he?" Nimmo sniffed.

"Look, Nimmo, given your . . . *background*, a bit of cynicism is understandable," Reach cautioned him. "But you should show more respect. They did what they did to keep you safe. Don't forget that."

As if I could, Nimmo thought sourly, thinking of the money he had just handed over. Money that went towards keeping his parents alive and unhurt.

Eighteen years before, his father had pulled off one of the most famous heists in history. He'd been a target for half the world's police forces ever since, including that of his native France. Quite a few of the world's mobsters wanted a piece of him too. An undercover operation run by the Gardaí in Ireland had finally tracked him down—but the woman who'd led it ended up falling in love with him, and helping him escape.

Twelve years later, they'd been living under new identities in Britain, with their young son. Then they were caught on another job, betrayed by those they were working with. Their true identities were still unknown, but the prisons that held them were no less secure despite this. They'd managed to keep Nimmo's existence a secret, but that meant they could never have direct contact with him. He'd been on his own in the world ever since.

"So how you been?" Reach asked in a softer voice.

"Things've been getting a bit complicated lately," Nimmo told him.

"Never a good thing, in your line," Reach grunted. "Somethin' I can do?"

"Know this guy?" Nimmo said, taking out his camera and

showing Reach the photos of the intruder from Veronica's apartment—the man's face and his tattoo.

"Name's Krieger—Frank Krieger," Reach rumbled. "A thief,
mainly, and a hustler—a bloody good one. Does a bit of violence
too. A real hard case. Steer clear of that one, Nimmo. You take
this while he was asleep or something?"

"Something like that," Nimmo told him. "He's done
time, right? That's a prison tattoo. Any way he could work for
WatchWorld?"

Reach raised his eyebrows slowly and then lowered them in
a frown.

"Nah, no way. They wouldn't touch him. They don't hire ex-
cons. Why do you ask?"

"I was wondering how he could have got this then," Nimmo
said, handing over the WatchWorld identity card he'd found on
Krieger. "I think it could be real."

On the surface, the card was a simple design: Krieger's photo
and real name were on it, along with a serial number and the
WatchWorld logo—the hands encircling the eye. But the real
ID information lay within the slim piece of plastic. A radio fre-
quency ID chip would carry every relevant fact about Krieger's
life, along with an encrypted identification signal that would give
him access to WatchWorld facilities. Tubby Reach looked at it in
bemusement, and then began rooting around in another drawer.
He took out several chocolate bars, some bags of tortilla chips, an
antique revolver and a hairbrush.

When he failed to find what he was looking for, Gort leaned
over and pointed at another drawer. Reach waved him away with

a snort of annoyance, but then opened the drawer and found a handheld RFID scanner. He held the card up to it and peered at the screen. Then he gave a low whistle, handing the card to his brother for him to see. Gort eyed it through his sunglasses, one of his implants providing him with a heads-up display of the card's contents on the lenses.

"A Level Three clearance," Reach said with an impressed wheeze. "I ain't seen one o' those in a while. It's real, all right. Or as good as real. Don't know nobody who's managed to forge one of those, but there's not a snowflake's chance in hell the law'd give one to Krieger."

"What can it be used for?" Nimmo asked.

"Get you into any public buildings, police stations, most of the WatchWorld facilities. You could get access to any of their surveillance installations. You could tap into the WatchWorld feed anywhere in the country."

Nimmo considered this for a moment. A professional criminal with the resources of WatchWorld at his fingertips.

"Krieger couldn't have set this up on his own." Reach interrupted the boy's thoughts as if he'd read them, taking the card back from his brother and passing it to Nimmo. "He's just a tool for a job on this level. This is way out of his league. Man, even I couldn't get you one of these passes—at least, not one that's made for you. A stolen one? No problem. A high-grade copy? Yeah, sure. I could even get you a blank one. But a personalized card with all the right ID stuff on it? No, man."

He gazed at the card in Nimmo's hand, and shook his head.

"I don't know what you're into, Nimmo. But you're up against someone with power—and if they're usin' the likes of Krieger, they're not playin' by any rules. You won't do no prison time for messin' with these—they'll just rub you out if you get in their way. You wanna get back beneath the radar. Low profile, my boy. Your mum and dad taught you how to work in this world—they'd tell you to read the writin' on the wall on this one, Nimmo. Walk away. I don't want to see you come to no violent end."

Nimmo didn't say anything at first. He was staring at the card in his right hand. He thought about the surveillance that would be closing around Veronica Brundle's life, about the ten blank credit cards that were supposed to be in her father's box, and Nimmo remembered her father's body, lying dead on the floor of his lab.

"Thanks for the concern, Tub," he said. "But I'm in this one till I'm done."

"Yeah, you had that look in your eye," Reach sighed, then his voice took on a harder edge. "I know better than to try and change your mind. Chip off the old blocks, intcha? Well, I'm here if you want help . . . to a point. Don't go makin' any more enemies than you can handle. And you know, you start mixin' it at this level, boy, you can't trust *no one*."

A hint of bitterness crossed Nimmo's face, but then it was gone.

"I never have," he murmured.

CHAPTER 17

CAUGHT ON VIDEO

FX SAT IN THE HIDE THAT FRIDAY MORNING, watching a video on one of his screens. A window on the screen beside it was scrolling down through hundreds of lines of code. It represented a program of his, looking for weaknesses in a firewall protecting a distant hard drive he wanted access to. On the desk to one side of him sat the phone that Nimmo had given him. The phone that the other boy had somehow taken from one of their 'competitors.' FX was not worried that the phone could be traced to this location, as could be done with any mobile phone nowadays. Nimmo had removed the battery when he took it, and once the door of the Hide was closed, no signals could get in or out unless FX wanted them to.

The owner of the phone had used the PIN number to lock it. It was a simple but very effective means of stopping anybody else from using it, or examining the content of the phone. Five wrong tries at inputting the number—there were ten thousand possible options—and the security settings would erase the content of the phone, making it useless to FX. There were ways around most security systems, but this one would either be really tricky, or really time-consuming.

According to Manikin, Nimmo had taken the phone from a man in Veronica's apartment. FX had decided to use that information. Most of the millions of surveillance cameras in London did not actually belong to WatchWorld—they were just privately owned eyeballs that fed into the wider network. So their security wasn't always the best. FX had cracked the Barbican's surveillance system a couple of weeks before, blinding the cameras so Move-Easy's men could do some job in there. He wondered now if it had had something to do with Veronica Brundle. But it meant that getting back in again didn't take long.

Once he had access to the camera feed, he was able to find the video file that showed Nimmo entering the flat, carefully hiding his face and disguising the way he walked. Minutes later, a man appeared in the corridor, wearing a security guard's uniform. He too opened the door and went inside. A few minutes after that, Nimmo came out again, still keeping his face turned away from the camera, and walking off.

FX made a copy of these video segments for himself, then corrupted the files on the Barbican's system. He found the cameras that had picked out the fake security guard and tracked the man backwards, to where he had first entered the complex of buildings. The man did not use his phone while he was in the Barbican.

A quick hack into the network of a small department store across the road, and the camera over their front door showed the man getting out of the passenger seat of a white Ford Transit van which had just pulled up to the curb. FX saved a picture of the van. From this angle, he could just make out the driver, and he froze the video and saved a blown-up copy of the pic to record the man's face. He would run both men's faces through his face recognition software and check them off against every database he could find to try and identify them.

The van drove off, and the fake security guard took out his phone, tapped the PIN number into its keypad, and made a phone call. FX couldn't make out the number from this view-point, but he saw there was a business supplies shop on the far side of the street with a camera that had a view over the man's shoulder. FX took note of the time of day on the video file. It took a few minutes for him to find that shop's network, not much lon-ger to crack it, then another minute or two to find the video file from their front door camera for the same time of day. Having found it, he watched the fake security guard tap the numbers "1972" into his phone.

"And that's a wrap, people!" FX said with a smile. He kissed the screen, and then picked up the stolen phone and tapped in the number to unlock it. "I love it when a plan comes together. Now let's see where that van came from . . ."

✿   ✿   ✿

Scope had set up a makeshift lab in a disused room in the old warehouse. Lamenting the poor working conditions, she cleaned it out as well as she could given the time constraints. Making sure that FX was fully engrossed in his digital world, she sat down at a scrubbed steel table to examine the contents of the plastic bags Nimmo had given her.

This was how she preferred it. Scope did like people—she found them fascinating. But they were also frustratingly irrational, emotional and prone to acting on impulse, rather than thinking things through. Especially in social situations. For Scope, it was a constant source of exasperation: what was the point in having higher brain functions if you continued to allow yourself to be governed by animal urges?

It was one of the reasons she liked Nimmo. If he was driven by animal instincts, it was difficult to tell, as he let so little of himself show. He seemed calm and deliberate in everything he did. He had thoughtfully labeled each of the small zip-lock bags of evidence: "Clothes Fibers," "Hair," "Under Fingernails," etc. At first glance, it didn't look like there was much to go on, though one of the bags of scrapings from Brundle's fingernails contained what looked like a tiny black seed. If he had snagged that off his attacker's clothing, it might provide some clue to their identity. There were some other hairs and particles that she thought could provide some useful information too. There was a faint smile on her face as she studied the tiny pieces of evidence.

Scope couldn't deny the pleasure she felt to be finally living up to her gran's hopes, analyzing the forensic traces of a crime, rather than faking them, as she did so often for Move-Easy.

There was also a data key with photographs on it. She had her console with her, and she linked the key in and looked through the photos. Scope clucked her tongue in disappointment at the poor resolution and lighting, but then resigned herself to making the best of what she had. It was a disturbing experience, seeing the body of a dead man—one whose life they were so busy sifting through in such fine detail.

Watson Brundle had died with his eyes half open. There was an expression of surrender on his face as he lay on his front, his head turned to one side. His left hand was under his neck, almost as if he had been lying his head on it; his right was stretched out towards the door. The only tell-tale sign that might hint at a cause of death was a slight bluish tint around the skin of his lips. There didn't appear to be any defensive wounds on the hands, no bruises or signs that Brundle had been in a fight with anybody. From what Nimmo had told her, Brundle hadn't been surprised by his attacker, but if it had been a professional assassin, they could easily have struck him down before he had time to react.

As well as the pictures of the body, Nimmo had also taken rather rushed photos of the lab, particularly the area around the corpse. They weren't enough to see anything in detail, but at least they gave her an idea of how the scene had looked. Something on the worktable next to Brundle's body caught her eye, and she put on her glasses and held the picture up to her one good eye. Lying on the table top, between a small toolbox and a large hard-backed notebook, was a packet of hazelnuts.

"Hm," she said quietly.

The way his hand was at his throat like that—could Brundle have just choked to death? Or maybe he'd had an allergic reaction to the nuts? Could he have been allergic to nuts without knowing it? Unlikely, but maybe Nimmo was wrong. Had he imagined a dramatic fight where there had been none? If Brundle had suffered a severe allergic reaction, he might have thrashed around as his windpipe closed up, effectively cutting off his oxygen. It would explain the blue-tinted skin around his mouth.

Scope shook her head. Nimmo must have seen the nuts, and would have commented on them if Brundle had a known allergy.

That got her thinking about Brundle's work again. There had been so little for her to go on. The man had published no articles in the past couple of years, and next to nothing had been written about him by other people. But from what she'd read, he had been obsessed with various procedures that repaired scar tissue.

According to Nimmo, Brundle was using some kind of micro-technology in his work, possibly RFIDs—radio frequency ID tags; the tiny transmitter chips that had replaced barcodes. But what was he using them for? Even the photos of his lab didn't offer any answers. Scope had no doubt that part of his motive was to help rid his daughter of that disfiguring birthmark.

She picked up the folder of documents that she and FX had compiled on Brundle. One of the sheets listed his employment history. His last proper job had been with Axis Health Solutions. Pharmaceutical companies were notoriously secretive, and Axis was no exception; their research files were stored on a very secure database. Keeping valuable new research out of the hands of corporate spies was a serious problem in the drugs business. FX hadn't managed to dig Brundle's file out yet—or he hadn't bothered.

Scope gazed down at the page, pinching her lip between finger and thumb. Axis was one of the world's biggest manufacturers of bio-tech implants—devices that could be installed into a human body. Devices that could be designed to perform any one of a huge range of functions. On impulse, she got up and went and found FX. He was still in the Hide, transfixed by his screens. It took a few moments for him to notice her, even after she opened the door.

"Hi . . . yeah?" He blinked, as if rousing himself from sleep. "What's up?"

There was a wet ring from his coffee mug on the desk beside him, and he surreptitiously wiped it away with his sleeve. She resisted the urge to roll her eyes.

"Axis Health Solutions," she said to him. "I think we need to know what Brundle was doing there. Not just his job, I mean, but what he was specifically working on. It might give us an idea of what he's been up to since then."

"That was, like, *years* ago," FX said to her. "How's it going to help us find the box? Look, I'm snowed under here. I'll get to it later, OK?"

Scope felt herself tense up with impatience, frustrated by his response. She had to remind herself that, unlike her, he was just trying to find the case, not solve Brundle's murder. Even so, it irritated her that FX wouldn't take her suggestion seriously. It went against her nature to ignore an avenue of investigation when it presented itself. She had thought that, like her, FX was afflicted by an obsessive curiosity.

"Oh, I almost forgot," he declared, reaching behind him for a few sheets of paper lying in the tray of a printer. "I pulled down the coroner's report on Brundle. Nothing mysterious after all. Cause of death was asphyxiation. Daft sod choked to death on a hazelnut."

"I thought it was really tricky to hack the WatchWorld system?" Scope asked, feeling slightly dismayed that her work had been done for her.

"Yeah, but the health service's database is like a bloody bus station. I got it off there."

Scope was positively disappointed—she had been looking forward to figuring this out herself. Taking the pages from him, she read through the description of the autopsy quickly, a frown materializing on her face.

"Not exactly what you'd call thorough," she murmured. "From the looks of this, he swallowed a whole hazelnut in one go. Who does that? I mean, they didn't even check his teeth to see if he'd tried to chew it. I don't think they even looked for another possible cause of death."

"Maybe they reckoned the *nut stuck down his throat* was a pretty solid bet," FX retorted.

"I've seen Nimmo knock someone out once, without leaving a mark," Scope persisted. "It's the kind of thing Coda could do too—anybody well trained in martial arts. Then it'd just be a matter of shoving a hazelnut down their throat and leaving them to choke on it. That'd be just the kind of thing Coda would do."

"Except Move-Easy obviously wanted something from Brundle and he still doesn't have it. It'd make no sense for Coda to kill him . . . though I suppose someone could have . . . Anyway, none of this is helping us. Time to move on to more box-shaped matters, I say."

Scope wasn't quite ready to agree with him. As far as she was concerned, the autopsy report had prompted more questions than answers. She was reading over it again as she headed back out of the door. Brundle's medical history was there too. Frowning, she checked the autopsy photos, then looked again at the medical file. There was something here that was strange—something you wouldn't notice unless you compared the two files. Stopping as she stepped out of the room, she swiveled back to look at FX, who had returned his attention to the screens in front of him.

"Brundle had an appendectomy when he was twenty-four."

"Yeah?" FX murmured.

"The operation left scars."

"Yeah, well it would, wouldn't it?"

"So look at these photos. There were no scars on the torso."

FX glanced over, shrugged, then turned back to his screen.

"Maybe they're poor quality photos. Keyhole surgery's really good now—they can do it with really small cuts. So what?"

"No, the photos are fine," Scope said, looking more carefully. "And according to the file, the appendectomy was botched— they had to go in twice. He ended up with four different scars. The coroner's description of the corpse doesn't mention the marks either. And he goes to the bother of mentioning vaccination scars . . . this is odd."

FX was sitting up straighter now. He tilted his head to look at the photos that Scope was holding up to him.

"Let's say Brundle was looking for a way to remove scar tissue," she went on, "without surgery. Nimmo reckons he was experimenting with implants. Somehow, he figures out how to regrow skin using some kind of micro-technology. Say that's what all the fuss was about. What if he decided to test it on himself, and managed to completely remove his appendectomy scars? Somehow he figured out how to *program* the growth of new skin without leaving a blemish. What do you think the pharmaceutical companies would do to get hold of something like that? I mean, that'd have to be worth millions, right?"

FX had a slightly winded expression on his face.

"Billions," he said softly. "Worldwide? Billions of pounds . . . or euros, or dollars, or whatever. That kind of thing would be like the Holy Grail for the medical industry. It'd be worth a bloody fortune."

That was when the two rat-runners realized just how much trouble they could be in. They knew too many people who would kill for that kind of money—kill without a second thought. And there had to be any number of powerful organizations who'd do the same to get their hands on such a piece of technology. Even Move-Easy could be out of his depth.

"No wonder Brundle was scared," Scope sniffed.

"Ah, balls," FX sighed. "OK, I'm just trying to track down this guy, Frank Krieger, that Nimmo ran into. I'll check out Axis after that, all right? What are you up to?"

"Going back through Brundle's file, seeing if there's anything we missed," she lied. "I could really do with checking out his lab. Anyway, I'm going to get back to it."

"Awrighty," FX chirped, turning back to his screens again. "I'll be right here." He thought about the kind of money that could be at stake, and the kinds of people they could be up against. He stood up, hitching up his loose-waisted combats. "Actually, I have to go to the toilet. But I'll be back here eventually."

Scope left him to his business and headed back to her makeshift lab. Picking up the little bags of evidence, she began looking at them one by one. She desperately wanted to be back in her own lab, with all her equipment. This was a puzzle she'd have fun solving. She cast a self-conscious glance down at the photos of the dead man on her screen. Perhaps 'fun' might be the wrong word.

CHAPTER 18

VAPOR

FX STOOD ON THE SEVENTH-FLOOR BALCONY of a derelict apartment building, looking down at the alleyway below, where the white van was turning a corner and disappearing from sight. Scope stood to his right, leaning her arms on the railing. It was nearly noon and the sun made hard sharp shapes of the shadows between the buildings. Across from the two rat-runners, on the other side of the alley, was a newly refurbished five-story office block whose near side was still encased in scaffolding. The scaffolding was wrapped in plastic, as it was being used by a sandblasting team who were cleaning the outside of the building.

"That's gotta be it," Scope said.

"What's the stuff called again?" FX asked.

"Garnet," she replied. "It's often used to replace silica sand in sandblasting operations. Fewer health risks for the guys using it. But it still makes a mess. Even with the plastic sheeting, bits of it are going to get everywhere. This has got to be the place."

FX nodded. He was still disappointed that he hadn't solved this himself, but there was no denying that she'd cracked it when he couldn't.

The phone Nimmo had taken from Frank Krieger had divulged only three phone numbers. There were no names listed. FX had found the service providers for all three numbers, and pulled the records. The positions of the phones had only been recorded intermittently across London—obviously these guys were careful, and pulled the batteries when they didn't want to make calls. But all three phones had been used in this part of the city a number of times, on the Greenwich docks, not far from the Blackwall Tunnel. That was as close as he could get to finding a specific location. When he had hacked into the city's camera network—the privately owned ones, not the WatchWorld installations—he had been able to follow the van carrying Krieger and his partner back to this area, but then they had disappeared. That had been *damned* odd, until FX discovered that camera feeds had been interfered with. There was a hacker working ahead of him, covering the tracks of the van. Any footage showing the van once it entered Greenwich had been edited out. FX found that a little bit scary. Impressive, but scary. These guys were *really* good.

Scope had found him sitting at his desk, staring at the phone. He had entertained such high hopes that it would provide answers. Instead, all he had were more questions. It was Scope who had thought to examine the phone itself. She had discovered a distinctive kind of dust in the grooves and buttons. Just looking at the phone, the stuff had been barely detectable to the human eye, but once wiped off and enlarged under the microscope, she had been able to identify it.

"Garnet," FX said softly.

Alluvial garnet grains were used for sandblasting the exteriors of buildings, removing the stains left by pollution. FX had checked the street cameras. There was only one building in that area undergoing sandblasting. As luck would have it, they had arrived just in time to see Krieger and his partner driving away down the alley in their van.

"So what now?" Scope asked.

"We take a closer look," FX responded. "Carefully. Really, really carefully."

"What about Nimmo and Manikin? This is more their bag, don't you think? Want to call them in?"

"Do you?"

Scope shook her head. She was tired of being stuck inside all the time.

"Right," FX said tightly. "Then let's go."

Manikin and Nimmo had both been out when Scope had made her discovery, so she and FX had taken this bit of reconnaissance upon themselves. Following the rat-runs through the city, they had found their way here to this condemned apartment block overlooking their target. From the sides of the building that had no scaffolding, they could see that the windows of the first three floors were barred, but the floors above were less secure. FX was confident he could get in on the fourth floor.

A two-and-a-half-meter-high hoarding surrounded the base of the scaffold, the top half of the boards coated with greasy red anti-climb paint. He and Scope would have to get over those boards to reach the scaffold. There was no easy way of grabbing hold of the scaffolding bars, since they were covered by the taut plastic sheeting. The plastic was filthy, nearly impossible to see through, but there was a rip in the sheeting at the level of the second floor, above the hoarding. It was small, but big enough for an agile twelve- or thirteen-year-old to push through.

The alley was about seven or eight meters wide, lined with the rear entrances of a row of cafés and other small businesses. Outside those doors were wheelie bins, and it was bin day. FX had checked.

"Here it comes," Scope muttered.

A garbage truck was slowly making its way down the alley, the bin men pulling two wheelie bins out at a time, hooking them onto the arms on the back of the truck. From there, they were lifted up and their contents emptied into the clanking vehicle. The two rat-runners turned and bounded through the broken window behind them into a kitchen that had long ago been gutted of its cupboards and appliances, then into the corridor beyond and down ten flights of stairs. They had found the room that suited their needs earlier. It didn't have a balcony, but one of the large windows was unlocked and could be opened right out. The garbage truck was almost beneath them as they reached it.

"Ladies first," Scope exclaimed, hopping onto the windowsill.

She poked her head out, gauged the distance, judging it to be about two meters. Checking to see that neither of the bin men were looking up, she leaped out onto the roof of the passing truck. The sound of her feet hitting the steel roof was drowned out by the noise of the hydraulic arms dumping two more bins into the truck's innards. FX followed a moment later. The next jump would be harder. The torn hole in the plastic sheeting was just out of reach, so they'd have to jump up as well as out.

"My turn," FX told her.

The truck set off just as he stood up to make his move. It was a bigger leap—nearly two and a half meters—and he was jerked sideways as he jumped. He thrust his hands through the hole, dropping them to catch the ledger—the horizontal bar running behind the sheeting. In one motion, he lunged up and through the gap, his body and small backpack just fitting without getting caught in the dust-covered plastic. He tucked into a roll, expecting to land on the boards that should have formed a floor beyond the ledger . . . but found himself falling into thin air instead. It was only his grip on the bar with his right hand that kept him from hitting the ground seven meters below. With a gasp, he got his other hand up to the bar, his feet dangling until he could brace them against the vertical bars known as standards.

Scope had been even more rushed in her jump, and there was shouting as she was spotted by the bin men. Like FX, she came headfirst through the rip in the plastic, but unlike him, she let go of the ledger before she realized there was no floor. She let out a panicked cry, her hands flailing, and FX just managed to catch her wrist as she fell past him. Her hand closed around his wrist in reflex, and his arm was nearly wrenched from its socket as he stopped her fall. She swung over onto the ledger below him, letting go of his hand, and hung there, breathing hard.

"Thanks," she panted.

"Don't mention it."

There were boards further along at FX's level, and Scope climbed up to join him as he scrambled over to them.

"Bloody vermin!" one of the bin men called from below. "You'll get yourselves killed, you fools! Why aren't you in school?"

But the garbage collectors left it at that. They saw plenty of rat-runners on their rounds, and knew they were the kind of trouble that was best ignored.

There was dust everywhere inside the scaffolding frame, the boards and plastic covered in it, spoiling the look of the freshly scoured walls. FX rubbed his hands; the palms were grazed from the rough, dried splashes of cement that coated the steel bars. There were ladders up through the scaffolding to the fourth floor, where the windows weren't barred. He and Scope scaled the ladders in no time, and on the fourth-floor boards, FX found a window he knew he could open.

Double-glazing was extremely difficult to break; it was easier to lever out the frame. Neither FX nor Scope carried a crowbar, however; a good way of inviting the attention of the police was to have a Safe-Guard spot one in your bag—it was hard to hide a steel bar from someone with x-ray vision. Using a crowbar also took a lot of strength, more than most teenage kids could normally bring to bear, and it could be noisy too. But FX had another way.

Fire services used a piece of hydraulic equipment called a 'spreader,' for prizing the pieces of a crashed car apart to get people out. The pincers could crush or spread metal with huge force. FX had made a much smaller, simpler version using a woodwork clamp. He kept it broken down to its component parts, so that it would be less obvious what it was. Some of those parts could also be used for other things.

Scope watched with interest as he quickly put it together and jammed the flat ends of the pincers in under the window frame. In his bag, he had a builder's sensor for finding electrical wires in walls. Looking through the glass into the space inside, he examined the frame with his eyes and then with the sensor for any sign of wiring for a burglar alarm, but didn't see anything. Then he slid a long screwdriver through the hole at the top of the screw to act as a lever.

"Couldn't you just use a glass cutter to make a hole in the window pane?" she asked.

"You mean with a suction cup, like in the films?" he snorted. "Try it. You can make a nice neat circle OK, but you can't pull the bleedin' thing out."

Gripping the screwdriver at either end with both hands, he twisted the clamp's screw and the frame was forced open a few millimeters at a time. After several turns, they heard a crack. Together, they got their fingers in under the frame and pulled hard. The latch finally broke completely and the window swung open.

They climbed inside and found themselves in what would probably end up as some kind of storeroom. There was no door in the doorway, so they moved on out into an office space, and beyond that to a corridor. It seemed that none of the rooms had been fitted with doors yet.

"That should make looking around a bit easier," Scope whispered.

FX nodded, and they set off down the corridor, peering into each room in turn. They weren't certain what they looking for, but were sure they'd know it if they found it.

"This could take ages," Scope said, after they'd checked out a number of rooms. "Let's think this through. If you were going to get up to something dodgy in an empty building, where would you do it?"

"Depends what I was doing," FX replied. "But probably where I'm least likely to be seen or heard—some room with no windows, or with the windows covered, either on the top floor or the basement. And if I'm using computer gear, I'd want to be as far from the sandblasters as possible. Probably the basement, but let's say we start at the top and work down?"

She agreed. The elevators were working, but using them would be stupid, so they crept up the stairwell that joined the floors at one end of the building. There were doors sectioning off the stairwell from the corridor on each floor. At the fifth floor, Scope was about to push through the door into the corridor when FX stopped her. He peered through the small square of glass in the door, then ducked his head back.

"PIR sensor," he muttered. "And it's working. They're not

very good at seeing through glass, so I don't think I triggered it, but there's no getting in that way. Not without a bit more preparation."

"There weren't any on the floor we came in on," Scope pointed out. "So what makes this floor so important?"

"Looking at the layout of this place, I'd say most of the rooms have windows," FX suggested. "Maybe these guys have been sloppy, and left some uncovered. Why don't we go up to the roof and find out?"

The only building directly overlooking the office block was the derelict building they had just come from, and all the other buildings nearby were lower, so the chances of being spotted were slim. FX assured Scope that there were no satellites overhead at that time of day—he had a piece of software that tracked their movements and sent updates to his phone—though he couldn't be sure about spotter planes or drones. They'd have to take the chance. A door in the corridor led to another that opened onto a flight of stairs that took them up to the flat, painted concrete rooftop. Around them, metal boxes for vents and air-conditioning units formed aluminum islands in the cream-colored concrete.

"How are we going to look in the windows?" Scope asked, wishing she'd brought her keyhole camera.

But FX had the next best thing. Taking a roll of stiff cable from his bag, he unwound it and attached one end to a small digital camera using a clamp he had designed himself. As with his improvised spreader, the pieces looked innocent enough, but it was how he put them together that made their use suspicious.

"Let's start with the side opposite the scaffolding," he said. "See what we can see."

"Right. Don't be too obvious, OK?"

He switched the camera to video, then plugged the other end into a small tablet. Nothing came up on the screen. He checked the camera was on, then tapped the screen of the tablet. Scope watched him tap it again. She sighed, putting a hand to her face.

"Bugger," he said. "Tablet's on. We should have the view from the camera. There must be a short in the cable. And the wireless doesn't work on this camera."

"We're supposed to be professionals here!" Scope said sharply. "Don't you *test* your gear before you use it on a job? I thought you were meant to be some hotshot brainiac?"

"The cable worked fine last time I used it!" FX protested. "There must be a kink in it . . . a broken connection somewhere."

"What—in the wire, or in your *brain*?"

"If we didn't have to keep our phones off here, we could—"

"Yeah, but we do, don't we?" Scope cut him off. "Come on, let's go downstairs and see if we can—"

FX held up his hand.

"Look, wait . . . I can just set it to record, lower it down, then pull it up every few meters and check out what it's picked up."

"We're not filming *hamsters in their burrow* here, FX. Given the psycho hit men we could be dealing with, I'd feel better if we weren't using kit that looks like it was made on *Blue Peter*!"

But when it came down to it, Scope didn't have any better

ideas, so she gave up and waved him on. He lowered the camera over the side of the building, until it was hanging just below the top of the fifth-floor window, where it could film what was inside. The cable was rigid enough for him to be able to keep the camera pointed in the right direction, though the breeze caused it to sway from side to side slightly.

There was nothing for Scope to do for the next few minutes. She walked to another corner of the building and looked down. With a grunt of interest, she went back over to FX and tapped his arm.

"There's a window open around this side."

FX wound his cable back up and looked at what he had recorded as they crossed the roof to the other end. The rooms he had filmed were empty. Reaching the parapet, he slowly and carefully lowered the phone again, paying out the cable until the camera was just below the top of the open window.

"Give it a minute or two," Scope said to him. "No more. We're pushing our luck as it is."

FX nodded and looked at his watch. After a minute and a half had passed, he raised the camera up and stopped it recording, switching it to play. They both gazed at the screen.

The room that came shakily into view was unlike any of the others they had seen. The camera had been hanging out in the daylight, looking into a darker room, so the light in the picture wasn't great. They could see tables set around the walls of the room, laid out with portable computer gear. Scope and FX both let out low whistles as they took in the laptops, servers and other pieces of hardware, impressed with what looked like top-end gear. A foldable satellite dish lay on one table, beside a bank of monitors, a selection of cameras and a bunch of other pieces of equipment they couldn't identify.

"See that?" FX murmured, pointing at a gun-shaped object with a dish at the end of the short barrel. "Think that's a long-range parabolic mike."

Scope nodded—she'd recognized it. It was a microphone that could pick up sounds from hundreds of meters away. There were wardrobe-sized metal cabinets in the room too. One stood open to show an array of assorted objects mounted on racks, ranging from an umbrella to a pair of boots, a rolled-up newspaper to a briefcase.

"Not sure what to make of those," FX grunted.

But in her time in Move-Easy's Void, Scope had seen most of these objects used in another context. Seeing them all together like this suggested only one thing to her.

"Weapons," she said. "I think they're all fitted with concealed weapons."

Then the camera's speaker, which up to now had just emitted the papery roar of wind across its mike, gave the hint of another sound. A voice. A man came into view, walking in through a doorway, speaking on a phone. He was a muscular, stocky man with long blond hair tied back in ponytail. He wore jeans and a black T-shirt emblazoned with the old death metal band, Absent Conscience, on it. His face was still in shadow, but he had rectangular, black plastic-framed glasses, and the stylized horror tattoos on his arms confirmed his death metal obsession. FX and Scope huddled around the camera's tiny speaker to try and hear what he was saying.

" . . . that's not whut he sayd," Death Metal's voice could just be heard saying over the sound of the wind. His accent was either Scottish or Northern Irish, it was hard to tell. The sound was being broken up by the interference on the mike: "He never sayd she *didn't have it*. He just . . . wuzn't *in hor apartment*. Whut? I don't know . . . ask him, why don't yeh? Huh? . . . moan all yeh like. Vapor paid this numpty, and he wants . . . give a damn about the cards. We do this . . . whut I mean? Performance-related bonus an' all that . . . got tae be worth a hundred gra— . . . Brundle didn't come cheap . . . wants his stuff, and he duzn't—"

At that point, the man's face turned towards the camera. There was still a shadow over his face, but they could feel his eyes staring straight out of the screen, seeming to fix FX and Scope in his gaze. He had spotted the camera. He froze and stopped speaking. Then he spun around and ran for the door.

"Jesus," FX swore, looking up.

They were watching a recording. Death Metal had run from the room nearly a minute before. Which was how he managed to be *right there now*, just three meters away from them on the roof . . . with a bloody great hunting knife in his hand.

Scope dived and rolled, coming to her feet behind him as he lunged forward. The knife came at FX, but he stepped to the side and whipped the cable at the man's face. It only distracted the man for an instant, but it was enough time for FX to duck under his swinging arm and start running along by the parapet. Scope was just ahead of him, looking back just once to make sure he was with her. FX detached the little camera from the cable and slipped it into his jacket pocket. He heard heavy feet accelerating along the roof behind him.

Scope reached the side of the building covered in scaffolding—the scaffolding that was entirely encased in tough plastic sheeting. There was no easy way in. She turned and jumped onto the parapet, running full tilt along it, pulling her small multi-tool from her pocket and unfolding the blade. Aiming for one of the open spaces of plastic, free of steel bars, she leaped forward onto it, skidding along it on her backside. She dug the blade in as she slid, cutting a long gash through it behind her. FX was right on her heels, and with one bound, jumped over the parapet and punched feet-first straight down through the hole, tearing it wide open. Scope was now sitting with her feet over the side of the slippery sheeting, and rolled backwards before she could lose her tenuous grip.

Death Metal had switched his sights from FX to her, and now he was up on the parapet above her as she came up against it. He made to grab her, and she dragged the nails of her left hand down his arm, drawing blood. He snarled, but it hardly slowed him down at all. She scrambled back out onto the plastic, and turned to look at him. Death Metal was glaring down at her, his eyes warily judging the strength of the sheeting, unwilling to put his greater weight on it. It probably wouldn't even hold *her* for long if she wasn't spreading her weight by staying on her hands and knees.

"Don't be stupid," he said in a reasonable voice, motioning her towards him with his empty hand. "You could fall, kill yorself. I'm not going tae hort yeh—I just want tae ask yeh a few questions."

OISÍN McGANN

"The feeling's mutual," she replied in a shaky voice, holding up the fingers she'd used to scratch him. "But you've got a much bigger knife. And I've got everything I need right here."

Then she plunged headfirst down through the rent in the plastic. She had a grip on a transom—one of the cross-bars across the top—as she tumbled through, and controlled her fall to touch down neatly on the boards below. As her eyes found FX, she jumped towards him, seeing what he was about to do. Death Metal and his huge knife came crashing down through the plastic, landing heavily on the boards where she had been standing a moment earlier. Then FX yanked one of the boards from the other end, dislodging it. The cement-covered plank fell from under the guy, who lost his footing and let out a shout as he fell, one leg dangling down through the gap.

Scope and FX slid down the ladder to the next level, but then had to dive aside as a grunt of effort and a rain of dust from above made them look up. FX gasped as dust got in his eyes, but he was already out of the way of a second heavy board as it clattered down. Scope had to throw herself forward and, rolling over, she looked up again to see their pursuer drop straight down through the wider gap in the floor above. Death Metal let out a snort of satisfaction as he landed beside FX, stamping on the boy's left calf hard enough to make him cry out. Probably just a dead leg—but FX wouldn't be running anywhere for the next few minutes. Scope was standing under another gap in the boards above her, and she jumped, just as the hunting knife slammed into the boards where her foot had been a moment before. Like a monkey, she scampered up one of the poles hugging the wall of the building, ending up back on the level above, where they'd started.

"Come on dine, sweetheart," Death Metal called. "I don't hurt kids as a rule, but it'll go bad for your friend if you don't get yer arse dine here right nye."

Scope closed her eyes for a couple of seconds, trying to get control over her breathing. Damn this bloody dust—she was covered in it, and it was causing havoc with her lungs. But she couldn't slow down now. She crouched down, unzipping the pockets on either side of her jacket. There was an inhaler in each pocket—a blue one in the right, and a brown one in the left. Looking down through the cracks between the stout bare planks, she could see him watching her. She would only be a dark shape against the light, but it was enough for him to follow her.

"Come on nye," he said in a softer, more confident voice. "Yer breathin' don't sound too good, love. Asthmatic, are we? You need to get out of here, before it gets any worse."

Scope coughed, and exaggerated the sound of her wheezing as she shook both inhalers. Taking a blast of the blue one, she held her breath, slipping that one back into her pocket.

"All right," she said, coughing again. "Don't hurt him. I'm coming down, OK? I'm coming down."

Checking his position through the cracks between the planks, she jammed her right foot between a board and the ledger. Then she swung the top half of her body down through the gap and sprayed Death Metal in the face with her brown inhaler. This one was highly pressurized—it wasn't designed to ease one's breathing.

Death Metal staggered back from the blast of the aerosol, rubbing his eyes and gagging. He drew in a huge breath and let out an almighty sneeze, and then another. The force of the sneezes caused him to bend forward. Scope pulled herself up, released her foot, grabbed hold of the transom and swung like a gymnast, bringing her whole body feet-first down and under the bar, and slamming the soles of her trainers into the top of Death Metal's head. He cried out and tumbled backwards.

FX was already on his feet, rubbing his eyes, but he could only limp towards the ladder that led down to the next floor. Scope let him go ahead of her, then slid down the ladder after him. Above them, they could hear Death Metal sneezing help-lessly, cursing and groaning as he struggled to breathe, or even open his eyes. FX let out a grunt as he jumped off the ladder, taking some weight on his bruised leg.

"What the hell was in that thing you hit him with?" he asked.

"Pepper, some Indian Unani powder, a little ammonia and a few other things," she replied. "A little potion I mixed up for this kind of thing. Keeps the lads at bay back in Move-Easy's."

They descended another ladder and strode along the boards to the hole in the plastic where they'd first come in, on the sec-ond floor. This was the section of scaffold without any boards; there should have been a ladder here, but it was missing. They dangled off the transom and were about to drop down to the first floor, when they heard a clatter from above. A sneeze turned into a high-pitched shriek, and they both let out yelps as Death Metal fell past them, hitting the ground below.

"Gaaaaaargh! Jesus Christ, me leg! Aaaargh! Jesus, I've broken me leg! Jesus!" he bellowed, and then started sneezing again, letting out roars of pain whenever he could draw breath, each violent blast of breath causing a spasm of agony in his broken leg, which caused more cries, and more sneezing.

The door in the tall wooden hoarding was locked, and they didn't want to climb down past Death Metal anyway. As Scope cut a hole in the wall of plastic sheeting at their level, FX found a length of rope, tied one end to a standard and tossed the other end out of the hole.

"Ladies first," he said.

Scope lowered herself out and abseiled carefully down past the greasy anti-climb paint on the hoarding. FX followed her down. His leg was loosening up, but he was still limping a little as they set off down the alley at a fast walk. They were breathing hard, shivering with a mixture of relief and adrenaline.

"So you hit him with sneezing powder?" FX asked, feeling restless, needing to talk.

"Yeah, but a pretty high-powered dose of it." She smirked, cocking her head as she listened to Death Metal letting rip, swearing and screaming behind them. "He'll calm down a bit in a few minutes, but he'll be sneezing for days."

"Cool!" FX laughed. "I'd have used tear gas myself. Or turned the bloody thing into a flame-thrower."

"The guys who were bullying me in Easy's?" Scope said, as she took a little zip-lock plastic bag from her pocket. "Most of 'em were too thick to be afraid of being hurt. I had to come up with a way of humiliating them—making the others laugh."

FX watched as she tore a toothpick out of a packet and used it to clean the blood from under the nails of her left hand—the blood and skin she'd scraped from Death Metal's arm.

"Move-Easy keeps files on every criminal his people ever come across," she explained to him. "He's got his own automated system for analyzing DNA, and a huge DNA database. For him, it's all ammunition he can use against them. I can even get Tanker to pipe me into the police database if I need to. This guy's DNA has to be on record somewhere. Give me a day or two, and I'll find out who he is."

"I'll race you," FX challenged her. "We've already got his voice recorded. Even that should be enough."

"Right," she said. "But what we really need now is his *employer*. Who is *Vapor*?"

After walking a few blocks, they both put their batteries back in their phones and turned them on. Scope's beeped immediately with a message. It was from Tanker. It wasn't good news.

CHAPTER 19

FOLLOWING

TANKER HAD SENT AN ENCRYPTED PIECE OF VIDEO to Scope's phone, with a message. As well as cracking online security for various dodgy purposes, one of Tanker's jobs was to download all the video files recorded by the miniature cameras carried by Move-Easy's people. Part of that task involved editing Coda out of any of these files. It was one of the conditions under which Coda worked for Easy—he was never to be recorded on film. Whenever he was caught on any of Easy's cameras, those images were to be deleted. It was a deal that Easy honored. Even someone like Move-Easy was wary of crossing Coda.

Tanker relished this part of the job, and Scope would often slag him about the man-crush he seemed to have on the enig-matic assassin. But she couldn't help a certain morbid fascination with the pieces of footage he showed her from time to time—the momentary glimpses the cameras picked up of the murderer at work. Tanker had just sent her one of those clips. It was a big risk to take; Scope winced at the thought of Easy or Coda finding out about her friend's indiscretion.

The piece of video had obviously been cut from a longer recording. On it, she could see three figures in balaclavas. The tiny camera was carried in a piercing on the face of a fourth villain. They were in the last throes of a raid, in what looked like a back-street implant clinic. In the gloomy swinging light cast by their torches, she could make out the features of the operating theater. She spotted two bodies lying still on the floor, as well as a woman tied up in the operating chair, her wide eyes watching the proceedings in terror.

A stack of boxes and packages stood next to a bundle of cash, all of these spoils waiting to be scooped into the last of three bulky black sports bags. An implant clinic . . . Scope was reminded of the job Punkin and Bunny had brought to Move-Easy. Sure enough, one of the figures lifted his mask to wipe sweat off his face, revealing Punkin's face long enough for any functional security camera to get a good clear look at him. He pulled the balaclava back down, shoved the remaining takings into the last bag and waved the others towards the door.

They found their path blocked by three Asian men—one large, one larger, and one gigantic. It seemed Punkin and his new posse had knocked over the wrong outfit. This place was protected. The first guy was a wide-boy in a glossy suit, armed with an automatic. The second was a muscular troll with a crew cut dressed in camo gear, the image completed by a thick cigar and a MAC-10 machine pistol. The third was an ogre in a track-suit wielding a TEC-9 machine pistol. Each man had the cold, hard eyes of a killer.

"You stupid wazzocks," Crew Cut snorted. "Don't you know who owns this place?"

In the first few seconds that they appeared on camera, gun barrels raised, there seemed to be no doubt about the grim fate of the raiders. But then, in the shadows behind the door, to the far left of Scope's screen, there was a smear of movement. The raiders had brought protection of their own.

Coda's face was visible for an instant as he moved out of the shadows. In a liquid flow of motion, he seemed to move faster than the video's frames could capture. Gliding from left to right, his body pivoted, his arms swirled and jabbed. A gunshot was heard, the muzzle flash overly bright, the camera struggling to adjust. The resolution came back, the picture cleared. Just over three seconds had passed, and now Coda was on the right-hand side of the screen. He had Crew Cut's cigar between his lips. He plucked it from his mouth and blew out some smoke.

The first man was collapsing, screaming, a bullet wound in his leg. The other two were sprawling to the floor after him, dis-armed, and either unconscious or already dead—it was impossible to tell. Scope stared at the screen. For the third time, she rewound it and watched it in slow motion . . . and Coda still looked fast.

Starting from the left: Wide-Boy became aware of Coda as the assassin stepped into the light. He swung his weapon, but Coda caught the man's gun hand in a move that looked almost gentle, sweeping it down as Wide-Boy's finger tightened on the trigger. By the time the shot was fired, the gun was pointing down at the man's thigh. In the burned-out flash of the shot, Coda stepped past, even as Wide-Boy's leg jolted under the impact of the bullet.

The camera's resolution was only starting to recover from the flash as Crew Cut reacted to this new threat. His arm swung around, but this time Coda ducked underneath. The heel of his right hand drove into Crew Cut's sternum, knocking him backwards, the cigar propelled from his mouth. Coda caught the cigar in mid-air, moving past towards the Ogre. He jabbed the burning tip of the cigar into the Ogre's hand, causing the man to flinch, letting go of his machine pistol. Coda caught the gun with his other hand and swung the butt back with a crack against Crew Cut's temple, dispatching the man as he tried to bring his gun up to aim at Coda's head.

The Ogre was quick for such a big guy, pivoting to face his opponent even before his friend fell . . . but he seemed to be moving through treacle compared to Coda. Coda yanked Crew Cut into the path of the Ogre's pile-driver punch. Instead of hitting Coda, the blow snapped Crew Cut's head to the side. Then Coda was sweeping past the giant man, the cigar jabbing up under the Ogre's chin. On reflex, the Ogre's head lifted away from the burning pain, leaving his neck and jaw wide open. Coda slammed the butt of the gun up under the man's jaw hard enough to break his neck, jolt him off his feet and drop him like a rag doll onto the floor.

The final image on the video clip was the look of arrogant

disdain on Coda's face as he glanced back towards the camera, exhaling cigar smoke. Then he disappeared through the door. Scope let out a long breath. Once again, she read the message Tanker had sent with the clip:

Easy's getting impatient. I think he's got Coda watching you. Mind yourself.

Scope was watching it again, carefully, and was so engrossed in what she was seeing that it took a few moments to hear Manikin's voice intruding on her thoughts:

"Incoming! Oi! Eyes on the road, girl!"

Scope gave a start, lifted her head, then jumped aside just in time to avoid the man in the clown costume who ran past, screaming, with his feet on fire. It was a magic trick that had gone wrong. The man could no doubt take comfort from the fact that he'd finally got the attention he'd been seeking from the cameras. Though he might be too busy trying to put his feet out to savor the moment.

She was walking through town with Nimmo and Manikin, and their route had taken them up Vauxhall Bridge Road, towards Victoria Station. There was a high concentration of WatchWorld cameras in this area, and it had become a popular area for people trying to get 'brasted.' A term drawn from 'casted for broadcasting,' it was used to refer to the people who desperately tried to draw attention to themselves in order to appear on the WatchWorld screens installed all over the city.

Anyone whose behavior succeeded in getting them brasted for more than fifteen minutes earned themselves a boon—a small payment—and the chance to be followed about their daily lives by the cameras. Online viewers could vote on who to follow, and the longer the braster could keep the audience's attention, the more money they could earn. Successful brasters could go on to become celebrities, and earn fortunes, but for most, it was just a chance to be famous, if only for a few minutes.

The paths of Vauxhall Bridge Road were teeming with hundreds of people, individually and in groups, struggling to get noticed. Some were professional street entertainers, some small-time entrepreneurs, but most were just attention-seekers, desperate to be famous for nothing in particular. The three rat-runners passed people dressed in all sorts of outlandish costumes, from *Star Wars* droids to orcs from *The Lord of the Rings*; a theater group performing Shakespeare's *Othello* in animal costumes; a man dressed in a deep-sea diver's suit, playing bagpipes; an English woman in an ethnic African dress, trying to convert people to some new-age religion; an inventor trying to sell virtual reality goggles for pets.

Manikin was approached by a young white man with quiffed brown hair, dressed in a suit whose trouser legs did not quite reach his socks.

"I bet you I can predict your thoughts," he said in a loud voice, hoping to be heard by the people around him. "Pick a number between one and ten, and I'll have that number written here on my left arm."

"Six," Manikin said in an uninterested voice.

"You say six!" he announced. "Let's see now . . . here it is!"

With a flourish, he pulled up his left sleeve to reveal the number six, which appeared to be written in marker on his arm.

"Brilliant!" Manikin said, smiling, reaching for his wrist as if to take a closer look.

Her hand closed around his fancy wristwatch, and with a shift of her thumb, she turned the dial that encircled the face of the watch. The six on his arm turned to a five, and then a four; then she twisted the dial the other way, and the number changed to a nine and a ten.

"A tattoo implant?" Manikin snorted at him. "I saw you flick the dial as you pulled up your sleeve. So that's it? That's your big feat of magic? What else can it do? A bunch of pictures, right? Or maybe you can type out words on your skin too? Bit of a one-trick pony, aren't you? Go learn some card tricks, ya loser."

The man scowled at her and hurried away through the crowd.

"Thought we were trying to keep a low profile?" Nimmo muttered.

"Are you kidding?" she retorted. "The only way to get noticed around here is to act normal."

Scope wasn't so sure. She was always nervous being outside during the day, between nine and four. Conscious of how young she looked, she always expected to have a copper or a peeper clap a hand on her shoulder and ask her why she wasn't in school. Maybe that was why the older two had chosen this route—there was so much going on, the city's watchers were unlikely to notice three kids minding their own business. But Nimmo wasn't about to make her feel very secure.

"Have you noticed the guy following us?" he asked her.

"What? No!" she exclaimed, but she was careful not to look

around her. Could it be Coda? she wondered. Had Move-Easy lost patience with them?

"It's the guy who was in the van with Krieger," Manikin said in a low voice, though that didn't make Scope feel much better. "About ten meters back, black guy with close-cut hair and a goatee. Wearing a dark gray suede jacket and tan jeans."

"Let's get a closer look at him," Nimmo said to them. "Quick, in here."

He ducked into a café, stopping just inside the door. Stepping to the side, he watched through the window, with the others behind him, as the guy passed along the path. Their tail must have seen them step inside, but he ignored them, making no attempt to follow them into the café.

"They'll have at least one other person shadowing us too," Manikin said. "Probably up ahead of us, waiting to switch with him. Let's stay here for a few minutes, see if we can make anyone who comes in."

Manikin and Scope got some coffees up at the counter, Nimmo treated himself to a sparkling water, and they went and sat down at a table against the wall near the door; a position that gave them a view out of the window. The noise in the café would make it difficult for anyone to hear, and they kept their voices low, and their heads close to each other across the table.

"We didn't have to come out here, y'know," Scope told Nimmo. "Why don't you just let me go back to Easy's? It's my base. I can do my tests there, and his people will help me give these guys the slip."

"I don't want you going back if we can avoid it," he replied.

"Move-Easy didn't want to let you out in the first place, and if he finds out we're attracting this kind of attention, he's liable to keep you in if you go back. Whatever gear you need, Tubby Reach either has it, or he can get it. The less contact we have with Easy, the better."

Right, Scope thought. And the less likely I am to tell Easy that you already have the box. She wondered if Nimmo trusted anyone at all.

"Things are getting complicated," Manikin said, sipping her coffee. "We could do with a round-up of the week's news. Here's how I see it:

"We're looking for a box that contains ten blank cards—credit cards of some kind. We know the box was in the possession of Watson Brundle. We don't know what the value of the cards might be, but Move-Easy's dead keen to get his hands on them, so they've gotta be worth a *bomb*. Based on what FX and Scope picked up when they were out, we think Brundle did a dodgy job for someone powerful—who we're calling Vapor—and the cards were Brundle's payment, or part of it."

"Whoever this Vapor guy is, he's a pretty serious customer," Scope took up the narrative. "Like, *scary* serious. Frank Krieger had WatchWorld gear on him when Nimmo flattened him. He's a well-known ex-con—he couldn't have been a real WatchWorld operative, but Vapor somehow has the means to equip him as one."

"Everything we know about Brundle suggests he didn't normally mix with villains," Nimmo put in. "We don't know what this job was, but Scope reckons it centers around the repair of scar tissue using some kind of implant. If her theory is right, Brundle could have come up with a way to . . . to *program* the growth of new skin—technology that would be worth an absolute *fortune*. We do know that Brundle was mugged a couple of weeks ago, and his case was stolen. If it was one of Move-Easy's trolls, it could explain how a street-level villain like Easy found out about Brundle's work."

"We can't be sure of that yet," Scope cut in. "But we know Brundle's behavior changed after the mugging. If Easy figured out what Brundle was working on, right there on Easy's territory, there's no way he'd miss out on grabbing a cut of that kind of money."

"And once Move-Easy took an interest," Nimmo added, "Brundle had a big problem. On one hand, he had Move-Easy demanding a piece of the profits, or maybe even wanting to take the whole thing over himself. On the other, Brundle has to satisfy this mysterious Vapor guy, who's possibly even more dangerous than Easy. So what happened? Did Brundle try and screw one of them over and get himself killed? And if we assume that the box of credit cards was his fee from the client, does that mean Brundle finished the job?"

"We know Vapor's lot have Brundle's daughter under surveillance," Manikin said. "Maybe they're looking for the box too. They could also be looking for whatever Brundle was working on. Maybe Brundle never handed it over. Or maybe he did, and Vapor's guys are just getting rid of loose ends to keep it all a secret."

"Whatever that secret is," Scope concluded helpfully.

"Still too many questions," Nimmo said, pressing his finger-tips against the cold glass containing his iced water.

"But it all really comes back to just one question," Manikin reminded them. "*Where's the box?* My money's on the daughter, but I'd still like to know where that kid went—the one who lived on the same floor as Brundle."

Nimmo turned to watch through the window as a half-naked man with nipple piercings hung an *Oxford English Dictionary* from each ring. Beyond the braster, Nimmo could see the black man with the goatee leaning against a lamppost on the far side of the street, not looking at the café.

"I'm sure he'll turn up," he murmured. "It's a big city, but it's hard to stay lost in it for long."

CHAPTER 20

CLOCK'S TICKIN'

AFTER THEY'D STAYED IN THE CAFÉ for over an hour, the three rat-runners decided to split up, to divide the men who were shadowing them. Manikin had to go and check out the nightclub and its surrounding streets, so she headed out first, turning left outside the café. Nimmo and Scope exited a few minutes later, turning right towards Victoria Station.

Once inside the station, Nimmo led Scope to an elevator, timing it so that they could get in alone. He pressed the button for the lowest floor, then, after the doors had slid closed, pressed the button for closing the doors three times, and then another three times. The elevator began to descend. It did not stop at the lowest floor, continuing on down another few meters.

"Move-Easy has one of these," Scope commented. "But only he and a few of his closest guys are allowed to use it."

"Reach has two, but he only ever uses the other one," Nimmo replied. "It's a cargo elevator. He wouldn't fit through this door. Listen, Scope, Tubby should be OK about us buying some time in his lab, but let me do the talking once we're inside, OK? Only answer a question if he or one of his brothers ask you directly. And try and stay out of the way of Gort—he's the one with the implants, and he's not as . . . *polite* as his brother."

The elevator doors opened into the corridor that led to the same well-appointed waiting room that Nimmo had so recently visited through. He and Scope passed the small group of people waiting for an audience with the King of the Getters. A ferret-faced woman with small black eyes and bright-red nail varnish sat in one of the chairs, reading a magazine filled with real-life drama. Nimmo drew in a breath, raising his left hand up as if to scratch the side of his head, hiding his face from the woman, as he walked past.

"That's Amelia Caper," he murmured to Scope, as he opened the door and closed it behind them. "She owns the apartment on the floor below Brundle's lab. What the hell's she doing here?"

"Maybe she's here to sell him a box of blank credit cards," Scope suggested.

"More likely chasing down the latest gossip in gangsterland."

Nimmo gave her a faint grin, as they were met by one of the women who acted as Reach's hosts. The pair of rat-runners were let into Reach's inner chamber, which still pulsed with music, its multi-level floor space and couched booths lit like an exclusive members' club. Tubby Reach greeted them warmly and exchanged a few civil words with Scope, his perceptive eyes reading much more from her appearance than she was giving him in words. Nimmo explained what they needed—without saying what for—and was surprised when Reach agreed without fixing a price.

Reach gestured to his youngest brother, and Gort stepped forward and gently took Scope's arm, leading her out of the room. Her eyes were looking back anxiously at Nimmo as she went through the door, but he nodded reassuringly to her.

"We would seem to have a problem in common," Reach said to Nimmo, as his brother and Scope left. "Namely, that tangerine psycho, Move-Easy."

Nimmo didn't reply at first. He was immediately suspicious. He hadn't told Reach that he was working for Easy, and if Reach was having him watched, Nimmo wasn't happy about it. He'd be even more unhappy that he hadn't spotted the watchers.

"Don't go all chilly on me." Reach held up his fat hands. "It's not you I was watchin'—it was this numpty."

The obese Asian crime boss had a screen built into his desk, and he tilted it to show Nimmo. A piece of video was playing on it. An operating theater being ransacked by three men and a woman, all wearing balaclavas. Reach froze the clip and pointed at one of the men, who was little more than a boy, hardly older than Nimmo. The idiot had lifted his balaclava to wipe sweat off his face, and had been caught by the hidden camera.

"His name's Punkin," Nimmo said. "That's about how dumb he is."

"I know," Reach grunted. "The girl must be his piece o' skirt, Bunny. And we've since found out those trolls he's with are from *Move-Easy*'s gang. Me an' Easy normally keep out of each other's way in the interests of avoidin' costly violence, but that's Punkin an' Co. knocking over one of my clinics, the one I told you about the other day. What you ain't seein' is Coda—you know Coda, right? He showed up just long enough to take three of my lads apart—one's dead, one's brain-damaged and one's got a bullet hole through his leg. Anyway, this little gang of trolls relieved my staff of a large wodge of my cash, and a batch of the latest implants from Axis Health Solutions—real state-of-the-art stuff.

"We got one new lot in that can change your eye color, even make 'em glow in the dark. People love that crap. Looks right spooky on the street screens. Got another kind too that can give you a false tan at the press of a button. Can make a white man black, just can't do it the other way. It'd work fine on your pale arse. You could do with a bit o' color."

"Maybe that's what Move-Easy was after," Nimmo said. "Sort out his skin problems."

"Yeah, maybe. Me, I'm just waitin' on one that'll turn you thin."

"Nah." Nimmo shook his head. "You just need one that'll make you give up your mum's cooking."

Reach laughed. "That kind o' science don't exist!"

"So how did *you* get these Axis implants? You steal 'em?"

"Not me personally, y'understand. I just happened to know some boys who hijacked a van takin' 'em from the lab to the airport."

"And now somebody's stolen them from you."

"Right, some people got no respect, y'know? Anyway, it was this Punkin who led the raid. Took my fellas a few hours to find the little monkey, and we've been watchin' him ever since. Move-Easy should know better than to knock over one of my operations—neither of us wants a turf war—but maybe he didn't know. Doesn't matter now. What matters is that I get my stuff back, or I get back at him—preferably both.

"A couple of my girls were following Punkin when he and Bunny ran into you and that one, Manikin, who you were with that time. You done 'em up nicely, I hear."

"That was nothing," Nimmo said uneasily. "Those two gombeens were trying their luck, that's all. I'm doing a job for Move-Easy, I don't have any trouble with him."

"No, Nimmo," Reach told him. "If you were all peachy with that Cockney Oompa-Loompa, he wouldn't have *Coda* shadowing you."

Nimmo felt cold air against his skin.

"What? What are you talking about? I haven't seen any sign of Coda."

"That's 'cos he don't *want* you to see him, boy. Guy's unnatural, Nimmo. Killed a man with a light bulb once—just for laughs. Move-Easy don't let that dog off its leash unless he's intendin' to *use* it, you get me?"

Nimmo avoided Reach's gaze, staring at the wall behind the fat man, but he nodded in agreement.

"Whatever you're into, it's high stakes," Reach said. "I know there's four of you rat-runners mixed up in it, that Easy has you lookin' for something, and that you're up against Watch-World . . . or somebody who's in with WatchWorld. And it's got something to do with a dead man named Watson Brundle. You're out of your depth, Nimmo." Tubby Reach leaned as far forward as his massive torso would allow, his expensive green silk shirt failing to hide the way his man-boobs created folds over his blubbery belly. His eyes were hard and eager. "But if you've got a line on something Move-Easy wants this badly, then I want it too—so let's us do some business."

Right, like there aren't enough villains involved already, Nimmo mused.

"Let me get back to you on that," he said.

"Yeah, well, don't take too long," Reach warned him. "Coda's got his eyes on you, boy. Clock's tickin'."

CHAPTER 21

GETTING TECHNICAL

TUBBY REACH HAD A LAB SETUP that put Scope's to shame. She struggled to contain her excitement as she explored the five rooms that made up the lab complex, looking around at the stereomicroscopes, the electron microscope and the thermal cycler. He had a gas chromatograph—and a mass spectrometer! His hackers also had a line into the WatchWorld DNA database. After Gort had made it clear to the two lab technicians that they were at her disposal, they offered to do the DNA work for her, but she wasn't about to leave it to someone she didn't know. From the looks on the faces of the man and woman, both in their forties, she could tell that they had their doubts. But Scope was used to that. This wasn't the kind of gear you'd normally let a kid anywhere near. But then, there weren't many kids like her.

"You sure you know what you're doing?" Gort asked.

Scope didn't reply as she sat down at the control console for the thermal cycler, took Nimmo's bags of samples from her backpack and laid them on the counter beside her. She took a sealed pack of small plastic vials from her bag—not trusting theirs to be clean enough—and began dealing out the samples. These included the blood and skin she had scraped from under her own fingernails after scratching the guy who had chased her and FX onto the scaffolding.

In the last few years DNA analysis had become almost entirely automated so, using their equipment, she could run all the tests herself in a matter of hours. It took a couple of minutes to sort the samples in their test tubes. Each sample would then have to be replicated in the thermal cycler before the tests could be run in the analyzer. She programmed in the instructions and got the machine running. In the meantime, she took some of the other forensic samples over to the bank of microscopes to take a closer look at them.

"Mind if I take a peek?" Gort said, still hanging like a night-club bouncer at her shoulder.

Scope did mind, but didn't want to offend him, fearing that he'd throw her out. She had heard enough about Gort, from listening to talk in Move-Easy's Void, to know he wasn't naturally curious about science. She also knew something about his array of implants. He had a plastic eye in his left socket, fitted with a camera, put there after his real eye had been damaged in a fight. Scope self-consciously put her fingers up to her own blind right eye. She didn't know what that camera could pick up, or what it might be recording. His closeness scared her too. She could smell the curry on his breath, his aftershave and the expensive soap he had used on his hands. Too close. No matter how much time she spent around violent people, no matter how well she thought she understood how their minds worked, she never got over the niggling fear that she would do or say something to set them off.

"So what you doing anyway?" he tried again.

Scope had picked up some glass slides, and now paused, wondering about the best way to get rid of him. Describing her work tended to do it for most people.

"Well, first the machine over there uses a polymerase chain reaction to amplify the DNA samples thousands of times over," she explained, speaking in a quick, breathless voice. "The fragments of DNA will then be separated and detected using electrophoresis. While that's going on, I'm going to put this trace evidence on a slide and stain it, dividing out the histologic specimens from the rest, in order to examine them for contaminants, toxins, et cetera. I'll then identify, categorize and determine the source of the remaining trace evidence, and see where it takes me."

She saw the two lab techs turning away, trying to hide their smiles. Gort noticed too.

"You bein' funny?" he asked.

"I'm sorry, I don't have a sense of humor that I'm aware of," she replied, looking up at him with big innocent eyes.

"Sounds like you don't think I'd understand this stuff," Gort said. "What stuff?"

"You know . . . *science* stuff. Forensics and all that."

"I wouldn't say that," she said. "I don't know anything about you."

"You will, sweetheart. Someday, *everybody's* going to know my name."

Bit of a stupid ambition for a criminal, Scope thought, but she didn't say it out loud.

"They'll write books about me," Gort went on, running his hand through his hair. "Tubby's a good manager, but I got flair. It's not enough to make the money if you want to be big these days. You gotta cut a dash—be a bit of a showman, you know what I mean?"

"Absolutely," Scope responded, trying to turn her attention back to her work.

He leaned his face in close to hers, his chin nearly touching her shoulder. She felt in her left trouser pocket for her inhaler— the one that contained the sneezing gas. His large hand closed around her pocket, gripping it like a vice, trapping her hand. She was close enough to tell the difference between his plastic eye and the real one. The real one was ever so slightly bloodshot.

"You work for Move-Easy, don'tcha?" he said softly. "Don't deny it. You may not know much about me, but we weren't going to let you in here without checking you out. You're the one who makes the fake evidence for him—you help him *blackmail* people. And now you're *here*, in *our place*. Nimmo's taking a bit of a chance with you, isn't he? What's your little pack of vermin up to then?"

"That's not how we treat our guests, Gort." Tubby Reach's voice cut across them. His huge form filled the doorway, looming over Nimmo, who was standing just inside. Reach dismissed his brother with a sideways tilt of the head. Gort gave a smirk and a shrug of his shoulders, as if he and Scope had been caught sharing a guilty joke. Reach stood aside to let him leave, and then turned to Scope. "I trust you have everything you need?" he asked. "How are you getting on?"

"Well, first the machine over there uses a polymerase chain reaction to amplify the DNA samples thousands of times over," she explained. "The fragments of DNA will then be separated and detected using electrophoresis. While that's going on, I'm going to put this trace evidence on a slide and stain it, dividing out the histologic specimens from the rest, in order to examine them for contaminants, toxins—"

"I've no idea what all that means." Reach held up his hands, turning to leave. "But it sounds great. Carry on."

He barely fitted through the doorway, and Scope could still hear his wheezing breathing as he trudged heavily down the corridor, but she had the definite impression that Reach's mind was infinitely more agile than his body. She suspected that nothing she could say would baffle him. Scope returned her attention to the slides she had started to prepare. Nimmo leaned back against a countertop and watched for a few minutes as she worked.

"Think you'll be finished before we have to do this thing tonight?" he asked.

"Hard to know," she muttered. "You never know what this stuff is going to say, once it starts talking to you."

"Hope it uses shorter words than you do," Nimmo chuckled, gazing around the lab, his eyes taking in the two technicians, who were trying to look engrossed in their work.

"Don't act the ignoramus, Nimmo, it doesn't suit you."

"The ignor-what?"

Scope frowned, increasing the magnification on the microscope she was looking through. The specimen she was peering at was the seed-like object Nimmo had taken from under Brundle's thumbnail. She had hoped that it would be some unusual seed, something that could be used to narrow down who Brundle's killer might be. But now, looking at it magnified two hundred and fifty times, she could see that it wasn't a seed—at least no seed she'd ever come across before. It had a surface like a colander, and she could see that there were more structures inside, but couldn't make them out. It looked organic, like it had been grown rather than made. There was some kind of marking on it. Turning the knob on the microscope, she increased the magnification.

What she saw made her lift her head and step back away from the counter in surprise.

"What's up?" Nimmo asked.

"It's man-made," she gasped. "It's got a bloody serial number on it. I think it's an implant, or an RFID tag."

"What?"

"This thing," she said, pointing at the microscope. "The seed thing you scraped from under Brundle's thumbnail. It's a piece of bio-tech. It's *really* advanced. I think it could be some kind of bug. If it is, it had to be planted by Vapor's people. I can't tell if it's transmitting anything, but we've both been carrying it around with us—we've had it with us almost since the start. If somebody's reading it . . ."

Nimmo took a quick look through the scope's eyepiece at the slide, then drew the slide from the clips. Taking a piece of tinfoil from his pack, he wrapped the slide up. It looked like a folded piece of chewing-gum wrapper. The foil would hopefully prevent it from sending out or receiving any signals. He slipped it into his jacket pocket.

"This can't change anything," he said. "Finish what you're doing. We know we're being watched. We know these guys are serious operators. This is a race, Scope. We have to figure *them* out before they crack *us*."

But I'm not in the racing business, she thought. She didn't like being rushed, and she was definitely wary of going up against people she couldn't identify, people with frightening power. Whatever that seed thing was, it was more advanced than anything she'd seen before. When you couldn't even make sense of the technology your enemies were using, you had to ask yourself how far you were willing to go.

Scope decided she'd go a little further.

Nimmo left her to it, and she lost track of time as she steered the computers through the DNA analysis and used the lab's equipment to examine the other forensic samples. Under the microscopes, she had learned nothing new after hours of study. But when the analyzer finally chimed to alert her that it had completed its task, she found herself with an identifiable segment of DNA. One of Reach's hackers helped her get into WatchWorld's DNA database, where a profile was kept on almost every adult in the country. It didn't take long to find a match.

The man she'd come to think of as Death Metal, because of

his tattoos, had a real name—and a face that matched the one she'd seen on the roof of the building in Greenwich. He was Paul Cronenberg, and he had a criminal record. A look at the court records online told her that Cronenberg had been convicted of developing and selling weapons. Bio-tech weapons.

Scope shivered slightly as she thought of the seed thing Nimmo now had in his jacket pocket.

CHAPTER 22

A FRIEND SHE HASN'T MET

VERONICA BRUNDLE OFTEN SPENT FRIDAY NIGHTS at her dad's because she liked to hit one of the clubs in town, and her mother took a dim view of her staying out late in general, and underage drinking in particular. Her father's views weren't quite as firm, though he wasn't above giving her the odd lecture on drinking responsibly. And she'd be guaranteed a few sharp words if she showed up at his place looking as if she'd spent several hours on a wildly spinning fairground ride— an appearance that came over her from time to time. But she was his little girl, and he never stayed mad at her for long.

There'd be no more lectures now; no more sleepovers at Dad's. Veronica Brundle was out for a night on the town, underage, overwhelmed by grief, itching to cut loose. She'd deal with her mother's outrage when she got home.

Club Vega was situated in a basement in Soho, under a building that housed a number of solicitors' offices. The narrow lane that led past it was a throughway between streets of all-night internet cafés, late-night pubs and dodgy nightclubs. Its sleaziness gave it an air of cool for the students who hung out there, flashing fake IDs that matched their carefully casual faces.

By 11 p.m. there was already a queue to get in, the smartly dressed young things chatting and flirting, hemmed in along the wall by a row of brass poles threaded with a red rope.

Manikin stood on the other side of the laneway, making no attempt to keep her eyes on Veronica, who stood about halfway up the queue. The girl had changed her appearance since the photos they had on file had been taken. Her hair was longer, and had streaks of a coppery orange running through it.

Manikin was tucked into the shadow of a doorway of a small feminist bookshop, talking into her mobile phone as if having a girlie conversation with a friend. She was a blonde again, but with multi-colored hair wraps giving her an Aussie backpacker look. Her black denim jacket, purple punk T-shirt with a peeling image, short black skirt and black tights all contrasted with a wide, studded pink belt that loosely encircled her waist. The pink Doc Martens she wore had a funky look she loved, but they were also comfortable enough for running. She was going to need them. This had to look convincing; FX was fast on his feet for a little nerd.

There was a white Ford Transit van a little way up the laneway to her right. She recognized it from a clip of video that FX had shown her. There were two men sitting in the darkness of the cab.

Manikin's 'friend' on the phone was Scope, who was talking to her via a secure line FX had set up over the web. Actually, Scope was doing very little talking, as most of what Manikin was saying was teenage gibberish:

"And then she was just, so, like, OH MY GOD!" Manikin gasped in a voice of utter disbelief. And he was going, y'know, like, what-EVER, and all that. So then they broke up!"

"Fascinating," Scope cut in. "You'll have to fill me in on the rest of that some other time. FX is all set to go. The cameras in the street are down, and there's no peepers for four blocks in any direction. This is our chance. How's our girl?"

"She's just, like, SO ready for it," Manikin said, in the same gushing voice as before. "Four meters from the front of the queue—next to a girl with purple hair and silver boots. The bag's hanging off her right arm, just inside the rope. Our guys in the van haven't moved. Let's do it."

"OK, he's off," Scope informed her.

Scope was back in Brill Alley, coordinating things. The rest of them were out here on the street. FX appeared from around the back of the white van. Manikin knew he had just placed a device of his own design on the van's back doors. He had a baseball cap low over his eyes and a pair of big square-framed glasses on that distorted the shape of his face. He had wanted to wear a mustache or goatee, but Manikin had convinced him he'd look ridiculous, on account of him being a baby-faced short-arse. Walking down the lane with his hands in the pockets of his jacket, he made his way towards the queue of teenagers.

"Here he comes," Manikin said into her phone, pulling out a hands-free earpiece from her pocket and fitting it into her ear.

The phone went into her pocket, and she started across the lane as if to join the queue for the nightclub. FX passed in front of her, from left to right, walking down the length of the queue towards the door of the club.

Two things happened almost at once. First, all the doors of the white van locked and its alarm started going off. The crowd in the queue turned and started to point and laugh as Krieger and his mate found themselves unable to get out, and unable to switch off the alarm. At the same time, FX was walking past Veronica. Moments after the alarm went off, he seized her red leather handbag and broke into a run, sprinting away down the laneway. He'd had his leg stamped on earlier that day, but it didn't seem to be slowing him down now.

"Oi, you little fart!" Manikin roared, and set off after him.

Veronica tried to follow, but high heels on a cobbled road soon brought her to a frustrated, stumbling halt. Two young guys took off to try and catch the thief, egged on by others in the queue.

"We've got a couple o' heroes," Manikin said into her earpiece, her legs pumping to keep up with FX.

"Nimmo's on it," Scope told her.

FX darted around a corner, and then another, racing down an alley with Manikin close on his heels. At another corner, they passed Nimmo, who was standing at the back door to a restaurant, among some wheelie bins. As soon as they'd gone past, he grabbed one of the bins and pulled it out into the alleyway. The two would-be heroes came around the corner at full tilt, and ran crashing into Nimmo and his bin. Three bodies and the large plastic container tumbled and sprawled over the cobbles.

Manikin cast a quick look back, hearing Nimmo bawling abuse at the two unfortunates, demanding to know what they were doing flouncin' around like a pair of chimps on a bouncy castle at this hour of the night.

FX's flight took him into the rat-runs, away from the cameras and sensors of WatchWorld and all the other businesses that fed into the network. He bounded up onto the back of a street bench and leaped over a wrought-iron fence into a small park. In the shadow of some bushes, he emptied the contents of the handbag over the ground. Manikin arrived a few seconds later. They were both breathing hard. Their route had been chosen carefully, but there was no telling how much time they had before a Safe-Guard wandered into the area.

Manikin examined the stuff from the bag, sorting through the scattering of mundane things every girl carried around with her. The only unusual things were a copy of Orwell's *Animal Farm*—the one with the mad illustrations by Ralph Steadman—and a set of keys adorned with the most key rings Manikin had ever seen in one bunch.

FX used a small blade to cut a couple of stitches in the seam at the bottom of the bag. He inserted a disc no bigger than the nail of his little finger, then sealed the tiny hole with a bead of superglue. Manikin handed him the SIM card from Veronica's phone and he slipped it into a scanner attached to his own phone. Having cloned its number and downloaded its files, he handed it back, along with another tiny disc. Manikin fitted both back into the phone. A third bug was quickly concealed in the lining of Veronica's wallet, and a fourth under the photo of her and her dad in a plastic fob on her key ring.

"OK, get out of here," Manikin whispered, gathering everything back into the bag. "Time for me to get into character."

"Break a leg," he replied, and then he was gone.

"Won't go that far," she said, reaching up to tear the collar of her T-shirt, and rip a small hole in her tights over her left thigh. "But I do want to look the part."

A quick application of some make-up made her look as if the corner of her mouth was slightly swollen. She could have got FX to give her a real split lip—he'd done it a few times before, not always with her permission—but there was no need. To an amateur like Veronica, in the atmospheric lights of a nightclub, Manikin would look every bit the conquering hero.

CHAPTER 23

THE POST-MUGGER LOOK

VERONICA AND HER FRIENDS WERE STILL STANDING outside the nightclub, discussing what had happened with expressions of shock and excitement. The bouncers, who had shown no sign of chasing after the thief, were still chivalrous enough to let the girls have some time out of the queue to wait and see if the pursuers had any success. When the two guys came back, the girls groaned their disappointment, but applauded the lads for having a go. Veronica was quite upset—an early state of drunkenness making her all the more dramatic. Her face had gone pale beneath her make-up, contrasting with the purple-red birthmark down the left side of her face. She wanted to give up on the night and go home, but her friends were all trying to persuade her to come on into the club.

Then Manikin showed up with a tired, triumphant smile on her face, holding the handbag in the air for the whole crowd to see. There was a chorus of cheers and whistles.

"Oh my God!" Veronica gasped, gratefully taking back her bag. "You did it! You absolute star! Honey, whoever you are, I owe you, big time! I'm Veronica, but everyone calls me Nica. Who the hell are you?"

"Georgina—but I bloody hate the name. Call me George," Manikin replied. "It was no problem. The little weasel threw a hissy fit when I caught him, but he was more scared of getting caught on camera than anything else. He took off when I started shouting for help. No big deal."

"No big deal, she says," Nica scoffed as she exchanged looks with her friends and tugged on Manikin's torn collar. "Well, you're my knight in shining Docs, George."

High on the excitement, they were all hugging Manikin and whooping like a team that had just scored the winning goal. Then, turning to the bouncers standing at the door, Nica announced:

"She's with us. And I'm paying her admission."

The club was already nearly full with bodies, hot and stuffy and pounding the customers' brains with drum and bass that Manikin could feel in her bones. She heard a voice just over the music, but couldn't hear what it was saying. Turning, she found Nica pointing at her leg.

"Hey, your tights are torn!" the girl shouted in her ear, offering a bottle of beer.

Manikin looked down at the hole in the fabric covering her left thigh. Taking the bottle that Nica was handing to her,

Manikin put it to her mouth. She acted as if she was taking a long slug of it, but took hardly any at all. She rarely drank and anyway, she'd need her head straight for this job. Then she handed back the drink for a minute, reached down, tore a few more holes in her tights, and took back the bottle.

"Cool!" Nica laughed. "Makin' a fashion statement, huh?"

"Yeah, it's the post-mugger look!" Manikin responded, clinking her bottle against Veronica's. "Let's make a toast to our useless bloody police!"

Nica's face fell suddenly, and there was pain in her eyes. Manikin wondered if she'd pushed it too far—the girl *had* to be angry that the authorities weren't investigating her dad's death. But Manikin felt a shiver of guilt at reminding Nica why she was trying to cut loose tonight.

"Yeah." Nica nodded, as she said in a colder, harder voice: "I'll drink to that. Here's to the fuzz!"

Despite the noise, other people heard her and laughed, raising their drinks and joining in the toast.

"To the fuzz!" they roared.

Manikin was concerned now that she'd spoiled Nica's mood, but the girl seemed all the more intent on partying. Manikin joined in for all she was worth, surreptitiously letting drink spill from her bottle when anyone wasn't watching. The gang welcomed her into their circle, and she played her part just right: a girl out for a good time, without looking like she badly needed friends. As the night passed, she found herself liking Nica and her mates, part of her envying their normal lives. But then she would see a troubled shadow cross Nica's face and think of the girl's father, and Manikin would remind herself that there was no such thing as normal. Every now and again, the hair that covered the left side of Nica's face would slip to one side and she would self-consciously put her hand to her face, brushing the hair forward to hide her birthmark as best she could.

Manikin knew Nimmo would be in here somewhere now, and her eyes occasionally looked around for him—and for any other watchers. But she didn't spot anything until a remix of an old seventies hit came over the speakers, and an Oriental man strutted out of the crowd onto the dance floor. He was dressed in a white suit, complete with waistcoat, and a black shirt and shoes. Christ, she thought—it's Coda. Shorter than most of the men around him, he still grabbed everyone's attention as he took over the center of the grid of lit squares that made up the dance floor.

Then he started to move.

The girls in the room hollered and whistled their appreciation as Coda twisted, flowed and rippled across the floor, each dance step executed with perfect coordination and grace. Within the first twenty seconds, eight girls had joined him, and he allowed them to gather around him, like a lead performer on a stage surrounded by chorus girls. Manikin found herself staring at the spectacle with her mouth open. Coda met her eyes every time he turned in her direction, the arrogant smile on his face contrasting with his stone-cold gaze.

He pirouetted his way across the floor to her, and before she could react, he had taken her hand, pulling her out through his chorus line, some of whom threw jealous stares her way. Behind her, Nica and her mates cheered her on.

Manikin considered herself an accomplished dancer, but Coda had to tone down his moves so that she could keep up. She felt the steel-like strength in his fingers when he touched her, the power and agility of a panther in his gyrating body.

"You're taking too long," he said to her, pressing him to her as they took a sliding walk across the floor. At first she thought he meant her dancing, but then he went on: "Mister Easy shouldn't have to involve me in this, but he's not seeing any results. He's getting impatient."

"It's only been two days," Manikin retorted. "He gave us three. He didn't hire us for a smash-and-grab job."

"You can have until Sunday," Coda snapped at her. "Don't forget you've got a debt to pay off. If you don't find that box, he'll have to find other ways of getting his money out of you."

He grasped the little finger of her left hand, folding the digit in on itself so hard into his own fingers he began to crush the joints. She twisted sharply in his arms, trying to escape the agonizing grip. With a flick of his hand, her arm locked out straight, pain shooting from her hand to her shoulder, causing her to gasp as he whirled her away from him like a whip. Coda spun her around and dropped her back into her seat beside Nica. She gritted her teeth and rubbed her aching finger, flexing her arm as he danced away from her. Then he turned to stride off the floor as the tune changed to a heavier, broodier number.

"Jesus, she can dance too!" Nica shouted. "George, you're a goddamn star!"

Manikin didn't reply, just shrugging and forcing a smile as she squeezed the throbbing joints. Coda had crushed that finger deliberately, sending her a very clear message. One of Move-Easy's apes had broken that finger a year ago—the last time she and FX had failed to make a payment.

The night wore on, and Manikin stayed sober as the others got drunk, though she maintained the appearance of drinking as much as they did. As their conversation grew more manic and repetitive, Nica became more withdrawn, resisting the attempts of her friends to include her in the banter. At one point, she got up and wandered off. Manikin gave it a few minutes and then pretended to get up and go to the toilet, taking her bag with her. Casting her eyes around, she found the other girl sitting in a dark corner, next to a pile of coats. Nica had her phone out, and she was looking through some photographs. Manikin sat down beside her, offering Nica a swig from her bottle, but Nica shook her head.

"Sorry, you want to be on your own?" Manikin asked her.

Nica shrugged and shook her head.

"Just don't feel like talking. You can sit where you like."

"That's OK," Manikin said. "I get that sometimes."

She let her bag fall to the floor, and it tipped over on its side, spilling some of its contents. It was a move she'd practiced to ensure it would fall the right way. Her purse ended up on the floor, along with a lip gloss, some keys and a book. Manikin gave Nica a furtive look, and hurriedly shoved the objects back into her bag.

"Hey, I saw that!" Nica lifted her head, giving her new friend a sly smile.

"What?"

"Don't act the innocent—I saw the book. Come on, let's have a look."

Manikin checked that nobody else around them was looking, and took the book from her bag, slipping it discreetly into Nica's hand. "Just keep your voice down, OK?" Manikin said into her ear.

"Are you kidding? Who's going to hear us in this racket?"

It was a comic-book edition of *Fahrenheit 451*, a novel about a society that burned books, where anyone found in the possession of one could be imprisoned in a mental hospital, or have mechanical hounds sent out to hunt and kill them if they ran. *Fahrenheit 451* was the kind of book that could get you all the wrong kind of attention from WatchWorld.

"It's in really good nick," Nica said.

"It's my brother's. He's completely anal about looking after his comics."

"I could get a lot of money for that if you wanted to sell it."

"Dunno, maybe. I do a bit of dealing myself," Manikin said, taking the book and putting it back in her bag. "Ask me another time—let's see if we can do a bit of business, yeah?"

Feeling that she had earned a bit more of Nica's trust, she took a peek at the girl's phone. The screen showed a picture of Watson Brundle.

"He looks a bit like you," Manikin observed. "That your dad?"

"Yeah," Nica said. She brushed her thumb across the screen, the movement sliding another photo across. "He died this week."

"Jesus, I'm sorry. I lost my dad years ago. There's nothing anybody can say, is there? It all just sounds like crap."

Nica nodded. She slid another picture of her father across,

and another. She didn't say anything, but she didn't try to hide the photos from Manikin either. It was as if she wanted to show Manikin her father: who he was, what he was like.

"They say his death was an accident," Nica sniffed. "But I don't believe it for a second. He . . . he got mixed up with some nasty people. Nobody else . . . nobody else knew about it, but I knew. He was terrified. There's no way he died the way they say."

Manikin was about to try and prompt her for more on her father's death, but then frowned as a new photo crossed onto the screen.

"I think I've seen that guy before," she said in an offhand way, pointing at the picture. "Who is he?"

In the foreground, Watson Brundle was holding up one of those Petri dishes—the shallow, flat-bottomed containers used for growing bacteria in a lab. There was a proud smile on his face. Behind him, a young man was walking through a door, his face just visible over Brundle's shoulder.

"Oh, that's nobody," Nica muttered. "Just some guy who lived in Dad's building, helped him out sometimes. His name's Chuck. Chuck Farley."

CHAPTER 24

EVERY SYSTEM CAN BE PLAYED

NIMMO FOUND HE OFTEN FELT AT EASE perched at a height somewhere, with a clear view around him. When he needed some peace and quiet to think things through, he sought these places out. It was an instinct that clashed with his professional need to be inconspicuous. So it came as some surprise to Scope to find him sitting on the windowsill of a castle tower in the warehouse in Brill Alley, his feet dangling about ten meters above the floor of the huge room. She didn't know if the set had ever been used in a film, but Nimmo resembled some vagabond who had climbed the tower looking for the princess he loved, and discovered her missing.

"Rapunzel, Rapunzel, let down your hair!" Scope called up.

Nimmo gave a reluctant smile, gestured to his close-cut scalp and shrugged an apology.

"How about you come down then?" Scope asked. "Manikin's up. Either she's hung over, or something's really pissed her off. Whatever it is, she's in a rotten mood."

"How can you even tell?" Nimmo muttered, rolling back through the window.

Manikin had come back late, and though they were all still up, she had insisted on going to bed before sharing anything that she had learned. She had been worked up about something, but not even FX could say why. This was exactly the kind of thing that caused Nimmo to work alone most of the time. He had grown up working with adults, and had little time for other kids, particularly moody teenagers.

He climbed down the scaffolding that made up the back of the fake stone tower, and followed Scope back to the kitchen, where Manikin and FX were sitting at the table, steaming mugs of coffee set in front of them. Manikin was looking tired but alert, dressed in a T-shirt and jeans, with her dark hair tied up at the back. She lifted her head to regard the other pair as they walked in, but didn't greet Nimmo. FX had his laptop hooked up to a large screen on the wall, so that they could all see what he had up. It was a selection of the photos, video files and documents they had put together on Veronica so far.

Scope sat down, but Nimmo stayed standing by the door, leaning back against the frame with his arms folded.

"Awright," said FX. "That bit of video me an' Scope got of Cronenberg in that building we checked out? I ran it through some editing software and cleaned up the sound. Here's the full recording."

He hit a button on the keyboard and the sound of a Northern Irish voice could be heard, still distorted by the noise of wind across the microphone, but much more audible than they'd heard it before:

" . . . that's not whut he sayd," the man's voice could be heard saying. "He never sayd she *didn't have it*. He just sayd it wuzn't *in hor apartment*. Whut? I don't know, you ask him, why don't yeh? Huh? . . . Look, you can moan all yeh like. Vapor paid this numpty, and he wants what he paid for. He duzn't give a damn about the cards. We do this right, those cards could go missing, know whut I mean? Performance-related bonus an' all that . . . I don't know, do I? But they've got tae be worth a hundred grand, maybe more. Brundle didn't come cheap, I know that much. Vapor just wants his stuff, and he duzn't—"

"And that's where he spotted the camera," FX told them. "Thanks to Scope, this guy now has a name—Paul Cronenberg, a dealer in bio-tech weapons. And he uses them, as well as selling them. And we know the man Nimmo ambushed in Veronica's apartment is Frank Krieger."

FX brought up the photo he had of the man driving the van, a long-faced black man with tightly clipped hair and a goatee.

"I was able to use face recognition software to do a search on the mug of this other fella in the van. As if things weren't difficult enough, we now have a new psycho to add into the mix. That right there is Harvey Benson, a.k.a. 'Hector.'"

"Can't be." Nimmo shook his head. "He's doing ten years in Belmarsh for assaulting a peeper. He worked for Tubby Reach as a hacker, but he's a real nasty piece of work too. Good at making sneaky weapons. Anyway, he only went down last year. There's no way he's out."

"Believe it," FX said. "I checked up on him. Released on a technicality. New evidence discovered by WatchWorld themselves."

"What new evidence?" Nimmo frowned. "He was caught by the peeper trying to hack into a WatchWorld surveillance post. He went nuts—did the guy serious damage before he was pulled off by two coppers. Put the peeper in hospital for a month. It was all recorded. The coppers were able to watch every thump and kick in slow-bloody-motion."

"Yeah, well he still got off," FX said. "Something about the peeper's gear not being calibrated properly. Thing is, *Frank Krieger* was up on charges of manslaughter around the same time, and he got off for a similar reason. Cronenberg got out of his conviction too. This Vapor guy has to be doing this, and if he is, he's really high up."

"More like it's the whole of WatchWorld that's in on it," Manikin muttered. "How could one guy play the system like that?"

"Because every system can be played," Nimmo replied, with FX nodding in agreement. "So we're up against a thief, a hacker and a bio-tech expert—each one with a history of violence. But how many more are there? It's the ones we don't know about who worry me most."

"Yeah, like maybe this kid who was living on the same floor as Brundle," Manikin said, glancing over at Nimmo. "He's supposed to be some harmless homeless guy that Brundle took in, but nobody's turned up anything on him. He might be working for Vapor . . . or even Move-Easy and Easy's not telling us, or he could be a nobody who just took the box and ran. We don't know."

"Except he told the Safe-Guard about the murder as soon as he discovered it," Scope said. "And he helped Brundle out when he was mugged."

"Doesn't mean anything," Manikin snorted. "Saving him from the muggers could have been part of the plan, right, Nimmo?"

"Maybe," Nimmo said carefully. "Did you learn anything from Veronica last night? We couldn't hear much from your mike because of the music."

"She had some interesting things to say."

"You going to share them anytime soon?"

"I dunno. I dunno if I want to share anything with you." Manikin leaned forward, holding him in a hostile stare. "I dunno if I want you in our *home* any more. Seein' as the last guy who shared his home with you ended up *dead*. So, what *have* we learned, *Chuck*?"

Nimmo unfolded his arms and went to stand up straight. Even as he did so, he saw his own face come up onscreen, along with all the details of his life as Charles U. Farley.

"Give us one reason why I shouldn't send this to Move-Easy right now, complete with your last known address," FX said in a tight voice. "You working for Vapor too, Nimmo? Or maybe it's Tubby Reach? Or are you just messin' with us until you can get this box for yourself? It's just that, if I remember right, the last guy who tried to con Move-Easy ended up in a cement mixer. And if he finds out that you've pulled a fast one on him, and if he even suspects *we're* in on it, we'll be rolling around in there with you."

"They're right, Nimmo," Scope said. "You need to be straight with them. You owe them that much."

"You mean *you knew*?" Manikin glared accusingly at her.

"I only found out Thursday afternoon—and don't give me that look, Mani. You're scanning our eyeballs on the sly, and God knows what else, so don't go acting all offended. We're not in a very trusting business here."

Manikin snorted, but then turned back to Nimmo. FX and Scope also fixed their attention on him. Nimmo stared at them all, standing lightly on the balls of his feet as he weighed up his options. They weren't an immediate threat to him, although he couldn't be sure what security measures FX and Manikin had set up in here—ones he *hadn't* spotted. He was confident he could get out of the building if he needed to. So there was no reason to give them anything. But if they did shop him to Move-Easy, he'd have to be gone from London by the end of the day, and he could never come back. That wasn't the end of the world. He could work in other places. Maybe it would be better than trusting them—letting them any further into his life.

Except his business here wasn't finished yet, and it would be a damn sight easier to get it finished if he could convince them to keep helping him. But it was asking a lot.

"All right," he said uneasily. "Brundle was a decent guy; I don't know if I could call him a friend—it wasn't that straightforward. But he let me live in his place, no questions asked, and we talked sometimes and did each other the odd favor. I liked him, and I trusted him . . . up to a point. I know he was murdered, and I figured I owed it to him to find out who did it. When he realized the Safe-Guard was coming up to his lab that day, he gave the box to me to hide. At least, I assume it was the same box—I still haven't looked inside."

Nimmo didn't mention that he had first hidden the case back in Brundle's lab. He was still feeling ashamed of pulling that trick on his old landlord.

"I don't know if he was killed for the box; it could just be a coincidence, but I doubt it. Yes, I've got the bloody thing, but I don't want it. As far as I'm concerned, it belongs to Nica—unless it's liable to just ruin her life. But I think it's the key to finding out who killed Brundle, so nobody's getting it until I figure that out. Not you, not Move-Easy, not Vapor and these fake Watch-Worlders, whoever the hell they are. Not even Nica. Nobody.

"Now you can threaten me, set Easy's apes on me, or you can even try and take me yourselves. But I've handled a lot tougher than you and bigger psychos than them and I'm still here. So the worst that's going to happen to me is that I end up having to leave town. And that box will be coming with me. On the other hand, if you help me put together the rest of this story; help me figure out what happened to Brundle and why, I'll hand that box over to whoever you like. Move-Easy never has to know. It's up to you."

There was a moment of silence while the others digested all of this. But it didn't take long for Nimmo to have his answer.

"You want to get between Move-Easy and something he wants?" Manikin said in a bitter voice. "Have you forgotten *who he is*? I'll tell you what: we'll give you two hours before we hand over everything we know to the *mass murderer* we're working for. That should be more than enough time for you to cop yourself on, or get your arse out of the city. It's up to you."

Nimmo looked for a reaction from FX and Scope, but their body language just backed up what Manikin had said. He was about to say something when a mobile sitting on the table began to ring. She looked at the screen:

"It's Nica . . . Veronica. I gave her the number for this phone last night. We set it up just to take her calls."

They all exchanged looks, but then she shrugged and took the call.

"Hello? Oh, hi, Nica! How's it goin'? Yeah, my head's bursting too. What bloody poison were we drinkin' at the end there last night? What? . . . Jesus, really? Bloody hell. No, I'm not doing anything . . . Yeah . . . Yeah. Sure, of course. I can do that. OK, I'll see you then."

Manikin rang off, and there was a troubled expression on her face as she looked at her phone for a few seconds before saying anything.

"Nica went home on her own last night. She had a fight with her friends—just a stupid drunken row. I stayed out of it. Turns out she was attacked on her way home. Again. The mugger took her bag. Again." Manikin gave a humorless chuckle, looking over at her brother. "She said it wasn't the same guy as last time. And obviously he didn't get her phone.

"But she did have a copy of *Animal Farm* in her bag—you know, the George Orwell book? Probably wanted to impress her mates. It was her mother's most valuable book, and she's worried

sick that her mum's going to find out she took it. I let her know
last night that I did a bit of book dealing, so she's just asked me if
I could get hold of another copy. I said I'd meet up with her and
see what I could do."

"She's a quick bonder, isn't she?" FX commented.

"Shut up, this is serious," Manikin sighed. "This doesn't fit.
Move-Easy's guys would have taken *her*, not her bag."

"And Vapor's lot wouldn't have to mug her," Nimmo said.
"They're smart operators; she wouldn't see them unless they
wanted her to. And if they were sending her a warning for some
reason, they'd do it so that she got the message. Maybe it was just
dumb luck she got mugged twice."

"Right. Anybody believe that?" Scope asked.

Nobody did. FX was already on his laptop, bringing up the
control windows for the bugs they had planted on Nica.

"The bugs in her bag were only short range," he said. "But
I've set them up to piggy-back on the mobile phone network,
using the same kind of roaming signal that a mobile uses—"

"Spare us the nerdisms. Can you find the bloody thing?"
Manikin snapped at him.

FX glowered back at her. "It was only meant to help us tail
her, or *record her voice*, or let us *listen in* when we were *nearby*,"
he said sullenly. "The signal's weak, but I can show the path it's
taken since it was stolen and, if the bag's close enough to two or
more antenna towers, I can locate it to within a few meters."

"What are you *waiting* for then?"

"I'm waiting for you to stop giving me *a great big pain in
my arse*."

"Let's find the bag then, shall we?" Scope gasped in exasperation.

FX tapped a few more keys and then his eye fixed on a point on the screen.

"OK, I've got it coming away from the club last night, and then it makes a sudden change in direction a few hundred meters away. Whoever took it followed one of the rat-runs away from the scene. It stops at this city center address for an hour—nice part of town . . . *not*—and then it takes off again."

"I know that building," Manikin muttered. "Punkin lives there with his parents. That figures."

"Do you think his folks know what he and Bunny get up to?" Scope asked.

"I think they know," FX replied. "His dad's in prison for beating Punkin unconscious with a handbag. Punkin'd nicked it from his own granny. Anyway, *Nica's* handbag continues through town until it ends up here. We lose the signal there. About four hours ago, it either went where it couldn't get a signal to a tower, or somebody damaged the bug."

He stabbed the screen with his finger, indicating the name of the complex where the signal had been lost. They all looked at it, and Manikin groaned. The label read: "Ratched Hospital." Below which lay Move-Easy's underground Void.

"Well, she won't be getting that back," Scope sighed. "If it was Punkin and Bunny, they were probably just trying to impress Easy—he might not have told them anything about our operation. I don't think this changes anything."

"Ah, actually, it might," FX said, wincing. "The bug I used

in the bag? It was one of the ones Nimmo took off Krieger. The WatchWorld bugs."

The others looked at him in shock. Scope let out a low moan, Nimmo closed his eyes for a few seconds and Manikin slapped the back of her brother's head.

"It's lovely kit, and I just figured . . . well, it was recycling, y'know?" he protested.

"If those two wazzocks walked into Move-Easy's Void carrying one of those things," Scope said, "it'd be detected at the door. And it would take Tanker all of five seconds to realize where it was made."

"But if Move-Easy figures out who hid it in the bag . . ." Manikin began.

"He's going to think we're working for WatchWorld," Nimmo finished. "Even if we told him where we'd got it, he's so paranoid he'd condemn us there and then. Just the suspicion would be enough. He's probably having pieces of Punkin and Bunny flushed down the sewer right now."

"So let's hope it stops there, and he doesn't figure out who really put the bug in the bag," Manikin said, standing up and grabbing a dark blue puffer jacket from a hook by the door. "If Easy thinks WatchWorld is onto him, we're out of time—he's going to turn nasty. I'm off to see Nica, and tell her to keep her head down, because Easy's going to stop tiptoein' around now. If he doesn't get that box soon, he's going to come lookin' for her and her mother." Manikin jabbed a finger in Nimmo's direction. "Two hours, Nimmo. Then we tell Easy everything. Don't piss about."

The door slammed behind her. Nimmo's eyes moved from the door to the floor, avoiding the others' gaze.

"There's no way around this, Nimmo," Scope said to him. "We need that box."

"All right," he sighed at last. "It's hidden on the roof of Brundle's building. I need an hour to get it. I'll meet you at the hospital, and we can bring it in together."

"No, I think we'll go with you the whole way," FX told him. "Just to be safe, y'know?"

"Right—just to be safe." Scope nodded, getting up from her chair. "And maybe we could pop into Brundle's lab while we're there. I'd really, really like to see what the hell he was doing that's got everybody so worked up. I have to say, I'm fascinated. From everything I've seen of his stuff, it doesn't look like anything illegal. At least, not technically."

"Funny, that's what Brundle said," Nimmo sniffed. "Just before someone murdered him."

CHAPTER 25

KEPT IN THE DARK

PUNKIN AND BUNNY DID NOT KNOW WHY they had been beaten up and thrown into the dark, bare concrete room, but it obviously had something to do with the stupid bloody handbag they'd stolen from that Brundle cow. All right, so Move-Easy hadn't told them to lift it, but they'd seen the opportunity and grasped it with both hands—much as they'd done the girl and her handbag. It was a philosophy that had served Punkin well enough in his relatively short life, and Bunny normally trusted his judgement, so they'd just gone ahead and done it. Only it seemed Move-Easy wasn't too keen about his minions acting on their own initiative.

The unfortunate pair didn't even get as far as seeing the boss. They were welcomed by one of his hard men, a bald giant named Hasan, more often known simply as "the Turk," though no one could say why, as everyone knew he was Greek. Apart from being built of pure brawn and spite, he had implants in his knuckles that could deliver electric shocks. And he enjoyed using them.

He welcomed Punkin and Bunny into the Void with a pair of other enforcers. The massive, muscled mound, smiling out from under his handlebar mustache, joined with his colleagues in surrounding the visitors. They then proceeded to punch and kick the pair until they were writhing in pain on the floor. After being thoroughly beaten, Punkin and Bunny were hauled up and dragged down the corridor to a steel door, which was opened just long enough for them to be thrown inside. Punkin swore and spat some blood from his mouth, before rolling onto his back. He didn't bother to check if Bunny was OK. He'd seen her take much worse than that from the grandad and granny who'd raised her. She'd just need a good bout of foul language and she'd be back on her feet in no time. He took her hand and lay there, cursing the pain that throbbed from various parts of his body.

"What the bloody hell did we do?" she whimpered, sniffing back the blood that dripped from her nose. "I mean, the poncey little hag was . . . was askin' for it, walkin' along on 'er own like 'at, in the middle o' the night. Move-Easy—'e wants to know about 'er movements and 'at, yeah? An' you . . . you gotta figure, you wanna find summink out about a girl, you look in 'er 'andbag, right? Didn't we do good? Like . . . those trolls just laid into us wivvout even sayin' what we done wrong!"

"We're bein' kept in the dark about something, luv," Punkin told her, wincing as he felt the swelling coming up on the side of his face. "But we've got to keep our 'eads. We're at the bottom of the food chain right now, but if we play things right, we'll work our way up to the big time—we've just gotta be patient, luv. We just gotta keep cool. Someday, I'm gonna be a serious villain like Move-Easy, and you're gonna be right up there with me."

"You've got such big dreams, darlin'," she sobbed in a tender voice, squeezing his hand. "An' you know I believe in yaw wiv all of my 'eart. But we're in up to our necks, 'ere, Punkin, and I fink one of those kicks broke a bone in my arse."

"Stick with me, sweet'eart," he said with a grimace. "Someday we'll be able to buy you a whole new arse if you want it."

"Gawd, you say the sweetest fings, Punkin," she said, smiling as she wiped a mixture of blood and snot from her nose.

They both flinched as the light came on; a key turned in the lock of the door, and it swung open. The Turk walked in with a steel-framed wooden chair and set it down on the floor. Then he stood aside and in walked Move-Easy himself. The fake-tanned mob boss sat down on the chair and crossed his legs. The Turk took out a cigar, clipped the end of it and handed it to his boss, then lit it with a match. Easy took a long, long drag and blew out a lazy cloud of smoke. He gazed at the two rat-runners, his eyes showing no more expression than if he'd had a pair of ball bearings set into his sockets.

"You two," Easy began, "must be, by far, the thickest pair of sewage-brained fungus-spraying goat-farts ever to stain the cobbles. I've seen motorway tarmac with more mental agility than I've seen from you. I've got a pair of greyhounds whose crap has a higher IQ."

Punkin was about to retort that perhaps Mr. Easy was taking it a bit far, but thought the better of it.

"It's not enough that you bring a pack of exploding money into my 'ome, the first time we let you in," Move-Easy went on to say. "Then you cook up a raid on an *implant clinic*, which turns out to belong to none other than *Tubby Reach*. That's the kind of 'assle I could've done wivout. But sod it. That blubbery scrote can drown in his own fat for all I care.

"Now, however, you two 'avin' been accepted into my employment, you show up with an 'andbag you were not instructed to lift—your task bein' merely to observe and report. Said 'andbag was found to contain not one, not two, but *three* transmitters in it. Tanker, my little computer wizard, has examined these devices, and reckons they're *WatchWorld* gear."

What little color was left in Punkin and Bunny's faces drained away at this. Bunny's teeth started chattering, and Punkin felt sobs rising in his chest. They looked anxiously up at the Turk, who smiled down at them, the room's single light bulb causing one of his gold teeth to gleam.

"Needless to say, in the world of Move-Easy," said Move-Easy, "this level of offense means you'd be food for the swine on my pig farm. Partial to a bit of dense meat, they are."

Bunny squeezed Punkin's hand, and they shared a doomed-lovers look that would not have looked out of place on the bow of the *Titanic*.

"However, as luck would 'ave it," Easy continued, taking another drag on his cigar, "your stupidness is your saving grace."

The doomed lovers perked up.

"Given your complete lack of mental faculties," he declared, "the boys an' I can truly believe that this was an accident. And there's no way WatchWorld would engage the services of a pair of dog-snots like you. So, the pigs can go wivout for the moment. And 'avin' knocked you about a bit, the boys feel that they've expressed their grievances at your distressin' lack of care in observin' the security of our 'ome. 'Opefully, you will have learned your lesson. There won't be a third lesson."

"We're . . . we're d-d-d-desperately sorry," Punkin stuttered. "It won't . . . won't happen a-a-a-again, Mister Easy. I s-s-s-swear it."

"*We* swear it." Bunny nodded frantically. "We'll never do anything this stupid again."

Move-Easy expressed his doubt with a snort, but then blew a smoke ring and fingered the medallion hanging amid the hair on his orange chest, visible beneath his white silk shirt.

"The question of how those bugs might've got in that bag remains, however," he said. "Per'aps you can enlighten us."

"It must have been Manikin an' FX!" Punkin exclaimed. "They did a fake mugging outside the nightclub—FX lifted the bag an' Manikin brought it back. They must've planted the bugs then. And there was two guys in a van watchin' what was goin' on then too. They could be in on the whole thing. D'you think it's WatchWorld, Mister Easy? D'you think FX an' Manikin are workin' for the law?"

Move-Easy leaned back in the chair and blew smoke at the ceiling, watching the curling fumes make shapes against the light.

"Or is it even the real law?" he murmured, almost to himself.

"Can't take the chance either way. Best to just get rid of all concerned, I think. I'm done bein' subtle. It doesn't suit me." Easy turned to the mountain of a man standing by the door, taking a last puff of his cigar. "Time to clean up shop, Turk. Find out where Coda's disappeared to; tell him to find the two guys in the van and deal with them. Then go pick up Brundle's little girl. Let's see if she knows what Daddy's done with Uncle Easy's stuff.

"Find Scope. My Little Brain's not gettin' out of here again—*ever*. Seems she can't be trusted to remember where her loyalties lie. And as for the rest of those vermin—whether they've got that box or not, I want their bodies hangin' in my fridge by tomorrow lunch time."

CHAPTER 26

VISITED IN THE NIGHT

MANIKIN HAD ARRANGED TO MEET NICA in an outdoor café set in the Barbican complex, on the terrace next to the small man-made lake. The complex was littered with surveillance cameras, but Manikin wasn't carrying anything illegal, and she was in character as George, foiler of muggers and dealer of dodgy books. She often felt safer disguised as someone else when she was out in public. She was wearing the same pink Doc Martens she'd had on in the club, and the same blonde wig with the Aussie hair-wraps. A stonewashed gray denim skirt, black tights and a purple hoodie completed her look. She had a small, scuffed backpack slung over one shoulder—the type with a pouch for a mobile phone on the strap—and a pair of shades pushed up onto her head. A little make-up had given her the swollen lip she'd allegedly picked up from the mugger the night before.

Her eyes swept the terrace as she walked out onto it. She spotted Nica sitting at a table near the water, but the girl had not seen her yet. Manikin took the opportunity to check out the rest of the people sitting out here.

Her heart gave an extra-hard thump as she saw the Greek giant known as the Turk sitting with three of Move-Easy's apes at a table near Nica's. The men hadn't recognized Manikin, but she was bound to catch their eyes once she sat down with Brundle's daughter. Swearing under her breath, she hesitated. Her aim had been to warn Nica that she and her mother might be in danger from Move-Easy. Now there was no 'might' about it. The Turk wasn't the kind of man you used for discreet surveillance. If he was here, Nica really was in trouble.

"George, hey!" Nica shouted, turning and waving to her. The girl's own pair of sunglasses failed to hide the bags under her eyes as Manikin drew closer. Her voice dropped when Manikin sat down at the table. "Thanks for coming. I'm really brickin' it here. If Mum finds out I've lost that book, she's going to skin me alive. It's her contact who gets the books, so I can't go looking that way to replace it."

"No problem," Manikin said, smiling and shrugging. "I'll see what I can do. I've got a friend near here who specializes in Orwell. We can just get out of here, and head around to . . ."

Her words faltered; Nica had just noticed the four men sitting nearby. They were looking over at her. From her expression, it was clear that she recognized them.

"Listen, I . . . I . . . just . . . I can't go anywhere right now," Nica said. There was a quiver in her voice. "I'd really appreciate your help with this, but I need to go now. Could we meet up some other time? We could—"

"Nica," Manikin said to her in a firm tone. "Nica, listen to me. Stop looking at them and listen to me for a minute. I know those men. I know what they are. But how come *you* know them?"

Nica pushed her sunglasses up her nose, but they could not conceal the barely suppressed fear on her face. She turned her head away, pretending to look up at the high buildings above them, or watch the reflections on the lake.

"Talk to me, Nica," Manikin tried again.

"I only recognize that big one," came the terse reply. "Or at least, I know his hands—those scars on his knuckles. He's got implants. Those guys are gangsters. They're looking for something my dad was working on. He's . . . he's a—he *was* a scientist, a biologist, and he had this project he'd spent years on for some private client. He never told me much about it, but he told me if he got it right, he'd be able to fix my . . . my birthmark." Her hand unconsciously brushed the side of her face. "Anyway, some gang boss found out what he was working on, figured it was worth a fortune, and just told my dad to hand it over when it was done, and to hell with the client who was paying all the bills.

"When my dad said no, that big guy there, the ogre with the bald head and gold teeth, came here in the middle of the night, broke into our apartment, sat down next to my bed. He took a . . . a picture of me sleeping, with his hand stroking my hair. They . . . they gave it to Dad—he . . . showed me the picture when I last saw him. That's how I recognize the hands. He told me about this a few days ago, and I wouldn't believe him until I saw that photo.

"Dad was terrified," Nica went on. "He told me he'd do whatever they wanted. He couldn't take the chance that they'd hurt me. But I reckon he didn't give it to them before he died. I . . . I think that's what really happened to him. I think . . . I think he refused to give it to them and they killed him for it. Don't ask me how. I know he's supposed to have choked on a bloody hazelnut, but that's just ridiculous. He *hated* hazelnuts. Those guys *must* have done it somehow."

Manikin didn't agree. She didn't want to say it, but if Move-Easy had wanted to force Brundle to do anything, he'd simply have taken Nica hostage. Killing Brundle wouldn't have got him what he wanted. Brundle was no use to them dead. And Move-Easy could always be counted on to do whatever it took to get his hands on the money.

"They're here for me," Nica said in a near-whisper, and Manikin was struck again by how stark and disfiguring the girl's birthmark looked when the rest of her face went pale. "I don't know what to do. How do I hide from people like that? No matter what I do, they'll find me."

Manikin stared over at the Turk, making no attempt to hide it. To hell with it, she thought. As far as she was concerned, Nimmo's time was up. There was no reason for Nica to get hurt, not when he had the box. This had gone far enough. But at least now they could clear this whole thing up. Manikin could worry about what Move-Easy had planned for them after she'd got out of here.

"I can help you, Nica," she said at last. "I know these guys, I can get them to back off if I can give them something they want. But you need to help me first. If this is to do with your dad, what was he working on, exactly? He was a biologist, working on fixing scar tissue, right? So what was he making?"

"I don't know," Nica sighed. "I was never really interested in the whole science thing, you know? And Dad hardly ever talked about his work. I just know he was working on something for this company, Axis something or other. Dad's part of the project fell through—it wasn't working, so they fired him in the end. But he found this private client to pay for the research, and kept going on his own. And he said it would sort my birthmark, and just before he died, he got really excited about something, and I reckon he'd cracked it, whatever it was. Anyway, that's all I know."

Manikin pressed her lips together in frustration, tapping her fingernails on the glass table. Had Move-Easy's men screwed up? Had they killed Brundle before they got their hands on the seed thing? Or had Vapor's men killed him to keep Easy from getting it? It didn't matter. What mattered to Manikin was handing over that box to Move-Easy, and keeping her and her brother alive— and Scope, Nica and Nimmo too, if it was possible.

"Listen," she said to Nica. "You're right, these guys will get you if they want you. You're not even safe with the police—the guy who's after you owns as many coppers as he does criminals. If you want to stay safe, stay out in public, stay in front of the cameras."

"I can't do that for ever!" Nica cried softly.

"You won't need to," Manikin said. "Just for today. Stay out of their reach for today. I'm going to take care of this."

Without saying anything more, she stood up, picked up her bag and strode over to where the Turk and his men were sitting, sipping their tea. Confident that they wouldn't try anything with so many witnesses around, she leaned over the table and locked eyes with the huge man.

"It's me, Manikin," she said in a tight voice. "We know where the box is. We'll have it for Easy within the hour. Leave her alone—she's no use to you, now that her dad's dead. Leave her be."

"Not for us to decide, my love," the Turk replied in a thick Greek accent, making a regretful face that was almost cartoon-ish. He held the knuckles of his fists a couple of centimeters apart on the table, and blue arcs of electricity crackled between them. "We do not make decisions. We just watch. We watch her, we watch you, we watch Brundle's lab, we watch Vapor and Vapor's fellows. Always we are watching."

"You know who Vapor is?" Manikin asked, intrigued despite herself.

"The boss does. He knows many things about many people. You scoot along and fetch box—bring back to us. Mister Easy is very reasonable man. I am sure he will listen to your appeal."

Manikin stood up straight. She prided herself on being a keen judge of human nature, on being able to read someone by their body language and tone of voice. She saw the way these four men were looking at her, with their chilly, uncaring stares, their closed-off expressions, their postures suggesting that they had no interest in what she said, that they were waiting for something else. In that moment, she became certain that these men meant her harm.

Turning on her heel, she strode off towards the nearest exit, needing to get out onto the road beyond the apartment blocks. It took all her self-control not to break into a run.

CHAPTER 27

BURNING TO KNOW

IT HAD BEEN AGREED AMONG NIMMO. FX and Scope that, before retrieving the box, the three rat-runners would search Brundle's lab for any last evidence that might provide a clear picture of his work, and an explanation for his death. They all figured the less time they actually had the case in their hands, the less risk they were taking.

They climbed up through the building without meeting anyone, including the inquisitive Mrs. Caper. It took Nimmo no time at all to pick the lock, and then they were inside. Nimmo had stopped to close the door again, so it was FX who walked past the pug dog toy sitting on the office desk. All three of them jumped in fright as it started barking and frantically nodding its head.

"Jesus, that nearly gave me a heart attack," FX said, taking a deep breath.

Scope let out a breath of her own and nodded. Nimmo grinned.

"I keep forgetting about that bloody thing."

FX picked it up, turning it over, but there was no off switch. The battery was sealed into it, so he just put it down by the door, where its infra-red sensor wouldn't detect them. Then they began the business of searching the lab.

FX went straight over to what Nimmo said was Brundle's main computer. It booted up quickly, and he set about exploring its files.

"Somebody's been on this since Brundle died," he told them. "They've wiped all the files, but they left the hard drive intact—too sloppy for Vapor's lot, so it must have been Move-Easy's trolls." It was very difficult to delete digital files properly without completely wiping the drive; most of what got deleted from a desktop could still be saved. "I'm going to try and retrieve as much of it as I can."

Scope was going through the research materials and lab equipment, looking for anything that might be useful, with Nimmo helping her. He watched as she looked at machines and dismissed them, switching on anything that could store computer files, or examining the contents of others.

"Implants," she said, studying something under a microscope. "Figured as much. He was using implants—and not just using them, I think he was *making* them. But there's nothing here I haven't seen before."

"He had a stash of notebooks," Nimmo told her. "Kept them in his safe. It's in the clean room at the end there."

"Really? He actually wrote stuff down on paper? And did he know you knew where his safe was?"

"It's not like it's well hidden." Nimmo opened the door into the clean room. "It's just built into the wall behind a set of shelves."

"Oh sure, that's hardly hidden at all."

"Anyway, if there's anything he was trying to keep secure, it'll be in there. What he probably didn't realize is that I knew the combination."

"How?" Scope asked, as she followed him through the airlock of plastic sheeting.

An air shower system would normally have been working to filter the impurities out of the air as anyone entering put on disposable coveralls in the airlock. Nimmo didn't bother with the coveralls. Scope was about to object, but then decided she'd just sound stupid. Brundle was dead, and they were in a rush.

"Because the numpty wrote down all his useful numbers on a sheet in his wallet," Nimmo sniffed. "I had a quick look at his wallet one time."

"Bloody hell! You've never just taken a quick look at my wallet, have you? Nimmo? Have you?"

"No," said Nimmo. "Not yet, anyway. You're not keeping any really personal secrets in there, are you?"

"That's not funny! Don't ever mess with my stuff! You hear me? Nimmo?"

There was more lab equipment in here, all immaculately dirt- and dust-free. Scope loved it. Brundle's lab was a lot smaller and not as well equipped as Tubby Reach's, or even Move-Easy's, but it had been perfectly fitted out for the needs of a biologist exploring bio-technology. Plastic vials lined the counters, and Scope looked at their labels, but it was some cataloguing system, and she'd need the index to figure it out.

The safe was set into the wall at one end of the clean room, where Brundle did all his micro-technology experiments. Nimmo swung open a set of aluminum shelves to reveal the door, which was as tall as he was. He gazed solemnly at the safe, which was clearly a serious affair. It had a keypad halfway up the left-hand side, and when Nimmo tapped in a six-digit number, it unlocked with a deep series of clicks, opening to reveal four shelves taken up with more plastic vials, and stacks of hardback, ring-bound notebooks, all wrapped in plastic to protect the work in the clean room.

"He kept handwritten notes," Scope muttered, smiling to herself. "How *traditional*. Move-Easy's got a stash like this somewhere. All the blackmail material he's got on coppers, judges. It's what makes him so untouchable. Old school, huh? Power in something as simple as the written word."

"Plus you can't hack paper and ink," Nimmo said.

"No, but it's easier to destroy," FX said from behind them, holding up a data key. "I've downloaded everything I could retrieve off the hard drive, but there's serious encryption on some of this stuff. Don't know if I'll be able to crack it. Looks like his back-up disks were nicked too."

Scope hesitated for a moment, then pulled one of the packages of notebooks out and tore off the plastic. Opening one, she scanned through a few of the pages.

"This is it—these are his research notes," she said. "Years of thoughts written down. Everything we need to know will be in here."

Out in the main part of the lab, the pug dog started barking.

The three rat-runners froze, looking towards the door. Nimmo strode over to the airlock, pushing through the zip-lock curtains, and peered out through the crack in the open door. Then he gently pushed it closed, and pressed the button that locked it.

"It's Krieger and Hector," he whispered.

FX swore under his breath.

"What do we do?" Scope asked.

"This clean room is also a safe room," Nimmo said. "Brundle took his security seriously. The door's solid steel, the walls are reinforced concrete. They can't get in here without heavy cutting equipment or high-grade explosives. We can just wait them out." He didn't look entirely convinced. "That's assuming they can't find another way in—or find a way of flushing us out."

They heard the handle of the door pull down and spring back up again. It was tried twice more. There was silence for a moment.

"What now?" FX said softly.

"We could just wait," Nimmo replied. "But if they're here for Brundle's research, everything they want is in this room."

Scope shrugged and looked through the pack of notebooks, trying to hide her nervousness. The books were dated, and she opened the most recent one and started reading.

Then the lights went out. A few seconds later, two emergency lights, mounted on a box on the wall, came on.

"They've cut the power to the room," FX said. "Those lights must be on a back-up system."

Nimmo strained his ears to listen, trying to guess what the two men were doing outside. He heard a scuffling sound in the external wall, the one that had once had a window in it, before it was sealed up. There was a ventilation duct in that wall at head height, and Nimmo put his ear to it.

"I think they've reached out of the window to block the vent up with something," he said. "I don't think there's any way to shift it from here."

"There should be fans running," FX said. "To feed air into this place." He found the switches on the walls, and flicked them on and off, but it made no difference. "How much air do you think we have in here?" he asked Nimmo.

"Less than ten hours, in a space this size," Scope told them, without lifting her head up from the book. "But we'll lose our ability to think clearly and function properly a while before that. Somehow though, if they want us dead, I don't think they'll be satisfied with hoping we suffocate."

"So, what, you'll be happy as long as you die reading?" FX gestured to the book.

"We all have our own ways of dealing with life-threatening situations," she said shakily. "I can think better if my imagination isn't given time to dwell on my impending doom."

Nimmo went back to the door through to the main part of the lab.

"The door's getting warmer," he grunted. "You're right, they're not waiting for the air to run out. They've set the lab on fire. Could've used any of the flammable stuff Brundle had in containers out there. Thought there was a sprinkler system, but maybe they've messed that up too."

"They're going to smoke us out," FX muttered, moving over to feel the door.

"No, it's a clean room—it's airtight," Scope pointed out, still keeping her eyes on the page. "There's no way for the smoke to get in."

"She's right," Nimmo said. "They're burning the whole place down, destroying the research . . . and us with it. I don't think the fire can get in here, but the whole place could collapse if the rest of the building goes up. Either way, we're going to bake like meat in an oven."

"Are you still reading?" FX asked Scope in amazement.

"Brundle got his prototype finished," Scope told them, pointing to a line of text. "It's an organic implant—he actually *grew* the thing. It can . . . it can be wired right into a human's nervous system! Do you know what that means? This is unreal!"

"That's fascinating," FX said to her in a level voice. "Have you heard that we're going to get cooked?"

"We have to get out of this room," Nimmo said, pulling the sleeve of his jacket over his hand as he hit the button to unlock the steel door. "We're in a concrete and metal box that's going to heat up fast." He pulled a tiny fire extinguisher off the wall. He doubted it would be much good against a room full of flames, but he might be able to clear a path to the front door. "Cover your noses and mouths with something, and keep low to the floor."

"Hang on," FX called, looking up at the sprinklers in the ceiling. "Maybe these still work. Our clothes'll burn slower if they're wet."

He pulled a lighter from his pocket, flicked it into life, and held it up to the smoke sensor. An alarm went off and a couple of seconds later, water began to spray at high pressure from the tiny shower-heads in the ceiling.

Scope let out a cry of dismay as the notebook she was holding became soaked, and the ink began to run. She closed it and tucked it into her backpack, along with the rest of that bundle. Then she began pulling more packages of notebooks from the safe, but there was no way she'd be able to carry everything. There must have been nearly two hundred books. As she took another lot out, the package split and dropped at her feet. One of the notebooks fell open and, picking it up, she swore loudly at what she saw.

"Bloody hell, we had it all the time!" she moaned.

The other two weren't listening. Nimmo was squatting down on the floor with FX beside him, a couple of meters from the door, as the sprinklers soaked their clothes and skin. In FX's hand was a piece of wire, the other end tied to the door handle. Nimmo held the fire extinguisher ready.

"Those scrotes could still be out there," FX warned him.

But Nimmo had felt the heat in the metal of the door through his sleeve.

"I doubt it," he said.

FX pulled down on the wire, and a blast of hot air slammed the door open. The lab beyond was ablaze, the desks, chairs, and some of the equipment already in flames. Crouching low, Nimmo held his breath and darted out, blasting jets of gas at the roots of the fires close to him. In less than thirty seconds, he had made it to the front door. Dropping the extinguisher, he covered his hand with his sleeve again and tried to open the door, but the lock was jammed. FX came up behind him.

"They've wrecked the lock!" Nimmo shouted to him, over the roar of the fire. "It's another bloody steel door! We'd need a blowtorch to get through it!"

"What about the windows?" FX called back.

"They're barred, and it's a six-story drop!" Nimmo growled, looking around in desperation.

The walls and ceiling were concrete—there was no way to get through them. The heat was intense, and the air was filled with fumes that made their eyes water and stung the back of their throats, making them gag and cough. In a matter of minutes, they wouldn't be able to breathe. Both boys looked down at the floor at the same time. It had a seamless vinyl covering from wall to wall, the kind designed to make lab floors easy to clean. There was a utility knife on the desk. FX grabbed it, slid out the blade and cut a right-angled slash in the vinyl. It was tough stuff, and it took both of them to dig up an edge and peel it back. Underneath it was riveted steel plate. The type you used to reinforce floors that had to take heavy lab equipment.

"Shit, we're going to die," FX coughed.

"Definitely, but not today," Nimmo said.

There was a cordless drill on one of the workbenches, and Nimmo grabbed it. Using the knife to cut away the vinyl to uncover the full plate—a square meter—he started drilling into the first of the twelve rivets.

"Man, we don't have time," FX muttered.

"Find a crowbar or a claw hammer to lift the plate," Nimmo snapped, as the drill bit shredded the head of the first rivet. "And get Scope!"

Sections of plaster were falling from the ceiling as flames crept across it. The smoke was making breathing unbearable. FX's head swam as he grabbed the fire extinguisher and bent double to try and find the cooler, clearer air near the floor. By the time he'd made it back to the clean room, the extinguisher was used up. Tossing it away, he crawled through the door on his hands and knees. Scope was still trying to bundle as many of the notebooks as she could into her bag. The sprinklers were still spraying; the clean room was clear of flames, and the air was still breathable.

"He wuh . . . wuh . . . was a genius!" she cried, when she saw FX coming through the smoke. Her voice was ragged and she was nearly choking, her breaths coming in short pants. "We . . . we can't lose . . . lose all this. Help me! We nuh . . . nuh . . . need these!"

"Scope, wake up!" he bellowed at her. "*The building is on fire!* The. Building. Is. On. Fire. Leave all that crap. We have to get out of here!"

She tried to push another book into her bag, but he grabbed her and dragged her back out into the chaos that was the main lab. There was a toolbox under one of the tables, and FX kicked it over, seizing a claw hammer from the contents that spilled

across the floor. The jerk of his body jolted Scope, who was trying to pull her inhaler from her pocket. The inhaler clattered
across the floor, and FX urged her on before she could grab it.
The vinyl was starting to burn, creeping across the floor from
the edges, forming a slowly tightening circle of flames. Nimmo
was coughing badly, his eyes filled with tears, but his hands were
steady as he kept his focus fixed on destroying the rivets that held
the plate to the floor. As the other two reached him, he finished
drilling the last rivet-head.

FX turned to vomit as far from the bare metal as he could,
then came back to help Nimmo get the claw of the hammer
under the edge of the steel plate. They worked the edge up and
got their fingers underneath. It was hot, but not yet hot enough
to burn them. Pulling it up and over, they exposed the steel
girders beneath. The undersides were covered by plywood, and
Nimmo covered his face with his sleeve, gagging on smoke as he
slammed the heel of his foot down between two of the girders,
smashing the plywood away. Four, then five kicks knocked the
plastered board onto the floor below, creating a ragged rectangular hole between the girders.

Scope was suffocating. Her asthmatic lungs could not draw
in air as her windpipe closed down; her chest felt as if someone
was tightening a belt around it. The smoke was close to knocking
Nimmo and FX out, but Scope was on the edge of death.
Nimmo dropped down through the hole, and FX lowered her
down to him. He was in the kitchen of Mrs. Caper's flat, and
she was staring in horror as he dragged this gasping, wheezing
girl across the floor, out of the way of the new hole in Caper's

kitchen ceiling. FX dropped down, his legs crumpling under him as he landed. Nimmo was searching through Scope's pockets. He found a brown inhaler, and was about to give that to her, but FX scrambled forward and stopped him.

"Don't!" he rasped through a painful throat. "It's a weapon, it's bloody sneezing gas. She needs her other one. She dropped it up in the lab, under Brundle's PC!"

Nimmo coughed and choked, swiveling to stare in dull determination at the hole in the ceiling. Then he staggered dizzily to the kitchen table, hauled it over until it was under the hole. He climbed on top, swaying slightly, reached up, and pulled himself back up into Brundle's burning lab.

FX watched the hole for what seemed like an age, listening to Scope's helpless gasps growing weaker and weaker, turning to see her face turning blue, her eyes bulging, half conscious. He could hear sirens, but they weren't going to be in time. Scope was going to die, and Nimmo had been up there too long. He was gone.

Then he tumbled down through the hole, landing with a crash on the table. Two of its legs broke and he was sent sprawling across the floor. FX took the inhaler from his clawed hands and held it to Scope's mouth and pressed the plunger. He took it away, shaking it, waiting for an improvement that didn't come. He gave her another blast. Still her lungs sucked hopelessly against her blocked windpipes. FX had heard enough about these things to know that if an inhaler didn't work within the first few tries, it wasn't going to work. But he tried again. And again . . .

CHAPTER 28

A MATTER OF CONTROL

SCOPE SAT WITH HER BACK TO THE WALL of a garage in an alleyway a few blocks from Brundle's building. She had her head resting on her forearms, hiding the tears that streamed down her face. The inhaler's effects had kicked in after a few suffocating minutes. Her breathing had recovered in time for her two friends to drag her out of Caper's flat and away from the emergency services. She had enough experience of managing her asthma to know that the worst was over, though she was still at risk of suffering a new attack if she wasn't careful. Her windpipe had been damaged by the smoke, and she would have to take care for the next while that she didn't do anything to bring on another attack, like getting caught in any more stressful situations.

Yeah, right.

She had demanded that FX and Nimmo get her out of the building before the emergency services found them. The paramedics would have put her on a trolley, fed her oxygen and carted her off to a hospital. She had experienced that before, and hated the feel of the oxygen mask on her face, the chaos of the A&E ward filled with fearful, angry, impatient people. Everyone desperate for medical attention, but there never seemed to be enough nurses and doctors. Scope preferred to just get through this on her own.

So when they had taken to the rat-runs and put a safe distance between them and the burning building, she had flopped down on the ground, leaned back against the wall with her head in her arms and cried, because it was the closest she'd ever come to dying, and it had terrified her.

Nimmo and FX left her alone, seeing that she needed to get this turbulent emotion out of her system. The spot they had chosen was quiet; the rear of a garage in a row of garages and storage lockups built into the stone arches beneath a railway line. Empty steel barrels, crates and other junk provided plenty of cover. When Scope finally lifted her head, she wiped her eyes and gave them a half-hearted smile.

"I'm OK," she croaked through an aching throat. "Actually, I'm feeling pretty good, considering."

"There's no buzz like surviving," Nimmo told her. "You had us pretty scared there, Scope. No amount of notes is worth that."

"These were," she said, looking up at him. "I think I've cracked the whole thing. Brundle was a bloody genius. He was trying to create a nano-tech implant that could regenerate human flesh, particularly the epidermis—your skin. He didn't want to just grow new skin—that's been possible for decades—he wanted to be able to *program* it to adopt a specific form, so it could cover a wound, or a scar . . . or a birthmark, on any part of the body and seal it without any visible mark or flaw. But while trying to come up with something that could do that, he created a molecular assembler."

"A what?" Nimmo asked.

"It's a kind of nano-technology seed. It can build things at an *atomic* level. In this case, he's created a seed that can be programmed to grow things like microchips or electrical components inside the human body. And they develop as part of your nervous system. He reckoned you could control them with your mind."

"That's impossible," Nimmo said. "How could you *grow* something as complicated as a microchip?"

"How does an acorn create something as complicated as an oak tree?" Scope countered. "The ribosomes in your own body's cells are molecular assemblers of a sort—they manufacture proteins according to a kind of 'chemical program' called RNA. The theory of a molecular assembler like this has been around for a long time."

"Yeah, it's just that nobody's ever managed to do it for real," FX scoffed. "And he was trying to cure *birthmarks*? That's like trying to design the first hot-air balloon and creating a jet engine instead."

"Well, from what he's written here, I think he managed it," Scope said, shrugging. "He called it the brundleseed, and he really wanted to do the right thing with his work. Even at the level he'd intended it, this thing could bring relief to thousands, *millions* of people living with disfiguring scars, birthmarks or deformities. But the science applications of a real molecular assembler are . . . are . . . I don't know, it's a game-changer—a revolution. It could be the biggest thing since the microchip. And he wanted everyone to have it."

"But that wasn't going to happen if Move-Easy got his hands on it," FX sniffed.

"Or Vapor," Nimmo added. "You don't pay the kind of money he did and then heal the world for free."

Scope pulled one of the notebooks from her backpack and opened it up.

"Yeah, except Vapor didn't give a damn about people's skin," she said. "Or at least, it wasn't the main thing he was after. Brundle realized that he'd accidentally created something else with his implant. You see, the brundleseed can grow devices that can be controlled by a person's nervous system. But it could also be made to work the other way around. It could be used to create devices that *tap into* a person's nervous system. And if it was made to receive radio signals, *somebody else* could trigger it. It could be used against the person who's carrying it. That's what Vapor was after."

"Technology embedded in your body that someone else would control?" FX screwed up his face. "That's mental."

"What could it do?" Nimmo asked.

"Depends what it's programmed to do," Scope said in a shaky voice. "They could grow miniature cameras inside anyone who worked for them. Imagine Safe-Guards who looked like normal people, but had their technology built into their bodies. And it'd be organic material . . . *really* difficult to detect, even with instruments.

"But it's what they could do to innocent people that bothers me. They could grow microphones or radio receivers under your skin, so you're permanently bugged. You could be tagged like a criminal, giving off all the information you'd find on a biometric passport, but you might not even know it. Diagnostic sensors could reveal what's happening inside your body. Maybe you could even end up with embedded weapons that could hurt you, or paralyze you if those in control decided you were misbehaving. And this control can be targeted. Give ten people brundleseeds, you can choose which one you're going to paralyze with the press of a button. You could control the population of a city, even a country, with this stuff."

"But you'd have to implant this seed into a person's body first," Nimmo pointed out. "Sounds like a bit of a roundabout way of going about things. And as for ruling a country . . . that just sounds like some half-arsed science fiction story."

"It's nano-technology," FX said thoughtfully. "It could be programmed to find its way through your body. You could put it in somebody's food or drink and it could get to where it needed to go."

"Make enough of them, you could put it in the bloody *water supply*," Scope rasped. "It's about *control*. Making people do what you want them to do. Brundle realized what he'd created, and tried to hide it from Vapor. But by then, Move-Easy had found out about it too, and Easy went straight for the throat—Brundle had to hand the seed over when it was finished, or Easy would kill his daughter."

"And Vapor had Brundle killed before he could give it to Move-Easy," Nimmo sighed. "Here . . . Brundle was experimenting on himself, right? He must have had an implant in his own body. D'you think they somehow used his own invention against him?"

Scope shrugged. There was no way of telling for sure.

"So the cards we've been sent after, they were just Brundle's payment," Nimmo said. "It's the brundleseed they're all really after. Say Brundle had one inside him . . ."

"If Vapor's as powerful as he seems, he could have that one already," Scope said. "But it's no good to him. It would have grown into whatever it was programmed to become. And it would have been bonded to Brundle's system; even if it could be salvaged from his corpse, it would never work again."

"Probably for the best," FX murmured. "Christ knows what somebody like Move-Easy could do with tech like that. But if there's another one, could be nobody would ever find it. Something that size, you could hide it anywhere. Let's hope whatever was left went up with the lab."

Scope bit her lip, unconsciously clicking the fingernails of her thumb and forefinger together.

"Actually, it didn't," she said, coughing and looking suddenly uncomfortable. "Brundle made at least one other prototype, one he hadn't given to anybody. He had drawings of it in his notes. We've had the bloody thing all along." She gave the thumbs-up to Nimmo. "He had it hidden under his thumbnail."

❂   ❂   ❂

The four rat-runners sat around FX's computer, listening as he played back the phone call that his system had recorded from the landline in Nica's apartment. He had tapped the phone as a matter of course. This was the most recent call.

"Hello?" A voice that had to be Nica's mother answered the phone.

"Is this Mrs. Brundle?" a man asked.

"Ms. Davis," she corrected him. "Watson and I are . . . had been divorced for a number of years."

"Apologies, Ms. Davis," the man said. "This is Detective Constable Dibble. I'm not sure if you're aware of the fire that occurred at your husband's building this afternoon?"

"Yes, yes, I'd heard," Davis replied in a tremulous voice. "God, could things get any worse? Was anybody hurt?"

"No, ma'am, at least not that we know of," Dibble told her. "The blaze was pretty serious, but the lab had reinforced floor and walls, and that helped to contain the fire to the top floor until the fire service arrived. The building's been declared safe. However, your daughter had requested permission to go into the lab and apartment a couple of days ago, to collect some of her father's belongings. Obviously there's not much left now . . . but . . . well, it's become a crime scene again. We believe the fire was the result of arson. An investigation will have to be carried out. There will be Safe-Guard surveillance on the scene for the next few days to secure the site. Your daughter can still have access to her father's living quarters if she wants, but the damaged sections will be off limits."

FX stopped the recording there.

"A bleedin' Safe-Guard," he said. "Considering how quickly they lost interest in Brundle's death, they seem to be taking this arson pretty seriously. This whole cluster-funk is starting to attract official attention. Could be that they've cottoned on to what's happening. Like we didn't have enough problems. How the hell are we going to get at that box if there's peepers watching the place?"

"Maybe we should just forget about it?" Scope suggested. "It's the brundleseed everybody really wants anyway."

"And you think we should let them have it?" Manikin asked. "Vapor wants us dead, and I'm betting Move-Easy does too. Who do you even give the bloody thing to? I don't want to think about what could happen if either of them got their hands on it. And if you give it to one of them, the other one will come looking for our heads."

The others nodded in agreement. None of them wanted to hand over the implant, but they couldn't see any way out of this.

"We may just have to get out of London—out of the UK altogether," Nimmo muttered.

Once more, he was asking himself if he would be better off alone, free of these others. He had plans laid for escaping London in a hurry: alternate identities, places to hide, stashes of money and gear. He could survive better on his own.

"You're assuming we can even make it out," FX pointed out. "Easy's a London villain, but he's got a long reach. I say we get him that box—I mean, we need *something* to bargain with. But that still leaves Vapor's lot. We're too tangled up in this. They're not going to let us go now."

"FX is right, that box is the only leverage we've got," Manikin said. "I think we could use it as bait for all of them. The Turk said something . . . I think Easy knows who Vapor is."

"Really?" FX piped up. "D'you think he'd tell us?"

The others regarded him with incredulous expressions.

"No," he murmured. "Maybe not now."

"Anyway, Easy knows Vapor's an enemy," Manikin went on. "If we could find a way to set those two on each other—maybe we could take their sights off us long enough for us to get clear."

"We're not giving them the brundleseed," Scope insisted. "Just promise me that, all of you. Neither of these maniacs is getting hold of this thing. Look, I know we're no choir of angels, but this is just too important. Too many people could be hurt by this. I'm deadly serious. It's more important than any of us."

Looking around the room, she met each person's eyes, measuring up the conviction of each of these young criminals. Each one met her gaze and nodded back. No matter what, this dangerously powerful thing that they now possessed must not fall into the wrong hands.

"So . . . how do we get this bloody case then?" Manikin put the question to them. "How do we get in and out of a place surrounded by villains that's going to have Safe-Guards and who knows what other kinds of surveillance on it? Anybody any ideas?"

There was a long pause, as she waited for an answer. Then Nimmo spoke up:

"Me an' Scope have been talkin'," he said. "The way I see it, there's no way any of us can get in there, and come out safely

carrying that case. There's just too much chance of being caught
by somebody. But Scope reckons she's figured out how to program this brundleseed."

"Yeah," Scope said, glancing over at Manikin. "It could
be the key to getting inside. It's just that it'd be a little
bit . . . well . . . *experimental.*"

Manikin sat up straighter, not liking the sound of this. "Why
are you both looking at me?" she demanded.

This is a stupid idea, Manikin thought. I can't believe how stupid
this is. Lying back in a chair that was eerily like a dentist's chair,
she let her body fit into its contours and tried to relax. Nimmo
had led the other three into Tubby Reach's Void. Reach owed him
a whole bunch of favors, and now Nimmo had called them all in.
Though when Reach heard what they wanted, he said he'd do
the job just to see the brundleseed at work. The tone in his voice
hinted that it would take that level of proof for him to believe
in this fairy-tale piece of technology. Manikin had no doubt the
King of the Getters was already dreaming up uses for this fairy
tale if it turned out to be real. They hadn't told him there'd only
be one shot at getting this stuff to work, and it would be useless
for anything else once it had been implanted.

"This is a really stupid idea," Manikin said aloud. "You know,
this thing is too good a deal to waste on me, don't you think?
Really, I'm not worthy."

"We've talked this through already," Scope responded from
somewhere behind her. "The case is the only thing we can

bargain with. This is the only way we can think of getting the case. Besides, as far as we're concerned, the brundleseed has just been a theory up until now. Actually seeing this one in operation is the best way to find out how it works."

"A theory. Right. So what if *I* end up dead? Then this thing will be lost to the world, won't it?"

"Yeah, so don't get dead. You don't want to let the world down, now, do you?"

Manikin realized that this conversation was pointless. Scope had discovered from Brundle's notes that the brundleseed could be made to reproduce itself once it was implanted in someone's body, but those new ones could then only be used in the same body—and had to be implanted immediately. Scope had put the one they had in Manikin's forearm and used it to grow three more. Long before they went anywhere near Tubby Reach, Manikin had become a human test subject for this bizarre new technology. It was too late to argue about it. Now these three would be removed. Like organs for transplant, they had to be put back into her body quickly, before the flesh they were made of began to die. Lying back in that creepy chair, Manikin was in an argumentative mood.

"How do you feel?" FX asked, from somewhere else in the room, where he was monitoring her vital signs. So far, the seeds had had no effect on her, except that she'd been able to relieve the itch their presence caused in her flesh without scratching it. Which was much more unsettling than having an itch.

"I feel like throwing up over the next person who asks how I'm feeling," Manikin snapped.

"Oooh, touchy," FX murmured, presumably in a voice that she wasn't supposed to hear.

"Give it a rest," Nimmo's voice whispered, also intended to be beyond her hearing. "There's no telling what those things could do to her. She's taking a big risk for all of us."

"I heard that!" she barked at him. "There better be some *major* appreciation at the end of this, that's all I can say."

A thin man in a green surgeon's outfit leaned over Manikin.

"I'll give you a local anesthetic for the hair and skin procedures," he said, peering down at Manikin from behind the bright lamp shining into her eyes. "You'll need a sedative as well as the painkillers, but you have to be able to talk to me."

"I hope you're not sensitive to foul language," she said through teeth that were tightly pressed together.

"Honey, I've heard it all before," he chuckled. "Relax. You shouldn't feel any pain. After we've shaved your head, and planted the seed there, I think maybe you'll just feel a slight . . . creeping, tingling sensation." He paused. "Actually, to be quite frank, I've no idea what this will feel like."

"Thanks a bunch." She was crying now. She loved her hair, and she was devastated to be losing it, even if she was getting a 'new and improved version.' The surgeon pulled up his face mask and pulled a complicated-looking magnifying glass down over one eye. On the wall behind him, almost invisible beyond the light, a set of speakers played gentle classical music. Scope stood beside him, ready to assist.

I'm going to kill her when this is over, Manikin fumed to herself. And Nimmo too, if I can catch the slippery sod. This is a really stupid idea.

"You're sure you don't want me to install control nodes?" the surgeon asked for the third time. "If this works, I mean."

"You don't need any wiring or switches," Scope answered softly for her. "Remember, that's the whole point. You'll be able to control it all as if it's part of your body."

"Just so you know, I'm going to kill you when this is over," Manikin said to her.

"See you on the other side," Scope replied with a smile, and her voice grew watery and strange as the surgeon injected something into the back of Manikin's hand, and the music playing in the background became longer, and stretched, and mixed in with her thoughts until she couldn't tell what was coming from outside, or what was being dreamed up inside . . .

CHAPTER 29

DECEPTION

MANIKIN WALKED THROUGH THE FRONT DOOR of Brundle's building, trying to slow her breathing and her pounding heart. There was no point having a disguise so good it could fool a Safe-Guard, if every biological sign she was giving off was spiking as if she was being electrocuted. She had to calm down.

Passing a mirror in the lobby, she checked her reflection.

"Oh, crap."

To the human eye, she looked the image of Veronica Brundle. The disfiguring birthmark on her face—made from high-quality simu-skin—would distract most people's eyes from the fact that Nica had a rounder face. Her skin was slightly darker than its natural hue, she wore clothes to match items that Nica owned, and Manikin had practiced the girl's voice and mannerisms. Contact lenses had colored her eyes to match Nica's.

The disguise was almost perfect, except for the fact that Manikin's new hair was slowly turning green.

"Crap!"

She turned down a corridor, finding a small alcove where she could take out her compact mirror and fix her hair. Concentrating, she watched it change from green, through blue to black, and then, with a wince, she managed to get the coppery streaks to appear through it, to mimic Nica's. Satisfied that her appearance was restored, Manikin closed her eyes and took some deep breaths. Her mind went back to earlier that day. She could hear FX as if he was standing next to her, briefing her on the tech stuff, and for once, he had her complete attention.

"The Safe-Guards have one major weakness," he reminded her. "All of their information comes from the Controllers. Your disguise won't fool a digital facial or voice recognition system, if WatchWorld has Nica on their files. And you know a peeper can x-ray your teeth and identify you from your dental records.

"But if they can't contact Control, if their communications link is down, then they have to go with the information they're carrying on their own hard drives, which is pretty minimal. And that link is basically just a mobile phone signal, which I'll be able to disrupt for a few minutes. Peepers lose signal more often than WatchWorld is willing to admit, so it shouldn't look too suspicious.

"So as long as you look and sound enough like Nica to fool the people in the building, you should be able to fool the peeper.

Your fake ID will pass too, as long as the peeper can't verify the chip online."

That was FX's part in this. To cut the Safe-Guard off from its base long enough for her to fool its technology. But getting past the peeper was only half the challenge.

"The box is taped into a ventilation duct on the roof," Nimmo explained. "But you don't have to go up to the roof to get it. The duct runs down behind the wall in my old flat. There's a cord hanging down from the package, that you can reach through a vent in the hallway. Pull on the cord, and the package will fall right into your hands.

"Then you have to get out," he continued. "That's the *real* problem. Because we can get you close to the building before you change into Nica. And we reckon both Vapor's and Easy's lot will let Nica go inside—everyone wants to see what she's going to bring out. Everyone thinks Nica is the key to getting hold of the box, or the brundleseed, or both."

"But then I have to get out," Manikin said.

"Yeah," he grunted. "You have to be Nica to *get in*, but if you *come out* looking like her, *somebody's* going to snatch you, whether you've got what they want or not. And the same goes if you come out looking like Manikin. So you have to look like somebody else—somebody who has no connection to this whole mess."

"But if the peeper scans you and finds you carrying anything that looks like a disguise, like a wig, or prosthetics or even something that would cover your face, it's going to get suspicious. You have to be able to change your appearance without carrying a disguise with you. You can throw stuff away, but you can't really add anything."

"And that's why you need the brundleseeds," Scope said.

Standing in the corridor of Brundle's building, Manikin checked her appearance again. Her hair was fine now; she was getting the hang of controlling the color, though it had already caught her out several times. The same went for her skin color. Both were now adjustable, thanks to the implants grown using the brundleseeds. These organic implants could not be detected by a peepers x-ray vision. And there were no controls anywhere on her body, because the implants worked as part of her own nervous system. She could control all of them just as she could her own fingers. Another implant in her throat enabled her to manipulate the muscles there to raise and lower the pitch of her voice beyond anything she could do naturally, all of which gave her a means of changing disguise that was undetectable.

As soon as she had the box and was clear of the Safe-Guard, she would switch. She'd rip off the simu-skin birthmark. Her jeans were reversible, blue on the outside, gray on the inside, and she would ditch her jacket. Her high heels would be thrown away, to be replaced by the pair of plimsolls she had in the plastic bag clutched in her hand. Plenty of girls carried a comfortable pair of shoes for the commute to and from work. She'd change her hair from black to deep red and darken her skin until she looked Asian. The intention was to resemble another girl they had found who lived in the building. Then Manikin would walk out into the street, and right past all those watchful eyes. At least, that was the plan.

A few more deep breaths, and she had composed herself. Her pulse had calmed down, and she no longer felt as if she was standing on a bridge, working up the nerve to do a bungee jump. This was a job, like so many other jobs. This was what she did, what she *was*. It was time to go to work. Stepping back into the lobby, she climbed the stairs to the top floor.

The Safe-Guard was there, standing in the middle of the corridor, as if it had been waiting for her all this time.

Manikin let her nerves show a bit. People got nervous talking to Safe-Guards. It was the combination of law-enforcer authority and the lack of a face behind the visor that freaked out most people.,

"Hi . . . er . . . I'm . . . I'm Veronica Brundle?" she said, as if she was checking her identity with the tall figure, rather than informing it. She held out her ID card. "I'm here to pick up some of my dad's things."

By now, FX would have disrupted the peeper's communication signal, so it should be flying solo, without guidance from the Controllers. It scanned her card and took a moment to reply in its asexual, monotone voice.

"Yes, Miss Brundle. You have been cleared to enter the living areas on this floor. There is no access to the laboratory area."

Manikin nodded. Nimmo had walked her through the layout of this floor, so that she would look familiar with it. He had given her keys to both apartments. She was amazed that Brundle had trusted him with a key to his home. Perhaps he and Nimmo really had been friends—unless, of course, Nimmo had stolen that too.

She walked past the peeper and let herself into Brundle's

apartment. As Nimmo had assured her, there was a collection of backpacks and bags in the cupboard by the door. Picking out a small backpack, she transferred the plimsolls into it, tossing her plastic bag in the bin. Wandering around the apartment, she took some objects at random, putting them in the backpack. She could return them to Nica later, Manikin just needed this to look like she really was here for personal items. Coming out of the apartment after a couple of minutes, she tried not to look at the Safe-Guard as it watched her unlock the door to Nimmo's flat. The array of lenses behind the peeper's visor gave it the emotionless gaze of an insect. It made no attempt to hide the fact that it was observing her every move.

This was where things were going to get a bit iffy. She went straight to the vent in the hallway. With a small utility tool, she unscrewed the grille and pulled it off the wall. The peeper came to the door and stood watching her. This had to look suspicious, but according to the letter of the law, she wasn't doing anything wrong. If the Safe-Guard had questions, it must have been waiting for guidance from its Controllers, which it couldn't get.

There was a cord hanging down the aluminum shaft inside the wall, just as Nimmo had said. Gripping it with her right hand, she gave it a yank. With a soft clatter that echoed down the duct, the box, wrapped in layers of plastic, dropped into her outstretched hands. She pulled it out of the vent. Avoiding turning her eyes towards the peeper, Manikin opened the plastic and took a long look at the black leather case. It was sealed shut, and she didn't want to risk damaging it, so she pulled the cord and plastic off it and threw the wrapping on a sideboard. Then she slipped the case into her backpack.

Overcome with a desperate urge to run out of the room, she paused for a few seconds instead, keeping her breathing slow, and willing her heart to try and do the same. Was the peeper suspicious? Did it want to question her? Did the person behind that visor, as a normal person would, wonder what she was doing? Walking straight up to the Safe-Guard, she gazed unafraid into its inhuman face.

"What's it like for you in there?" she asked. "How does it feel, to be turned into this thing every day?"

But of course, it did not answer. Stepping past it, she walked out into the corridor and made her way towards the stairs.

CHAPTER 30

TAKEN

TROTTING DOWN THE STAIRS, Manikin planned out her next few moves. There was a utility room at the far end of the corridor on the fourth floor, where she could change disguise and dump the bits she didn't need. She was already taking off her jacket as she descended, which was how she happened to have it draped over her forearm as she reached the fifth floor and ran right into Frank Krieger. He was wearing a casual brown suit and shirt. Apologizing, he stepped back, reaching for his jacket pocket. Manikin tensed, ready to raise her hands in defense.

"Miss Brundle?" he asked, flipping open a police identity card. "I'm Detective Sergeant Pembry. Something's come up regarding the circumstances surrounding your father's death, and we need to ask you a few questions. Would you mind coming with me?"

Manikin hesitated. None of the rat-runners had expected anybody would try anything inside the building—not with the Safe-Guard so close. They weren't prepared for this.

"Would I mind coming where?" she asked, her mind racing.

"Just down to the station," he replied in an easy voice. "It won't take lo—"

She threw her jacket into his face, swung her foot up into his balls, then brought her knee up into his face as he doubled over. Grabbing him by the hair, she pulled his head past her and brought her elbow down between his shoulder blades. Then she kicked off her shoes and bolted for the next flight of stairs, taking them three at a time.

She heard Krieger saying something above her—calling somebody over a radio. Swerving around the turn in the stairs, she made it down to the fourth floor in time to see Hector charging up towards her. She could try getting past him—one on one, she might have a chance—but he only had to hold onto her long enough for Krieger to catch up and they'd have her. And whatever the scrotes intended doing, they obviously weren't too worried about alerting the bloody peeper.

Changing direction, she sprinted down the corridor. Passing the utility room she had intended to use, she reached the tall sash window at the end of the hallway. Wrenching it open, she looked out. She was four floors up and there was no way down. Manikin pulled the bag from her back and hurled it out.

Four stories below, Nimmo was there to catch it. Seconds later, he was gone, off into the rat-runs. Wonder if we'll ever see him again, she thought, her face twisting into a scowl. Manikin pivoted, her guard up, ready for a fight, but Hector and Krieger were approaching her cautiously, their eyes flicking between her and the window. They'd seen what she'd done. Breathing hard, she was bitterly aware that these men would have little problem beating a teenage girl. But she was going to make sure they got hurt in the process.

Then she looked past the two men, spotting a figure coming down the stairs beyond them.

"Mrs. Caper!" she called. "Mrs. Caper! Hi!"

The weaselly woman lifted her head and waved hesitantly. Veronica Brundle would not have normally been so eager to get her attention. Manikin walked past Hector and Krieger, not giving them a second glance as they exchanged looks, unsure of what to do. Perhaps they weren't as willing to take their chances with witnesses, now that they knew she no longer had the case. Manikin joined Mrs. Caper at the stairs.

"Hello, Veronica, love," Mrs. Caper said, in a friendly but curious voice, regarding the two strangers with interest. No doubt her nose for gossip caught a tantalizing whiff. "I didn't think I'd be seeing you again anytime soon. How are you, my dear?"

"Having a bit of a rough day, to be honest," Manikin responded. "I was just here to pick up a few of Dad's things. You know, after the fire. Horrible, seeing the place like that. What do you think happened? Are you on your way out? I'll walk with you."

"Of course, my love," Mrs. Caper said, eyeing the two men one last time, before continuing on down the stairs. "I was just popping out for my magazines. Yes, that fire was a terrible thing. It was a bunch of those rat-runner vermin who set it, you know.

Some gang of little thieves. Almost got themselves killed! Fell right down through the ceiling of my kitchen, don't y'know! I don't suppose you know if your dad's insurance is still valid, do you?"

Manikin cast a quick look back at Vapor's men, before turning to listen to Mrs. Caper's account of the day the vermin dropped in. Strolling down the stairs into the lobby, they made their way to the front door, with Manikin making all the right noises as she listened to Mrs. Caper rabbit on, and fended off the woman's attempts to learn more about Veronica's 'two friends upstairs.'

Pulling open the doors, they stepped out onto the path. Manikin hooked her arm into Caper's as they walked past the line of cars parked at the curb, heading towards the shop on the corner of the street.

Manikin had not missed the minivan with the darkened windows that stood at the curb with its engine running. She tensed, ready to turn and run at the first sign of a door opening.

"Wherever are your shoes, my dear?" Mrs. Caper asked, looking down at Manikin's feet.

On reflex, Manikin looked down too, and that was when Mrs. Caper struck her over the head with something hard and heavy. The door of the van slid open, and she was dragged semiconscious into the vehicle. With a screech of tires, it pulled out, and roared down the street.

FX stood, trembling in shock, as he watched from the bus stop on the far side of the road.

"That was the Turk!" he blurted into his phone. "Jesus, Scope, they've got Manikin. Move-Easy's got my sister!"

In the Hide in Brill Alley, FX sat on one of the chairs, face resting on the heels of his hands, his fingers clutching his hair. Scope watched him, her pale face making a lie of her attempts to reassure him.

"What are we going to do?" he moaned. "God, they're going to kill her! Move-Easy knows we've screwed him over for sure now. They're going to put her through *hell*, and then they're going to kill her."

"She's still got a chance," Scope said softly, struggling to hold onto the hope herself. "As long as they think she's Veronica, they won't hurt her—not for a while at least. Move-Easy will think she's just a little girl he can scare into giving him what he wants."

"Yeah, but what happens when he doesn't get it?" FX groaned through gritted teeth. "She's got to let him have one of the brundleseeds. Can she do that? Can they take it out of her?"

Scope didn't reply, because he already knew the answer. The seeds had grown into implants, and they couldn't be removed without an operation—even assuming a surgeon could work out how to separate one from her body. And it would be useless once it was taken out. And even that didn't matter.

Manikin's disguise wouldn't fool Move-Easy for long. And the mob boss would have ordered the deaths of the rat-runners by now. He might still spare Scope, but Manikin wasn't getting out of there alive.

"*Where the hell is Nimmo?*" FX snarled. "He should be back by now! If he's cut out on us—"

"There he is," Scope said, pointing at the screen that showed the view from the doorway in the alley.

Nimmo was approaching the door. Scope buzzed him in, and less than a minute later he was walking into the Hide.

"I tracked the van to Move-Easy's Void," he told them, taking the black leather case from his backpack and laying it on the desk where FX was sitting. "As far as I could tell, they still think Manikin is Nica. So long as she doesn't give them reason to check her fingerprints or her irises, that should keep her alive for a while."

"We need to take the case to them, try to trade it for her," FX said, laying his fingers on the box.

"That's not going to work, FX, and you know it," Nimmo replied. "Easy thinks we're working for the law, or for Vapor. We've been marked, man. We have to get Manikin out of there some other way."

Scope shook her head and picked up the box. "Let's see what all the fuss has been about," she muttered.

Taking a scalpel from her toolkit, she broke the resin seal around the edge of the case, and opened it. Inside the leather-lined walnut box were ten blue and gold cards held in a presentation velvet setting, each one with a credit chip embedded in it. Each card was emblazoned with the WatchWorld logo.

"They're boons," FX said in a subdued voice, reading the RFIDs with his phone. "This is how everyone who gets brasted by WatchWorld gets paid. If you put on a good show for the screens, they give you one of these." He looked at the readout. "But these are the highest denomination. Each card is worth twenty-five grand."

"Quarter of a million quid," Nimmo murmured.

"Small money, really, for what Brundle invented," Scope

commented. "But maybe it *is* enough to buy Manikin back. For this kind of money, maybe Move-Easy'd be willing to forget all about us."

"Enough to make him forget about the brundleseed?" Nimmo asked. "Because as long as he doesn't have that, he's never going to let us go. And d'you want to see his surgeons trying to dig one out of Manikin's body?"

Scope was looking closely at the box. "There's something else here," she muttered, picking up her scalpel again. "Somebody's tampered with the bottom of this case."

Cutting around it, she peeled back the layer of leather that covered the walnut box. A hollow had been cut into the underside of the box, covered by a thin panel of the wood. Scope prized it open. Nestled neatly into the bottom of the box, held in place by clips, were five small plastic vials. Scope took one out and held it up to the light. Floating in some kind of clear solution was a dark speck, much like a small seed. As the others watched intently, Scope took a magnifying glass from her toolkit and examined the tiny object.

"I think it's a brundleseed," she said, a look of wonder on her face. "We've got ourselves five more brundleseeds."

"We can get Manikin out!" FX exclaimed excitedly. "Bloody hell, we only need *one*, and we could trade it for her!"

There were a few seconds of silence as they all considered this.

"How could we know for sure he'd leave us be?" Nimmo wondered aloud. "The guy does treachery for a living. And then what about Vapor? Do we do the same for him? We don't know anything about him, or how far he can reach. Even if we handed the rest of these over to him and made a run for it, how far would we get? And is this what we want to be doing with what could be the most dangerous technology on the planet? Givin' it to the likes of Easy or Vapor? Seriously? This doesn't solve our problems. If anything, we've just raised the stakes."

"I know it's a crap choice," Scope snapped. "But what else are we supposed to do?"

"I'm tired of letting all these scrotes decide the rules of this game," Nimmo said, a hardness setting in his eyes. "And I'm done bein' on the defensive. Let's take these bloody implants and use them to do like Manikin said—draw Easy and Vapor out. Let's play this our way, and see what happens."

CHAPTER 31

TO BE CONVINCING

MANIKIN SAT IN THE BARE CONCRETE CELL, her back against the wall, her arms resting on her knees, her head resting on her arms. The only light came from the cracks around the steel door, which did not have a keyhole on the inside. Her wrists were bound by manacles, a twenty-four-centimeter chain between them, and another, longer one, attached to the ring in the wall over her shoulder. She had gone through the worst of the terror at her situation, and it had subsided to a cold dread, which at least allowed her to think clearly.

The Turk had questioned her for a little while, intimidating her, but not hurting her. They still thought she was Veronica, and trusted to the abject fear she would doubtless feel to get the truth out of her. But she hadn't been able to tell them anything useful, and sooner or later they were going to get impatient. Then they'd start hurting her. Manikin didn't know what she'd say then.

The cell was cold and damp, and she shivered, though it might not have been the chill that caused it. FX would be going out of his mind right now. Scope would be a bit more removed, trying to think it out. Had Nimmo come back? Manikin had her doubts. But even if he did, she couldn't see how any of them could help her now. She had brundleseeds in her body, which meant that Move-Easy had them, even if he couldn't use them when he took them out of her. If Nimmo had come back, then he and the others had the case, but that wouldn't be enough. Manikin wasn't kidding herself. Move-Easy wasn't about to let her go—and if he found out who she really was, he wasn't about to let her live.

Manikin had one desperate play left, but if she blew it, she'd be dead for sure. For even the sliver of a chance of getting out of here, she'd have to time it just right. Her head jerked up as she heard footsteps in the corridor outside. A key turned in the lock, and the expression of fear on her face as the Turk walked in was not as fake as Manikin would have liked.

"I have more questions," he said to her, his gold teeth and his eyebrow piercing glinting in the dim light, that light also forming a cold halo reflected off the bald dome of his head. "In particular, I would like to know, please, your relationship with a girl called Manikin, and her rat-runner friends."

"I don't know anyone named Manikin," she replied automatically.

"You know her as George, but that is just her play-acting," he grunted, crouching down so that he could look into her eyes.

"She was pretending to be your friend, fooling you to get what we are after. I need to know if she and her friends got this thing, the brundleseed. You can tell me. They will not harm you. They will be dead soon, so there is no need to be afraid of them."

No, she should be afraid of him instead. But he didn't have to say that.

"How could I know if they have it?" she asked. "I don't even know who they are."

"We cannot know this for sure," he replied, shrugging. "You must convince me. If you do not, I must convince myself. Believe me when I say that you do not want that."

Nimmo heard the ringing tone and felt a tightness in his throat. This was it. Nearly four hours had passed since Manikin had been abducted. It had taken nearly half that time for FX to locate Paul Cronenberg's phone number. The remaining two hours had been spent waiting for him to switch on his phone. A few seconds after it started ringing, he answered.

"Cronenberg, you don't need to know who I am, but I have what you're looking for, so listen up. I've got the cards and one of the brundleseeds too—one that works."

There was a pause, no doubt so that the man could wave one or both of his mates over to listen in.

"So why are you callin'?" he asked in his Northern Irish accent.

"Because Move-Easy has a friend of ours, and he's liable to kill her if we don't get her away from him. We need your help to do that."

"Is that right? And whut are yeh offerin'?"

"You can have the lot, pretty much. We just want to take a couple of the cards for traveling money, and we want out. We'll leave London—the whole bloody country if we have to. We're out of our depth and we know it. We just want out. But we're not leaving without our friend."

"And whut? You want us to take dine Move-Easy for you? Yer jokin', right?"

"No. We have a way to get in, and get her out. What we need is for a couple of fake coppers to show up at just the right time . . . just to distract *your* competitors for a few minutes, so we can get clear. Do that and you can have the cards and the brundleseed."

"How do we know you even have the seed?"

"You don't. You'll just have to take the chance."

There was another pause—a longer one this time. Then:

"All right, let's hear it. Where and when?"

When Nimmo finished his call, he put the phone's handset down in its cradle and looked at Tubby Reach, who was regarding him with amusement.

"Well played," Reach chuckled, his belly starting a wave of shakes that rose all the way to his soft jowls. "My people are almost done with Scope and FX. You ready for your turn?"

"No," Nimmo replied in a tense voice. "To be honest, I'm still not sure I want your bloody surgeons putting me under."

"Hey, it was *your* idea. Don't you got *no* faith? I ain't tried to take one of these seeds off you, 'ave I? And you know I could if I wanted—but your old man saved my life once, so you get special dispensation. Besides, I like what you got goin' here. You got trust issues, boy. Where's the love? You've known me your whole life."

"That's why I've got trust issues."

"Ooh, that stings! OK, enough stalling. I'm doin' this on the house 'cos you're takin' on my biggest competitor and I'm happy to sponsor the match. Now, what is it the Yanks say? 'Get your game face on,' boy. You gotta get tooled up."

Nimmo nodded and took a deep breath.

"How do you rate our chances, Tubby?"

"You must be goin' soft, Nimmo, to be askin' me questions like that. But since you ask, I'd say it'll be like throwin' three hamsters into a pit of hungry dogs. Still . . . should be good for a laugh, eh?"

CHAPTER 32

A BREACH OF TRUST

WALKING ALONE INTO RATCHED HOSPITAL, Scope made her way down into the maze of utility tunnels in the basement level, where she was intercepted by one of the many sentries who wandered around in the guise of porters, security guards or cleaners.

She was handed a pair of blacked-out contact lenses before being led inside, as if she was a stranger to the Void. Putting the first one into her left eye, she made to put the second one in and dropped it, cursing, and looking around the floor for it.

"Ah, sod it," she grumbled. "I'm not using it if it's dirty anyway."

The troll frowned at her and went to take another set from his pocket, but she gave him a pained look and gestured to her right eye.

"Look, I'm *blind* in this one, remember? Easy's made his point—I'm on probation, OK? Come on, let's go."

With her left eye covered, she shouldn't have been able to see a thing, so she let herself be led as if she was blindfolded. As they walked, she tested the extraordinary zoom lenses of the camera that had grown inside her right eye socket. With perfect clarity, she watched, and recorded, the troll as he tapped in the four-digit access code that unlocked the door to the Void. The numbers 9491. But there was so much more that she could make out in her surroundings. She could tell where she was by the smells around her. She could identify the functions of the rooms they passed, even the kinds of cleaning fluids that had been used to clean them, right down to their chemical make-up, along with anything else she breathed in through her nose.

As she walked, a read-out appeared in the vision of her right eye, detailing a complete breakdown of her guide's breath and body odor, his aftershave, deodorant and hair gel. The chemical analyzer that had formed in the roof of her mouth could give her a comprehensive analysis of any concentration of molecules it found in the air. This new digital 'sense of smell' made her a human bloodhound—or at least it would, when she learned to use it properly.

All the corridors into the Void linked up and channeled you through the security checkpoint. She was stopped there, as her body was being scanned, x-rayed. They would be searching for any hidden means of recording information of any kind, any way of transmitting signals. This was where she felt her first real cold dart of fear. If her new implants were going to be spotted, it would be here and now. It took every bit of self-control she had not to tremble as they walked her through the scanners.

But then she was ushered on, down the echoing corridor. The pungent aroma of cigar smoke was thick in the air of Move-Easy's audience chamber. Waiting until she was instructed to do so, she took out the single lens and handed it to the troll, who then left the room. Sitting on one of the couches in the sunken area of that 1970s throwback of a room was the orange-skinned villain himself. He stared up at her with those icy, empty eyes of his, through a thin cloud of smoke.

"My Little Brain," he said in the tone of a fond but disappointed father, taking the cigar from his lips. "I've been worried about'cha. I fink you been led astray, love. Those vermin've bin fillin' your head with strange ideas."

"What do you mean?" She frowned, acting a little hurt. "I was just doing the job you sent me out to do. When I heard the Turk had grabbed Veronica, I figured you didn't need me on it any more, so I came back. And here I am. What did I do wrong?"

Move-Easy's face was impossible to read. He took another puff of his cigar and gazed at her some more.

"What did you do wrong?" he repeated, as if pondering the question. "What did you do wrong? It's a matter of principle, darlin'. A breach of trust. These vermin 'ave turned out to be wrong 'uns and no mistake, and it seemed to the boys who was watchin' that you fit right in. I wonder if you've forgotten where your loyalties lie. I don't feel like I can trust you no more."

"Funny, that's what *they* said about me too. Which is ironic, considering."

"Considering what, darlin'?"

"Considering it was *Nimmo* who reesed them."

Move-Easy sat up a bit straighter, laying his cigar in the ash-tray. He clasped his hands together and leaned forward.

"How so?" he rumbled.

Scope kept her eyes level, not quite meeting his, but not avoiding his stare either. She had lied to Move-Easy before, but never at the risk of her life. The fear was almost enough to dissuade her from what she had to do next. But then she lifted her head slightly, and met his eyes. As she did so, the powerful zoom lens on her eye-mounted camera focused tightly on his right iris and took a photo. She would need that soon.

"He had the box all the time, but he'd kept it hidden. He was Chuck Farley. But we only found out afterwards that he had the brundleseed too. That implant—the one you're looking for. The one *everybody* seems to be looking for. He's done a runner with it. And when he did, Manikin and FX told me to sod off. They didn't trust me. So *I'm* getting it from all sides. And Nimmo's got the cards, and the implant."

Easy picked up his cigar again, but didn't take a drag.

"This implant—this . . . brundleseed—you know what it does?"

She nodded.

"Reckon you could figure out how it worked?"

"If I had an unused one—or one that was still working in someone's body. But they'd have to be *alive* for me to be able to use it."

"And Nimmo has one?"

"Yes."

Easy sat back and took a long, long drag before blowing out a lungful of smoke.

"You're back 'ome now, luv, but you're on detention, you 'ear me? You're stayin' in for the next few days. No access codes for the doors, no goin' outside and no surfin' the bloody web or phone calls to the outside, you got me?"

Scope nodded.

"Good. It'll be safer for you that way. Things is about to get violent, darlin'. Don't want you gettin' caught in the crossfire, now, do we?"

As soon as she was dismissed, she hurried to her lab. She had almost made it to the door when Tanker came out of his computer room. Dressed in his usual cargo pants, hoodie and a red baseball cap, he looked delighted to see her. Her heart sank—he was the last person she wanted to run into.

"Scope, hey! Jesus, long time no see. How was life out in the sun?"

"Blinding," she replied. "Sorry, Tank, I've got a job to do for Easy . . ."

"What, you can't take a few seconds to say hello? Come on, tell me what the hell's been goin' on? I know about the brundleseed, Scope. Easy told me, but nobody's fillin' me in on what's happenin'. This is huge . . . *massive*! It's so bloody unfair I'm being left out of it! Come on, girl—let me in on it!"

"Look . . . later, OK?" She waved him away. "I promise, I'll tell you all about it later."

"I heard Easy's got Brundle's daughter in the cells—is that true? Tell me that much at least."

"Yeah, yeah," Scope told him, nodding. "He's got his daughter."

"Maybe I should talk to *her* then," Tanker sniffed.

"Maybe you should keep out of it, Tank," she replied. "Easy's letting the dogs loose on this job. I'd keep my head down if I was you."

Stepping into her lab, she closed the door behind her and took out her mobile. There was no phone signal, of course—communications with the outside world were tightly controlled by Tanker and Move-Easy's other tech people. But the wireless connection that could link her phone to her computer was switched on. She left it that way, and waited, her heart pounding.

CHAPTER 33

TECH-HEAD

FX APPROACHED MOVE-EASY'S VOID just as Scope had done, and was met in the utility tunnels by one of the trolls. He told the man with the cruel eyes, the bad teeth and the tattooed hands that he needed to see Easy—that he had something the boss wanted.

The contacts blocked his vision very effectively, but like Scope, FX had grown new senses. Inside his skull, one brundleseed had grown into a processor that could read anything with wireless connectivity. With a thought, he could access any RFID around him, which supplied him with masses of information on the objects and equipment in his environment, including the villain's clothes, half the contents of his pockets, and the signs at each junction of the corridor. Right now, he was in corridor AI, block 13.

His guide also had the wireless function on his phone switched on, unencrypted, so FX was able to examine the files on the phone's memory. There were a number of Wi-Fi signals down here, and if he'd wanted, FX could have surfed the web. He couldn't quite make phone calls with his head, but he was going to work on that.

They might have covered his eyes, but he had a wireless camera tucked into the side of his mouth. It wasn't an implant, it was just small. He would only need it temporarily. A second brundle-seed had given him a hyper-sensitive microphone, based on the ones the Safe-Guards used. It could pick up sounds beyond the range of any human ear. With his eyes covered, he had to be able to pick up any cue that these villains might be about to reese him.

When they stopped, and he was told to wait, he made sure his new processor wasn't transmitting, then poked the tiny camera out between his teeth. He watched on the video feed that had been grown into his optic nerve, as the man tapped in the four-digit access code: 9491.

The door opened, and FX was led inside. He quickly chewed up the rubber-cased camera and swallowed it. They'd never spot the crunched up remains on their scanners. The solid steel thud of the door closing behind him had a very permanent quality to it, here in this underground bunker. Like FX's Hide, no unauthorized signals could get in or out of Move-Easy's Void. From this point on, if FX ran into trouble, there would be no one he could call outside for help, and no way of calling them anyway.

FX closed his blind eyes, trying to keep his cool as they ran their checks on him. If they spotted the implants, things were going to get a whole lot more painful. He felt the movement of air over his face and hands, somebody waving a metal-detecting wand over his body, then he was searched roughly by strong hands, including his groin, his ass-crack and his hair.

They went through his backpack too, taking his console out. Ensuring it was switched off, they put it aside. He knew it would be placed in a metal basket beside the scanners, to be handed back to him when he left. If he left.

His chest and throat were tight with tension, and there was no hiding the sweat that soaked his skin, leaving damp patches under his arms and down his back, and caused his curly gelled hair to sag. But most people were nervous when it came to meeting Move-Easy, and FX had every right to be now. They kept hold of his backpack and led him on down the corridor.

As soon as he was clear of the checkpoint, he used the implant in his skull to connect to the wireless chip in a phone *inside* Easy's hideout—Scope's phone. He used the connection to send her the access code for unlocking the doors to the Void: 9491—just in case she hadn't got it. This would also serve as a message to her, letting her know he'd arrived.

The smell of smoke hit his nostrils, lingering from the dead cigar he saw in the ashtray on the coffee table, when he was told to take his contacts out. His backpack was sitting on the table beside it. He was standing, facing the orange mobster in Easy's audience chamber. Coda was leaning against the bar, dressed in a black suit and white shirt, his earphones in, his head nodding ever so slightly. FX turned up his hearing implant and identified the tune on the enforcer's player: "Every Breath You Take," by that old band, The Police. Though there were only the three of them in the room, his heightened hearing also detected the breathing of three more men just beyond the doors. It picked up his own pumping heart too.

"Let's keep this short," Easy said to him, lounging back in the sofa. "You say you have something I want—and from you, that can only be one of two things. So let's 'ave it."

FX was visibly trembling now. He clenched his teeth together so that they wouldn't chatter.

"It's in the bag," he said in a forced tone.

Move-Easy didn't budge. Instead, it was Coda who came forward, obviously listening past his music, and came down the steps to sit and open the bag. As he was doing this, Easy stared up at FX, who felt not unlike a bird sitting on the low branch of a tree, waiting to be brought down with a shotgun.

"Where's your sister?" Easy asked. "She's the action chick. It's normally her that does the legwork, isn't it?"

Coda emptied the contents of the bag onto the table. There was some of FX's normal gear, and the black leather case. Coda opened it, and held it up for Easy to see.

"There's two cards missing," the boss said immediately.

"Traveling money," FX replied, in a voice that was squeakier than he'd intended. "We want out. I mean . . . me an' Manikin, we want . . ." He took a breath. "Nimmo reesed us. He had the box. We caught him, we got it back off him, but . . ."

"But what? Spit it out, yeh little rat!"

"He's got Manikin. He told me he'd kill her if I didn't give the box back. I can't take him on my own. I need help. I have

— 281 —

something to trade. The brundleseed. I have one. You can have it if you help me get her back. And if you let us leave London."

Easy barked a laugh.

"You *bargainin'* with me?" he snorted. "'Ow about you give me the brundleseed or I get Coda here to pull yor heart out through your ribs?"

"Because you need me alive," FX replied. He tapped his head. "The seed's inside my skull. Right now, it's growing into a radio receiver. In a few days, I'll be able to receive radio signals with my head. But it'll only work while I'm alive. Kill me, and you destroy the seed."

"You put it in your own skull?"

"How else was I going to get out of here alive?" FX said, trying to keep his voice steady. "I didn't have to come here, you know. I could have gone to Vapor. We know all about him, how he's working from inside WatchWorld. How he paid Brundle to create the seed. You know Vapor has this whole place under surveillance, right? He'll have seen me come in, he'll know why I'm here. He's as powerful as you are. Maybe even more powerful. I could have gone to him, but I didn't.

"I brought the case to *you*, to show you Manikin and me want to make amends. None of this is our fault—we did the job you set us, but Nimmo reesed us. And now he's going to kill Manikin if he doesn't get what he wants. Vapor knows what I've got and he knows I'm here. Me an' Manikin just want out of this mess. Help me save her, and you can have the brundleseed."

Move-Easy gave FX a look like that of a scientist dissecting an animal. A long time seemed to pass, though it might well have been a matter of seconds.

"Vapor," he rumbled. "I've just about had it with that scum. No more bein' delicate, I think. Time that treacherous snake saw the inside of a cement mixer." He fell silent, staring at FX. "Aw-right," he said at last. "Coda, you're going wiv 'im. Take him down to Scope, have her check that seed's there like 'e says it is. Don't let him out of yor sight, got it?"

Coda nodded. And if lizards could be said to have expressions, Coda's was a perfect match. FX gave him a grim smirk and turned to follow the enforcer out of the room. As he did so, FX sent a signal from his new implant to his console, which still sat in the basket at the security checkpoint. The signal activated the small but extremely powerful battery FX had built into the console. The trolls should have known better than to put visitors' gear in a metal basket right next to the scanners. The electricity surged through contacts on the console's case, through the metal basket and through the metal case of the scanner next to it. It fried the scanner's circuits, along with the circuits of all the computer terminals it linked to . . . which included those controlling the bunker's alarm system. He sent another message to Scope to let her know. Time to get moving.

CHAPTER 34

SHAPE-SHIFTER

MANIKIN TRIED TO FIND A POSITION to sit or stand in that relieved her aching body, but failed. The Turk's patience had run out, and he had started hurting her. So far, he was just using his hands. He hadn't even resorted to those electrical things in his knuckles. But he seemed to have fingers like a Terminator, and knew just the right nerve points to dig into. She was already wondering how much more she'd be able to stand before she blurted out anything she thought he'd want to hear.

He'd left her to 'think things over,' and she was crouching down on her hunkers, stretching out her bruised thighs, when she heard voices on the far side of the door.

"I just want to ask her a few questions," someone said. It sounded like Tanker. "I'm not going to *do* anything to her. Maybe she'll tell me something she wouldn't tell the Turk."

Manikin's eyes flicked towards the door, and she immediately reached down to the waistband of her jeans. Unwinding a piece of stiff wire from around the metal button, she bent it into shape with weak, sore fingers and went to work on the locks of her handcuffs.

"I dunno, Tanker. The Turk's awful particular about who questions the guests. You know what 'e's like about someone tryin' to do his job for 'im. And he's not the type to go complain to his union rep about it, know what I mean?"

"Five minutes, that's all I'm askin'. What could it hurt?"

"Awright, five minutes and that's it."

Manikin had the first cuff open as she heard a key rattle in the door. By the time the door swung open, she had switched to the other one. A few seconds later, it released her wrist with a click, and she winced, hoping her new visitor hadn't heard.

"Hi, Veronica?" the silhouetted figure in the doorway said. "My name's Tanker. I work on the computers here. I'm not . . . I'm not going to hurt you. That's not what I do. I'm just a tech-head . . . a bit like your old man, I suppose. Can I talk to you for a bit? Do you mind?"

"What do you want?" Manikin rasped in a weak, hoarse whisper.

Tanker came closer.

"Sorry, what?"

"What do you want to know?" Manikin said again, in an even fainter voice.

Tanker leaned right in beside her—and she clamped a hand over his mouth, swung her leg to sweep his feet out from under him, and smacked his head off the wall. He collapsed to the floor and lay still.

She knew Tanker. He was about her height and build, their faces were about the same shape, and she could imitate his voice. This was the kind of chance she'd been waiting for.

Moving quickly but deliberately, Manikin slid out of her trousers and T-shirt. She pulled off his camouflage cargo pants and his dark blue hoodie. Slipping into his clothes, she handcuffed his hands behind him. Tearing a wide strip out of her T-shirt, she used it to gag him. Having done that, she ripped the fake birthmark off her face, hissing as the adhesive peeled away from her skin, and massaging it until all the glue had been rubbed away. Then she put on Tanker's shoes.

"God, I'm glad you brought a hat," she said, as she used her implant to turn her skin dark brown.

She could change the color of her skin and hair to match his, but she couldn't match the distinctive cornrows that had been braided into his hair. She just had to hope that the hat would be enough to hide the difference. Poor Tanker. He'd be severely punished for letting this happen.

"For what it's worth," she said in a low voice, "I always feel a bit guilty beating up nerds. It's like picking on somebody who's obnoxious but kind of, you know . . . disabled. It just makes you feel all wrong."

Pulling the cap on, she tugged the peak down low over her face. Then she went to where the door stood ajar, and stepped through.

The corridor she was standing in was lined with eight cell doors like the one she had just come through. Move-Easy's infamous 'guest rooms.' At the top of the corridor, a guy sat in a chair, reading a newspaper.

"Have it your way, you little cow!" Manikin snarled back into the cell, in her best impression of Tanker. "You'll be wishing you talked to me after the Turk's gone back to work on you!"

With that, she slammed the door and locked it. She strode up the corridor towards the guard, tossing back the key and wiping her nose with the back of her hand as she passed him, effectively hiding most of her face.

"Oh, you're a right villain and no mistake," the guard snorted without looking up from his paper.

But Manikin was already gone.

Scope walked down the corridor that would take her to the security checkpoint. Men and women ran past her. There was a slight sense of panic in the air. A woman, one of the tech-heads, asked if Scope had seen Tanker. Scope replied that she'd last seen him at the lab. From the snippets of sentences she caught as people passed her, she was able to make out that the checkpoint's computers had gone down, and the Void's alarm system with it. The bunker's cameras were down too.

Once she'd been working in the Void long enough to learn her way around this maze-like bunker, Scope had found there were a few different routes that could bypass the checkpoint. It was just that opening any of the doors on those corridors would normally have set off the alarms. And there was a guard on every door into the Void.

Scope took the bound bundle of money from her pocket. It was the bundle that Punkin and Bunny had brought into the bunker—the one Scope had removed from the throat of the cuddly caterpillar. The one she'd attached a magnet to. She opened a dusty, corroded steel door, breathing out with relief when she heard no alarm siren. Striding around a corner, she came to one of the main doors into the Void. A thug named Muntz sat at a small table near the door, playing Patience with a deck of playing cards with obscene pictures on them.

"Hey, Muntz," Scope said to him. "Could you do me a favor and hold onto this for me?"

Holding out the bundle of money, she held onto the magnet as he took it from her. His frown brightened into a smile as he realized what it was. Removing the magnet had armed the dye pack hidden in the bundle. Scope walked back around the corner, and a few seconds later there was a loud bang, a hiss of burning gas and paper, and a scream from Muntz. He came staggering around the corner, covered with pink dye and blowing on his burned hands. Scope stuck out her foot, and he tripped over it, falling flat on his face. Careful not to get dye on her clothes, she knelt on his back and used a hypodermic gun to inject a strong sedative into the side of his neck. A couple of seconds later, he was unconscious.

Scope went over to the door, and typed in the four-digit access code. The door slid back into the wall, and again, there was no alarm. Standing on the other side was Nimmo.

"We're cutting it close," he said, stepping inside. "Vapor's lot will be here any minute."

"We better hope we've timed this right," she replied. "The techs will have the alarm system back online in less than five."

CHAPTER 35

INTRUDERS

KRIEGER AND HECTOR SHOWED UP three minutes after Nimmo entered Move-Easy's Void. They found the door standing open, and on further inspection discovered the unconscious, dye-stained and slightly scorched body of Muntz. Both of them stood looking down at the sedated thug with guns drawn. The weapons were a risk—even for men with their connections. Guns could buy you a lot of trouble in a WatchWorld city. But Nimmo had asked them to fire off some shots once they'd got inside the Void, to create a diversion for the rat-runners. And even with the security system down, if you were going to trespass on Move-Easy's domain, being well-armed was a sensible precaution.

"The vermin weren't kiddin'," Krieger grunted with grudging respect. "They got inside. Want to see what we can find?"

"I still don't like this," Hector said. "There's nothing Vapor can do to protect us if we get cornered down *here*. We're in a right snake pit. If it wasn't for those pesky kids, we'd have had that bloody implant by now. I think we're bein' set up for something here. We should—"

"Did you really just say 'pesky,' Hector?" Krieger sneered. "You are such a bloody nerd, y'know that?"

"Bite my hairy ass, you gimp. Come on, let's see what there is to see."

"All right, but don't go too far into this pit until we know what's going on," Krieger said in a low voice as he looked around. "One of us needs to stay by the door—"

At that moment, the door slid shut, and the lock clicked and beeped. A light on the keypad beside it showed that the alarm system had been armed once more.

"To make sure we don't get locked in," Krieger finished with a dismayed voice.

"You can crack that lock, right?" Hector asked.

"Sure, if we had time," Krieger answered, taking the safety off his sub-machine gun. "But it sounds like time's somethin' we don't got."

From down the corridor there came the noise of several pairs of heavy feet.

Nimmo made his way carefully along the corridor. It was his job to find the cells where Manikin was being held. He was on a tight deadline, and he couldn't afford to be seen. Three different brundleseeds had been planted in his body to aid him in his task. All of the designs used to program the seeds were based on Safe-Guard technology. Nimmo had stolen the designs a couple of years ago. Just being in possession of them was highly illegal.

In the palm of his left hand, just beneath the skin, was a thermographic camera. Using infra-red radiation, its 'sight' was based on heat—seeing people and objects based on how much heat they gave off. Inside the palm of his right hand was an x-ray camera. With these two devices, he could see in the dark, through thick smoke, through solid objects. By looking through walls, he could effectively see around corners, so that he could spot security cameras before they spotted him. And he could search for Manikin without opening doors, or calling out for her.

A third implant had grown into one of the Safe-Guards' most useful devices: a key fabricator. Using his x-ray camera, he could identify a type of lock, and the fabricator built into the longest bone of his right index finger could then, in a matter of seconds, create a key to fit it. This was the technology that allowed peepers to go almost anywhere in the city.

Nimmo knew roughly where the cells were in Move-Easy's bunker, but he had to take a number of detours to avoid running into any of the gangsters. Like a shadow, he passed through the Void, slipping quiet and unseen through the maze of tunnels.

When he eventually found his way to the corridor leading to the 'guest rooms,' he ran his scanners over the wall at the corner. There was a chair at the top of the corridor, but nobody was sitting in it. There were people in some of the cells, but he wasn't close enough to tell if any of them was Manikin. Stepping silently around the corner, his eyes took in every detail of the drab gray-green-painted hallway. There was a door ajar at the end of the corridor—the only one of the eight doors that was open. He walked down the corridor, holding his hands out to the sides, his strange new technological senses checking each cell on either side as he passed.

There were prisoners here, but no sign of Manikin. He did not release any of the captives. Some might not be friendly, and they would all be released anyway, when the police raided this place.

"Look, I cocked up, all right?" a plaintive voice protested. "But she's in a locked-down bunker! Where the bloody hell can she go?"

"I dunno, why don't you go ask the *Turk*? You wazzock!"

He came to the cell with the open door. Inside, one of Move-Easy's thugs—presumably the one charged with guarding the cells—was unlocking the handcuffs of a boy who was chained to the wall.

The boy was Tanker, and he was wearing only a T-shirt and his underwear. Nimmo took in the scene in a couple of seconds. There was a blossoming bruise on Tanker's forehead, where he'd obviously taken a nasty knock. A pair of blue and gray reversible jeans that could have been Manikin's lay crumpled on the ground, as well as something that looked like the remains of her fake birthmark.

"Hey!" The troll looked up, his face twisting into a snarl. "What the hell are you doing here?"

He lunged at Nimmo, who calmly swung the steel door shut in his face, and locked it. Turning to head back up the corridor, ignoring the shouts from behind him, he let out a sigh.

"All right, but where the bloody hell did she go?"

CHAPTER 36

ENEMY AT THE GATES

THE RAT-RUNNERS' TIMING had been a bit off. FX wasn't brought to Scope's lab as quickly as they'd expected. They'd almost got it right—Vapor's men got locked into the Void just after the computers in the checkpoint went down. As soon as the intruders were spotted on the reactivated cameras, Easy's men assumed the Void was under attack. Which was all according to plan.

It was just that FX should have reached Scope by the time it happened. Instead, he and Coda were still making their way along one of the lengthy corridors.

"Oh Jesus, it's them, isn't it?" FX cried as he heard the sound of gunshots. In a pretty convincing show of terror, he grabbed Coda's arm. "Please, man, don't let them take me! This is it, they're coming in! They're gonna take me! *They're gonna take me!*"

Coda threw him a suspicious glance, and FX suspected that if he hadn't been the key to getting the brundleseed, he'd have been dead right then. Instead, Coda shoved him back against the wall and bound his wrists to a pipe with a large plastic cable-tie. Instead of heading in the direction of the gunfire, Coda strode quickly in the other direction. FX watched him go in frustration. He'd hoped the gunfight would get Coda out of the picture for a while.

Krieger and Hector were inside, and facing the wrath of a nest full of gangsters. Their deaths weren't a necessary part of the plan—the rat-runners had just arranged for them to be there so that the two men would be in the right place at the right time, when people started getting arrested. Right now, police would be surrounding the bunker and blocking off all the exits. Fifteen minutes ago, an email sent on timed delivery had plonked into every police inbox in the city, with a detailed layout of Move-Easy's Void, drawn up by Scope, along with information on all the operations going on down there. FX just had to stay alive until the coppers got inside.

"The law's outside!" someone yelled down the tunnel. "The bloody law's outside! They're everywhere! Where's the shotguns? Someone's gonna die for this!"

Now FX was struggling to keep his bowels from emptying into his pants. Because the gunfire was getting louder, and he was stuck to this pipe. Instead of just providing a few minutes of diversion, Vapor's men appeared to be killing their way towards him. And now that the police *were* here, one of the many igno-rant, violent nutters running past him might decide FX was a liability they could do without. There's no lock to pick on a cable-tie, and he had no means of cutting the toughened plastic.

"You!" a voice growled. "What the hell are you doing 'ere?"

It was Punkin. Speaking of ignorant violent nutters, here was the treacherous rat-runner who'd reesed them so he could get in with Easy's mob. The one who hated FX and his sister with a vicious passion. The dangerous little thug who *probably didn't know how important FX was to Move-Easy*. Punkin extended the blade from his wrist and held it to FX's throat.

"See? Like Wolverine's," he hissed.

"Wolverine has three blades," FX corrected him, unable to stop himself. "On each hand."

"You and your sister slipped a bloody dye pack into that caterpillar, you little fart," Punkin spat. "Nearly got me an' Bunny killed when we brought it down here. We still owe you for that one. And I *know* your sister nicked my wallet." He gave FX a nasty smile, swiveling the blade so it caught the light. "Now, look! Here you are, all gift-wrapped. Sweet!"

As usual, when FX got scared, his mouth developed a mind of its own.

"Really? She took your wallet? The thieving cow! Was that the time, y'know, when you, like, reesed us over for a caterpillar full of cash? That time? I'm sorry, man. That girl's just got no principles. Get me out of this and I'll give her a right tellin' off. Have it back to you in no time."

"Seems like stuff always goes pear-shaped when you're around," Punkin muttered. "There's enemies in the castle. Now, how did they get in, do y'think?"

"I dunno. Maybe they followed that *smell* your head gives off—ever since you shoved it up *Easy's arse*?"

Punkin's blade twitched, but then his arm was pulled back, twisted into a lock, and he was flipped onto his back. He hit the floor with a thud that knocked the air from his lungs. A black girl who looked a bit like Tanker, but without the cornrows, laid in a few more thumps while he lay there winded. Before he could recover, he was dragged over to the same pipe FX was attached to and bound alongside him. He swore loudly as he realized the plastic around his wrists was out of reach of the blade sticking out of the back of his hand. The girl gasped in exasperation at FX as she cut him free.

"'The smell your head gives off—ever since you shoved it up Easy's arse'?" She grimaced. "That's the only line you could come up with?"

"I had a knife to my throat! It was the best I could do under pressure."

Manikin looked up and down the corridor. There was no one coming in either direction.

"What's with all the shooting?" she asked.

"We tricked Vapor's gimps into coming down and got 'em locked in."

She looked at him with a puzzled expression.

"What, there weren't enough psychos down here already?"

CHAPTER 37

THE LAST DANCE

TRYING TO IGNORE THE PITCHED BATTLE that seemed to be taking place in one of the corridors a few hundred meters away, Scope walked towards the door into Move-Easy's living quarters, slipping the contact lens with the fake iris onto her right eye. She had made it using the photo she'd taken earlier of Easy's eye. Holding her face up to the iris lock that controlled entry to his living quarters, she allowed it to scan her contact lens. The door lock clicked open, and she stepped inside, leaving the door slightly ajar. Once in the corridor, she let herself into his trophy room, pulling off the empty backpack that hung from her shoulder.

It was not the rat-runners' plan just to rescue Manikin. Scope was standing in this large room, letting her eyes sweep across its contents, because the plan was to take down Move-Easy altogether, and hopefully take Vapor with him.

The trophy room housed all of the objects Move-Easy prized most: from a selection of works of art that his bands of thieves had stolen over the years, to film and music memorabilia. Some of these things were worthless, but had great sentimental value; others were worth a fortune, but Move-Easy would never allow them to be sold.

Scope crept past a group of manikins wearing old burlesque dance-hall costumes, down an aisle lined with display cases full of antique clocks and compasses. At the end of this aisle stood a red 1969 Mini Cooper S with two black straps over the bonnet and three big fog-lights mounted on the front. She let her fingers stroke its bonnet as she passed. It had been completely taken apart and reassembled to get it in through the doors. Beyond that there were shelves of video cassettes of 1980s movies, and a waist-high Jerzy safe with a hole drilled through the side of it—apparently a souvenir from Easy's very first armed robbery. Scope bent over the safe, inhaling air over her chemical analyzer, but didn't get a hit.

Hidden somewhere in this room was Move-Easy's 'insurance policy.' His power over London's underworld was not merely based on his small army of villains and the fact that he was a clever, violent control freak. Easy had amassed a large stash of dirt on a selection of high-ranking judges and police officers, not to mention many of his gangster competitors. It was this stash of blackmail material that had kept Easy out of the hands of the law for so long. The police would be battering down the doors of the Void by now, but Easy could still get off with little or no sentence.

Scope wanted to ensure he got what was coming to him. And more than that, she wanted to know who Vapor was. Because Easy knew, and that was the kind of information he kept safe for a rainy day.

Without his insurance policy, he was just a cunning thug. But she had no idea where in this room he had hidden the stash, and the room was so full of clutter, even if you had x-ray vision, you could search for hours. Which was why she needed her new technologically enhanced sense of smell. Painfully aware that she had little time, she forced herself to walk slowly up and down the aisles, letting her nose do the searching. If she was caught here, the boss's fondness for her wouldn't save her. He might even take her betrayal harder—with consequences she couldn't bear to think about.

The readout scrolling down across the artificial vision in her right eye told her what kinds of molecules were floating in the air. She was looking for a high concentration of cigar smoke, not suspended in the air around her, but hanging close to some surface in the room.

It was when she was walking down past the rear of the Mini Cooper that she found it. Move-Easy smoked cigars, and they left their pungent smell on his fingertips. Anything he handled regularly also picked up the smell. Scope bent down and put her nose close to the handle of the car's boot. Bingo.

She opened the boot and discovered most of the interior was taken up with a large, very impressive-looking safe. It had an old-fashioned combination lock. She swore under her breath, lifting her head and looking around. Easy kept a key on a chain around his neck, which she'd always assumed was for his stash. But, of course, Easy knew he was surrounded by criminals.

This wasn't fair—she should have had FX with her, and possibly even Nimmo. She could pick a fairly simple lock, but this was beyond her.

"Let me have a look," a voice said from behind her, causing her heart to thump the air out of her lungs.

It was Nimmo. He stood behind her, having approached without her hearing.

She punched him in the arm, hissing at him: "Jesus! You tryin' to scare the piss out of me?"

"Didn't want to spoil your concentration," he replied softly, gesturing towards Easy's stash. "Sorry if I gave you a start."

"No, you're not. Where's Manikin? Did you break her out?"

"She beat me to it. I figured there was no point wandering around trying to find her, so I came back to help you. Here, stand back."

Placing his right hand against the door of the safe, he used his x-ray camera to study the tumblers of the lock. Then he spun the dial clockwise, then anti-clockwise, then back clockwise again. The lock clicked open.

The door of the wide, low safe opened and they saw folders full of papers, compact discs, data keys and variously sized boxes arranged neatly inside.

"Grab the discs, keys and as much paper as you can get into

your pack," Nimmo told her. "Don't take more than you can carry while running."

She did as he said, and he quickly filled his pockets with whatever he could.

"Not bad, for vermin," a cold voice grated, making them both jump.

Behind them stood the Turk, leaning against one of the display cases. Scope experienced a horrible sinking feeling, and she could see even Nimmo had gone pale. The bald giant was holding an Uzi sub-machine-gun. He aimed it at them and pulled the trigger. They jumped again as the hammer clicked, but the gun did not go off.

"Out of ammo." He leered apologetically. Shrugging the strap off his shoulder, he tossed the gun away behind him. "Will have to switch to manual."

Raising his bunched fists, he held them a few centimeters apart so the rat-runners could see the electricity arcing between his knuckles. He took a step towards them. Even as he did so, there was a whistle from behind him. Swiveling to look around, he grunted as the strap from his Uzi whipped around his wrists, the loop pulling tight. A well-dressed Oriental man jerked the Turk's arms out straight, wrenching the giant off balance, then twisted the rest of the strap around the Turk's neck and flipped him head over heels onto his back. The Turk landed with his electrically charged fists tied up under his chin. His body thrashed and twitched for a few seconds and then fell still.

Nimmo and Scope both felt a moment of relief, before it gave way to dread at the sight of the stone-cold assassin who faced them.

Registering both reactions, Coda held up his empty but deadly hands with a modest expression, as if the two kids were an audience showing their appreciation for a performer.

"Great minds think alike," he chuckled, nodding towards Easy's stash. "That's just what I was looking for. I *was* wondering how I was going to open the *safe*—seeing as it was going to be a bit of a rush job. Thanks for sorting that. I've been following your progress, actually, ever since I first met Brundle. You're a bright bunch—you've got some moves on you. But these matters you're meddling in now . . . well, they're just not suitable for children." Scope glared at him. Coda was here, not to protect Easy's stash, but to steal it for himself. And as she realized this, she knew it wasn't the first time he had betrayed his boss.

"You killed Brundle," Scope spoke up. "You knocked him out, then jammed a hazelnut down his throat. That had to be you, right? It's your style."

"Yes," Coda replied simply.

"But Move-Easy didn't want him dead," Nimmo said. "Killing him made no sense . . . unless you're working for *Vapor*. That's why you had to kill Brundle—to stop him from giving the seed to Easy. But then what? Vapor thought his guys would just find the implant once he sent them in to search the lab?"

"Yes, well done. We didn't know Brundle had given the only remaining ones to *you*. Now, just hand that stuff over, and I'll let you run for your lives. We can worry about the brundleseed later. This place is about to become a war zone, so I'd be very surprised if you got out alive. But as long as you give me the files, I promise I'll let someone else kill you."

"Scope, take what you've got and go," Nimmo said firmly, brushing past her left side to stand between her and Coda.

She was about to argue, but knowing Nimmo, there would be little point. He'd made his decision. Besides, he'd just picked her pocket. She closed the flap on the pack, slung it onto her shoulder and backed down the aisle, away from Coda. The hit man watched her leave without any sense of urgency, as if there was nowhere she could possibly go to escape him. Then he put his earbuds in his ears.

"Catch up with you in a minute," he said, waving to her. Nodding his head to the beat of the music, he added to Nimmo: "Hadn't figured you for the self-sacrificing type. Thought you were smart."

"And I thought you didn't talk much," Nimmo replied, checking that Scope was on her way out. "You gonna rabbit on all day, or are we goin' to work?"

Coda drove his elbow down into the display case beside him, smashing the glass top. Picking up a long, triangular piece of glass, he raised his hands and did a little shuffling dance before taking a fighting stance.

"Time someone took you to school, boy."

"Yeah, I've been hearin' that my whole life."

Coda came at him fast, gliding like a dancer, striking with frightening speed. Nimmo dodged or deflected the first few blows of the glass blade, stepped inside a kick, but then took a punch to the ribs. A knee to his back caught him in the kidneys, and he staggered. The jagged piece of glass came at his neck and he blocked the strike with his elbow, the glass cutting a bad slash across his upper arm. But he was in close now, and he head-butted Coda on the chin—and then pushed Scope's brown inhaler into the man's face and squeezed. Coda gasped as the blinding spray blasted into his nose and mouth. He tried not to breathe it in, but it was too late. A fit of sneezing seized him, and his head rocked with each explosive burst of breath. Cursing and sneezing, he lashed out with both arms, trying to catch Nimmo across the head. Nimmo dropped, spinning as he went down, his swinging leg taking Coda's feet out from under him.

Coda fell flat on his back, but rolled and tried to get to his feet as soon as he hit the floor. Nimmo grabbed the Mini's door handle and whipped the door open, slamming it into Coda's head. He liked the noise it made, so he did it a couple more times.

Then he heard the sounds of battle coming up the corridor outside. Nimmo turned and ran.

CHAPTER 38

BROUGHT TO LIGHT

SCOPE'S ESCAPE ROUTE was via Move-Easy's private elevator. Only Easy and his most loyal lieutenants had the means of making it work, but she thought she had a way around that. If it didn't work, she'd reached the end of the line, literally. The door of the lift was at the bottom of a dead-end corridor. This lift had once been used by the hospital, but most of the doors had been walled up, and now it only opened into the car park where a getaway car was always kept waiting. The door on the car park level was concealed behind a false wall. Nobody else but Move-Easy's most trusted men used this lift.

Reaching the elevator, Scope pressed the button to open the sliding door and stepped inside. As she did so, she heard running feet coming down the corridor. There was nowhere she could go;

she had to hope she could bluff her way past whoever appeared in the doorway.

Manikin peered fearfully in, with FX popping his head around a moment later.

"Going up?" Manikin asked breathlessly.

"That's the plan," Scope replied. "But the lift is locked down. We need a code or a key—I don't know how to get it started."

"That's it?" Manikin exclaimed with an expression of disbelief. "Move-Easy and some of his dog-soldiers are about a minute behind us. This is a bloody dead end, and that's your big escape plan?"

"Sort of," Scope said, shrugging. "Come on, give us a boost."

As the door closed behind them, they helped her up onto the bar that ran at waist-height around the walls of the lift, and she opened the maintenance panel in the ceiling. Climbing out onto the roof, she turned to help FX and then Manikin up behind her. Even as they closed the hatch, they could hear voices approaching. Looking up the sheer shaft, they saw there were metal doors blocking the shaft less than three meters above them. There was no way to climb out.

There was a vent in the top of the ceiling panels, and Scope parted the slats slightly so that they could see down into the elevator car.

"Breaker says the coppers have closed down the hospital," someone said. "But they're not in the car park yet."

"We've been reesed, lads," Move-Easy's voice snarled. "Somebody's grassed up the whole operation. How could the pigs know where all the doors were? If they know about the lift . . ."

"We've got a camera in the car park," a third voice said. "The fuzz aren't there yet."

"I don't *trust* stinkin' cameras. My bloody life's at stake 'ere. I want someone to be lookin' out there wiv *their own eyes*. There's too much fiddlin' can be done otherwise.

"Anyway, when we get out of 'ere, we're goin' to hunt down this squealer and string 'em up," Move-Easy told them as the three men strode into the elevator below the three rat-runners. "I swear to God, I'm gonna cook 'em an' eat 'em."

In the dim lines of light from the vent, FX and Manikin glanced at Scope, but she avoided looking back. They all watched as Move-Easy took the key from the chain around his neck and fitted it into a keyhole in the control panel. Then he punched the grid of numbered buttons in a certain order, the door slid closed and the lift jolted into life.

As one, the three rat-runners lifted their heads and looked up anxiously at the metal doors blocking the shaft above them. They flinched, ducking down as the lift carried them quickly upwards, threatening to crush them against the doors, which only opened at the last second to allow the elevator car through. It glided up and up, the sound of the winch loud in the echoing shaft.

"I tell ya, lads," Move-Easy muttered in a voice that was almost vulnerable, his orange face raised towards the ceiling of the car. "This is a *bad* blow, a bad blow. But it'll be good to see the sun again after all these years. It's been too long."

The exits were welded shut on every floor they passed, until they reached a door that was still oiled and working. The three rat-runners watched the doorway slide down past them, and the lift came to a halt, then they lowered their eyes to peer through the slats of the vent.

The doors of the elevator car opened below them, and a stark white light shone through the doorway. But instead of the sunshine that Move-Easy so longed to see, it was the harsh glow of spotlights.

"*Armed police!*" A warning was roared from outside. "Put your weapons down and come out with your hands up *immediately* or we will open fire!"

One of Easy's men made to press the button to close the door, but a shot was fired and he was thrown against the back wall. As his body slumped to the floor, Easy and the other men reluctantly tossed down their guns. Raising their hands *only just* high enough, they walked out into the ring of heavily armed jump squad officers with defiant expressions set on their hard faces.

"What do we do now?" FX asked softly.

"Nothing we can do," Manikin whispered back. "Except wait. Though I'd suggest we get off this elevator."

And so they climbed off onto a ledge and waited, listening intently to the noises outside, as the police took London's biggest gangster away in handcuffs. Some jump squad officers commandeered the elevator and, closing the door, took it back down into the depths of Move-Easy's bunker to join the fire-fight that was raging below.

The rat-runners crouched on the ledge, looking at each other in the light of Scope's torch.

"Think Nimmo made it out?" Scope asked, finally voicing her concerns.

"Like he said a while back, it's what he does best," FX replied. "Avoiding responsibility."

They fell quiet again, each one lost in their own thoughts.

"So how long do we wait here?" Manikin spoke up. "How do we know when they're all gone from out there?"

"Dunno," FX grunted.

Manikin looked over at Scope, who shook her head and shrugged.

"Oh, brilliant."

FX used his wireless connection to examine the files on Move-Easy's data keys, working his way through one key after another, but there were thousands of pages of documents, as well as photos and pieces of video. It would take days to go through them properly.

The elevator shaft was dark and cold, but Manikin and Scope had still managed to fall asleep on the narrow concrete shelf beside him. Hours had passed since Move-Easy's arrest. FX had tried to look through the stolen paper files, but they didn't want to waste the battery on Scope's torch, so now he was examining the digital files. This was the fourth key he had gone through, the information appearing overlaid in 'windows' on his normal vision. He loved this, being plugged directly into the data. It was such a buzz, but so far he had found nothing on Vapor.

Finally, he found it. A file on WatchWorld personnel. Names, positions, and the places and dates of the various illegal or immoral activities they got up to. Except instead of having just one name he could nail down as Vapor, there was a list of possible candidates.

"Who are you?" he whispered. "Where are you?"

"Up here, looking down at you," an echoey voice called softly from above him, giving him such a start that he nearly fell off the ledge.

FX looked up to see Nimmo's face peering through a small hatch further up the wall of the shaft.

"Git," FX snapped at him, but smiling as he said it. "You do that on purpose."

"You lot ever going to come out of there?" Nimmo asked.

"We were waiting for the right moment," FX replied, as Manikin and Scope woke up beside him.

Nimmo held up his hands.

"This is it. Help from on high."

"What about the police?" Manikin asked him, rubbing her hands up and down her arms to get the circulation going. "You sure no one's watching?"

"Someone's always watching," Nimmo replied, as he dropped a rope down to them. "But there's plenty they don't see."

CHAPTER 39

A RATHER SLICK JOB

PUNKIN COULDN'T BELIEVE HIS LUCK. After Manikin had tied him to the pipe in the corridor—having rescued her brother—Punkin had been freed by one of Easy's other guys, so he could help make a stand against the army of police who had stormed the Void. Punkin had decided fighting a bunch of gun-happy coppers trained by the SAS wasn't such a good idea. So he'd run to the guest rooms, and locked himself into one of the cells.

The police had found him there, and held him for questioning. His story was that he'd owed money to Move-Easy, and that they'd imprisoned him there, underground, while they decided if they were going to kill him or not. After three days of questioning, the bill remained unconvinced by the story. But they still had nothing solid on him, except that he'd been in the Void. Charged with that relatively minor offense, he'd been released on bail.

Now he was back in Bunny's arms, as they lounged on a massive beanbag in the small tenement flat he shared with his parents, laughing at the wazzocks on WatchWorld TV and planning how they were going to nail Manikin and FX good and proper.

"We could tell Move-Easy it was them who grassed 'im up to the police," Bunny suggested.

"Nah, Tubby Reach is saying *he* did it," Punkin said sourly. "Besides, Easy's got no power on the street now. Every copper and judge in London has it in for him—most of the villains too. Word got out he's lost his stash. He'll be inside for the rest of his natural. An' 'is natural may not be too long, with all the enemies he's got."

"Maybe we should grass *Manikin an' FX* up to the police?"

"Don't be stupid, luv—they've got as much dirt on us as we have on them. More probably, seein' how devious they are. No, we're lucky we got free of the law so easy. We got to play this one smart, so they don't see us comin'."

There was a knock at the front door. Punkin and Bunny looked anxiously at one another. With all this talk of the law, neither was eager for visitors. Punkin struggled out of the beanbag and went out into the hall. He took a breath and opened the door.

It was Coda. He was as well-dressed as ever in a gray silk suit, light blue shirt and cravat. But his hair had not been combed, and he hadn't shaved in a couple of days. He didn't say anything, but Punkin stepped aside to let him in. As the hit man strolled into the living room, Bunny gave Punkin an alarmed glance, which he returned with a fearful shrug, not knowing what else to do. Coda sat down in the only armchair and crossed his legs.

"Have a seat," Coda said, as if it was his home, and not Punkin's.

Punkin sat down on the arm of the sofa, which was as far down as his trembling legs would allow him to sink without collapsing.

"It's interesting that you got free of the police so easily," Coda began, gazing coldly at Punkin. "I managed to get out of the Void without being seen. I gather they just let you go."

"They . . . they . . . eh . . . I . . . I . . . I was able to—" Punkin stuttered.

"That's not why I'm here," Coda interrupted him. "At least, not directly."

Punkin shut up. Bunny tried to sink deeper into the dark brown beanbag.

"Can I ask you, Punkin," Coda asked in a smooth, velvet voice that sounded horribly dangerous, "where you were last night?"

"Here," Punkin said quietly. "Here all night."

"You're quite sure?"

"He was!" Bunny blurted out. "He was here with me the whole time!"

Coda smiled at her; a slightly sad but approving smile.

"So loyal, my dear. So loyal!" the hit man continued. "You see, my apartment was burgled last night. Quite a feat in itself, given that the security in the building—which I outfitted myself—is tighter than a duck's arse. The thieves didn't take anything. They just cracked the encryption on my laptop and dumped the entire contents of the hard drive onto the web. I am now wanted by

WatchWorld, Europol, the FBI and half a dozen other national and international law enforcement agencies for various criminal and terrorist acts I've committed over the last few years. Once I'm done here, I'm going to have to leave London—possibly for good."

"Once . . . once you're done?" Bunny repeated in a slightly shrill voice.

"Yes." Coda reached into his jacket, and drew something out. "You see, when I set about trying to figure out who had carried out this rather *slick* job, the names of two idiots like you would not have been top of my list. But then I found this lying on the floor near my laptop. And this is just the kind of stupid mistake I'd expect you two to make."

And with that, he held up Punkin's wallet.

Punkin stared at it in astonishment for a moment before a look of realization blossomed on his face. Curling his hands into claws, clenching his teeth, he let rip with a frustrated, outraged cry:

"Those bloody rats!"

ACKNOWLEDGMENTS

My first thanks, as always, go to my family, for their encourage-
ment and support. They are the root of my confidence, but ever-
watchful in case I should get big-headed about having my name
on the front of a few books. They are my first 'outside eyes'—my
first readers and my most valued critics. I'm especially grateful
to my wife, Maedhbh, for her patience, her understanding, and
her constant reminders about how weird it is to live with me. I'd
disagree, but she'd say that's just proof she's right.

My brother, Marek, takes time out of his exploration
of the human experience to keep my website working
(www.oisinmcgann.com), discuss all things newfangled and technical, and answer my various random and awkward questions
about . . . well, anything that comes to mind, really.

A big shout out to all of those passionate and dedicated odd-
balls who populate the children's books industry and make it
such a fun business to work in—even if it sometimes feels like
we're heading into some bizarre science-fiction world. Please
support your local library and librarians! Times are tough and
we need them more than ever. Do you know any other branch
of your public service that welcomes you into its space and
encourages you to spend time there? One where every visit
doesn't automatically involve a) paying, b) form-filling or c)

speaking through a pane of glass? These places are ours, let's keep them that way.

Thanks to my wise and ever-vigilant agent, Sophie Hicks, her able deputy, Edina Imrik, and all at Ed Victor Ltd for their continued professionalism.

And finally, a special thanks to Emma Pulitzer and Tim Travaglini at Open Road Media, for their work on the US edition of this book, and for their diligence in making sure I was involved in, and kept informed of, every stage of the process.

With gratitude,

Oisín

ABOUT THE AUTHOR

Oisín McGann was born and raised in Dublin and Drogheda, County Louth, in Ireland. He studied art at Senior College Ballyfermot and Dún Laoghaire School of Art, Design & Technology. Before becoming an author, he worked as a freelance illustrator, serving time along the way as a pizza chef, security guard, background artist for an animation company, and art director and copywriter in an advertising agency.

In 2003 McGann published his first two books in the Mad Grandad series for young readers, followed by his first young adult novel, *The Gods and Their Machines*. Since then, he has written several more novels for young adults, including the Wildenstern Saga, a steampunk series set in nineteenth-century Ireland, and the thrillers *Strangled Silence* and *Rat Runners*.

A full-time writer and illustrator, McGann is married, has three children, and lives somewhere in the Irish countryside.